“Sta

Her savior mumbled, stepping tormentor. “Let the girl go.” He called across the chasm.

“No need to shout,” the deadly voice said. “I can hear you clearly.”

“It’s me you want, not her. Let her go and you can have me.”

“Really? You would give in that easily? She means that much to you?” Grace’s tormentor was clearly enjoying himself. “You’ve got it all wrong, you know. It’s not you I want. Grace is mine. I discovered her long before you, which gives me prior claim.”

Once again, something about the way the madman spoke sounded familiar to Grace. He must have been familiar to her helper, too, because he stared at the lunatic for a moment as if putting the pieces of an intricate puzzle together.

“You were after Grace all along. Why? She’s innocent. What can she possibly offer you? Unless…”

“You don’t even understand her true value, do you?” He let out a sinister laugh, pacing on the other side of the pit. “I’ve had the chance to poke around in her mind a bit. She’s strong like your Meg. I’m not letting her go. Which means you must.”

His arm flew out from his side, stretching like a giant rope across the gap in the earth and pulling her to his side.

Kudos for Amanda Uhl

MIND WAVES received a bronze medal in the paranormal category for the 2015 Rudy contest, second place in the paranormal category of the 2015 Central Ohio Fiction Writers Ignite the Flame contest, and honorable mention in the 2015 Music City Romance Writers Pitch Competition.

Mind Waves

by

Amanda Uhl

Mind Hackers Series

This is a work of fiction. Names, characters, places, and incidents are either the product of the author's imagination or are used fictitiously, and any resemblance to actual persons living or dead, business establishments, events, or locales, is entirely coincidental.

Mind Waves

Contact Information: info@thewildrosepress.com

Cover Art by *Diana Carlile*

The Wild Rose Press, Inc.
PO Box 708
Adams Basin, NY 14410-0708
Visit us at www.thewildrosepress.com

Publishing History
First Fantasy Rose Edition, 2016
Print ISBN 978-1-5092-0977-4
Digital ISBN 978-1-5092-0978-1

Mind Hackers Series
Published in the United States of America

Dedication

To my husband, Barry,
and my children, Simon, Samuel, and Ella,
with love
and in fond memory of many happy hours
gathering beach glass on the shores of Lake Erie.

Acknowledgments

Publishing a novel is an ambitious project. When I began, I had no idea it would take three years from start to finish to see the book in print. Yet, the actual journey began long before, as a ten-year-old, dreaming up stories in my head. ONE DAY I'll write them down, I thought. ONE DAY turned into one year, then five, and eventually, three decades, until one day, became THE DAY—the day I decided to set aside my self-doubts and write.

Nine months later, I stared at the final words in astonishment. In trembling fear, I gave it to Holly Ridgeway, the head of my department at work, who finished the book in one night. Her initial encouragement gave me the confidence to show it to others.

Thank you to all those who read and critiqued early versions: Darlene Hritz, Lynn Shirk, Stacy Helco, Jackie Hudson, Natalie Verardi, Barb Thuel, Janice Bartholomew, Ricketta Van Dress, Debbie Kessler, Judy Bartholomew, Johanne Bartholomew, Cheryl Young, Jon McKenzie, Jillian Petrocci, Debi Wehr, Audrey Haygood, Laura Baricevic, Joyce Caylor, Cathy Matuszak, Leslie Kessler and Tara Harlow.

To my editor, Laura Kelly, thank you for saying "yes" to Mind Waves and lending your incredible talent to the final version.

To those reading who have buried their longings deep, please don't let your fears stop you from pursuing your dreams. The first step is to believe.

May today be THE DAY.

~Amanda Uhl

Prologue

Three years ago

David, do you think we'll ever marry? She twirled her hair absently, a habit when she was deep in thought.

I don't know. Maybe. Why? Despite the fact they were in each other's minds, frequently sharing thoughts, he didn't always understand Meg's emotions. It was typically this way before the more critical missions. She grew introspective and questioned their life together.

I wondered, that's all. I mean, we're not getting any younger. Sophia met Brian when she was only twenty-five.

David took a precious minute to study her where she sat in the Cleveland office. Her long dark hair and oval face were youthful, giving her a dreamy innocence their dangerous line of work never seemed to mar. They had joined the ranks of the U.S. government's Cognitive Mind Unit, or CMU as they called it, when they were barely twenty. Now, some seventeen years later, they still worked side by side, he as the hacker and she as his trainer, infiltrating minds, implanting thoughts, and stealing secrets to protect the nation's intellectual capital. After all this time, David was intimately familiar with Meg's moodiness. He took a moment to calm her.

This is our last mission, I promise. There's plenty of time to plan for the future. What are you worried about?

I don't know. Meg shrugged, laughing it off. *Nothing, I guess. It's...sometimes I wonder if I'll ever lead a normal life. I'd like to have children someday, you know.*

David did know. Still, he quashed the urge he had to comfort her. They could not afford the delay. The others were waiting.

I understand. But we'll talk about this later. It's time to go.

She nodded. David closed his eyes and gave the signal. Instantly, the shimmering, orange energy portal she created appeared, allowing him to slip inside their target's mind undetected to find his crew waiting. They would not start without him, their leader. He had the most dangerous task of holding their shield in place. A controlled focus was required to draw on his trainer's powerful energy and maintain a steady flow of waves to mask their presence.

Although his men spread out, dodging and neutralizing the dark soldiers, almost immediately David sensed something was wrong. He felt the smallest tremor. That was the only warning he received. A massive energy wave burst upon him, destroying their protective shield and giving him mere seconds to react. Unthinking, he pushed outward, while at the same time pulling enough latent energy to propel himself back through the portal. He was safe! But his relief was short-lived. The orange doorway in the target's mind closed behind him, leaving the others trapped.

"No!" David tried desperately to force a spike in the energy field, but it was too late. His crew perished instantly, their life-force absorbed into the target's mind. Meg's light was sucked through the portal with them. "No!" He screamed, a deep agony filling him. Instinctively, he followed their special mental path, but he could not cut through the darkness.

She was gone. He had killed her.

Chapter One
The Interview

Present day

Grace Woznisky was about to con the CEO of a billion dollar corporation—or at least omit one tiny, but crucial, detail. She took a minute to wipe her clammy hands on her skirt, while staring at the shiny, glass office building of Cleveland's Gallant Enterprises. The giant structure appeared cold and sleek, like the high-tech, robotic parts manufactured there. Grace could not screw up this opportunity. Her bank account could not afford it.

With a deep breath, she gathered her courage, and for at least the twentieth time since she got out of bed this morning, rehearsed exactly what she would say to convince Brice Gallant she was the woman for the design job. Grace was fortunate to have been granted an in-person interview, a favor orchestrated by her ex-husband Greg, who had been high school pals with the CEO.

Making her way through the double doors, she caught a glimpse of her reflection. The girl in the glass had short dark blond hair and filled out the skirt and jacket with curves in all the right places. She appeared confident and professional. At least she looked the part. Now, if only Brice Gallant thought so, too.

"Hello." She smiled at the receptionist, who did not smile back. "My name is Grace Woznisky. I have a meeting with Mr. Gallant?" She hated how her words came out, like she wasn't certain she had an appointment.

"Certainly. Let me notify his assistant that you're here. Have a seat." The receptionist indicated the black, leather chairs in the waiting area.

Grace did not remain seated for long. As promised, the assistant arrived to escort her to the elevator, which took her to a large conference room with windows overlooking a sleek landscape design in the shape of a robot, next to a cascading waterfall. "Make yourself comfortable. It will be a moment," the woman said.

Grace had just sat in one of the sleek, black chairs when the door opened widely and in strolled a heavy-set and short Gallant, followed by a small army. Grace had not expected such a large audience. She had only brought materials for five.

"A pleasure to meet you, Grace. I hope you don't mind I've invited a few others along." Gallant indicated his companions, three women and two men, but did not make any further introductions, leaving Grace guessing at their roles at the company.

"Not at all," she said. "Thank you for giving me the chance to bid on the project."

"Of course. We're excited to see what you have to offer." The rotund Gallant waved one manicured hand toward her portfolio. "I've heard great things about you from Gregory Tilko. He reminded me you're a talented artist. We're looking for someone who can design the right artwork for our new building. The art we display is important to me, since that's the first thing our employees and customers will see. Which is why I've made it a point to personally meet with all those who are bidding on the project."

"Great. Well, I'm eager to show you my ideas."

"Let's see what you've got for us." He pulled out the largest chair at the head of the table and sat. The rest of the pack followed suit, until every chair around the table was filled.

That's when Grace noticed a third gentleman in the room. He must have been at the rear when the group entered, and so she had missed seeing him. His ebony hair gleamed under the fluorescent lights, and he took a seat slightly apart from the others, staring at his notebook with a stillness that stood out. Although he was not looking at her, Grace sensed he watched her carefully and, in fact, was already making notations in his notebook.

He turned his head toward her slightly to catch her staring, his eyes stabbing into her like a mouse singled out by a dangerous predator. Maybe it was her imagination, but they seemed to glow from within, like a cat in the night. His thick, glossy black hair contrasted dramatically with the chiseled lines of his face, which could have been carved from marble.

She peeled her gaze away from his with some effort and pulled out her samples. "I, I'm sorry. I didn't expect such a large group. I only brought five packets. Hopefully, some of you can share."

Handing them out hurriedly, Grace began her presentation. Having spent long hours poring over design ideas to create the mockup she was now showing, she knew it was some of her best work. The mural she would create with pieces of green, blue and yellow beach glass she had gathered mostly on the Lake Erie shoreline would dominate the south wall of the main entrance of the building, rising like a giant wave to greet its visitors. The biggest issue was whether she could pull it off. The yellow glass she would need was rare. And since she worked alone, she would have to hire plenty of help to bring the design to life. Grace was also not sure she could get the pricing she had indicated, which was where she would fudge a little. Once she got the job, she would convince Brice Gallant to up the budget slightly for materials.

After showing them her proposal, Grace was concluding her speech when she was interrupted by the intense man with the notebook. “How do you propose to obtain that much beach glass for your design? One of the colors you have specified is rare.”

His question threw her off, given Grace had the same thought only minutes before. She had a large collection to offer from years of gathering glass from the Lake Erie shoreline, but it would be likely she would have to buy off the Internet. She wasn’t confident local providers would have the colors she was after—many of them were her artist friends with their own projects involving beach glass. Grace studied him again carefully. How did he know about the rarity of certain colors?

“I have a few sources.” She forced herself to look at him directly, heart pounding. “If I can’t find what I’m looking for locally, I’m certain I can find what I’ll need on the Internet.”

“Ah, but that could be expensive. And besides,” her interrogator glanced at Brice, “didn’t you say you wanted only local products in the design?”

Brice Gallant looked startled for a moment, but quickly seized on the idea. "Good observation, David. Although it may not look like it today, Gallant Enterprises is a neighborhood company, started by my great grandfather nearly one hundred years ago. We pride ourselves on keeping our business in the community, hiring local workers and supplies as much as possible. I want to make sure the chosen design reflects our philosophy."

"Well, I'm sure I can find enough local sources for the artwork."

"What about labor?" The man, David, was persistent, his expression impossible to read. "This is a big effort and must be completed by the grand opening in November. How do you propose to get all the mosaic work completed in such a short amount of time? You'll need skilled assistants. Will those also come from the community?"

Sweat beaded on her forehead. He had her there. There were only a few other skilled mosaic artists who were local, and they were her competitors. They would be unlikely to assist her on the budget she had to offer. Grace had been planning to hire a few friends from art school who lived in New York City.

"I do plan to use art students at a local college. But as you pointed out, mosaic work does require skilled labor. I know several talented artists working out of New York City who could assist if I can't find the local talent. Also, I—"

"Great questions, Jenkins." Brice Gallant interrupted. "This is why I like to have you attend these things."

David chuckled, the sound grating on Grace's

nerves. "Happy to assist."

Brice Gallant rose from his chair and offered her a hand, indicating the interview was at an end. "Grace, it was a pleasure talking to you. We'll be in touch after we have a chance to consider all of our options. Thank you for sharing your ideas with us."

Grace had a sinking feeling she had lost the bid. What's more, she suspected the dark-haired David knew it, too. She squared her shoulders. "When can I expect to hear from you, Mr. Gallant?"

"We'll be in touch with you within a few days." Grace noticed the big man looked at David before responding, as if seeking his approval. *Weird.*

"Okay," she agreed, plastering on a smile. "I'll look forward to hearing from you."

There was nothing left to do but gather her materials, shake Brice Gallant's hand and the hands of all the others, and hustle out the door. Although she kept her head high, in her mind, it hung in shame. If she didn't get this job, she would have to call the bank again and beg for an extension on her mortgage payment. She might even have to move in with her mom and Glenn, until she could get back on her feet.

Chapter Two
Job Crusher

The bell over the antique door of *Coffersations* chimed as Grace entered. A wave of coffee shop aromas washed over her, and she breathed deep their rich warmth. The dark tang of roasted coffee beans eddied with the sweetness of fresh-baked apple muffins. Above the deep sea of venti caramel latte scents and cinnamon pastries circled the hushed conversations of the shop's patrons. Most were huddled over small tables this evening, coveting their steaming mugs and murmuring. A dry laugh pierced the monotone sounds like the cry of an angry albatross, sending shivers down her spine and causing her stomach to churn. *No way. It can't be.*

Her heart sank as her gaze alighted on a couple nearby. It was him, the Job Crusher—David Jenkins. The jerk who had watched her presentation with unblinking eyes this morning and kept scribbling in his notebook. What was he doing here?

Grace stood at the counter and studied him carefully under the guise of perusing the drink list. His clothes were more casual than this morning's suit, but he still cut a GQ figure, dressed in charcoal gray slacks and a black, button-down shirt. He didn't wear a tie, which was likely a good thing—she might be tempted to strangle him with it. His black hair looked exactly as it had this morning—perfect. Except, now there was a slight curl on the right side. *Ha!* So he was as vulnerable to Cleveland's summer humidity as the rest of the population. Nice to know he was human. She had doubted the possibility.

Her gaze shifted to his companion. The girl was young, maybe twenty-five, thin with straight, long blonde hair and a skimpy green dress. She spoke, her hands waving as if it were her primary form of communication and smiling, clearly doing her best to flirt. As far as Grace could tell, it wasn't working. Job Crusher looked bored. He nodded to his companion and seemed to turn his head deliberately to catch her staring.

"Dammit." Grace mumbled under her breath. She gave him a casual smile, but he showed no sign of recognition, so she looked away. When she looked back again, he was speaking to his companion, who laughed at whatever he said.

Did he even remember her? She had gone to great pains to look good this evening. She was supposed to be meeting an online date, but he had yet to show. Grace looked around and checked her cell phone. It was ten minutes past seven. She had been running late and figured he would be waiting for her. It concerned her he was not.

Could he have seen her arrive, picked her out from her photo on the dating site, and hidden in the bathroom? It didn't seem likely. They had been emailing for months and had a great deal in common. Neither liked the bar scene, which was why they had met online in a chat room. They had kept their identities secret, preferring to call themselves by a handle. She was Gigi. He was Brains. When he had asked her to meet him for coffee, she had agreed easily. *Sucker.*

With a sigh, she checked her watch again and glanced around. Looked like a no-show. A wave of insecurity overwhelmed her. By anyone's standards, she was cute, but no one had ever called her beautiful, like the slim blond with the Job Crusher, who reminded Grace a little of her sister, Claire. While Claire was white blonde, blue-eyed and leggy, Grace was small—standing five foot four inches in her bare feet—and curvy. Yet she knew she looked much younger than her thirty-five years. She should have no trouble attracting a date.

She spotted a favorite magazine nearby and scooped it up before making her way to the counter to order a latte. David still talked to the young girl. In her peripheral vision—she didn't dare get caught staring again—Grace saw her nodding her head at him.

She grabbed her latte. The rich smell of coffee beans and vanilla was mildly comforting. Her date was nowhere in sight. Taking the table and chair closest to the window, Grace opened the magazine and pretended to read, though all she wanted was to curl into a ball and cry. Was steady work and a little male attention too much to ask for? How could a day, which had started out so promising, become so depressing?

She frowned and turned to search out David, but he was hidden behind other customers. Why did she let his silence intimidate her? She should have reintroduced herself. Maybe she could have changed his impression.

Grace sighed and gazed unseeing at her magazine. The thought of looking into his cold gray eyes again unnerved her.

"Is this chair taken?" A deep, male voice startled her from her thoughts, skittering deliciously across her nerve endings. Was this Brains? She glanced up, hoping it was.

It wasn't.

David Jenkins was in front of her. Time seemed to speed forward. She took a deep breath and forced a smile.

"Oh, hello. I saw you earlier but wasn't sure you remembered me. You know—from our meeting this morning." She swallowed, her throat dry. What could he possibly want to talk to her about after his total lack of interest that morning and snub minutes earlier?

Part of her registered relief. She had another shot to change his first impression. Grace badly needed a client, any client, to pay her mounting debt. Saying goodbye to a husband and a corporate paycheck in the same year had not been favorable to her pocketbook. If she landed the Gallant job, she would stand to make ten to fifteen thousand dollars after expenses. A chunk of change compared to her normal commissions. "Please take a seat." She gestured to the chair opposite.

"Are you expecting someone?" He raised one eyebrow in query.

"No—I mean, I am, but it doesn't look like they made it. Go ahead and sit if you'd like." He did, casually crossing his long legs under the table. He stared at Grace intently. She reached a hand into her hair and twirled a strand. His eyes followed the movement. She pulled her hand into her lap.

"Gallant didn't do a good job with introductions. I'm David Jenkins. And you are Grace…?"

"Woznisky." She fiddled with the handle of her

coffee cup. Um…what exactly do you do for Gallant?"

"I don't work for Gallant. I'm a business consultant. From time to time, Gallant has used my services. I happened to be there today to talk about another matter and was asked to sit in on your presentation."

He placed one hand on his forehead, his long fingers caressing his temples. "So, how long have you been in business for yourself?"

Grace snagged her drink and took a swallow. *C'mon Grace. You won a staring contest with Luke Wilson in the third grade. You killed a humungous spider in the bathroom yesterday. You can do this.*

"A year." She managed breezily. "I was a graphic designer for a greeting card company for fifteen years but decided to pursue a career as a full-time mosaic artist when I was laid off a little over a year ago." When he didn't immediately respond, she added, "It was a good decision." She mentally kicked herself for adding the last part. She didn't need to justify herself.

"How did you get in with Gallant?"

His fierce eyes glittered, seeming to stab into her disjointed thoughts, compelling her to respond. At the same time, she noticed they were not gray, but green. Or was it a trick of the light? "Brice Gallant went to school with my ex-husband."

David nodded as if cataloging the small detail but remained silent. Grace fiddled with the magazine, a *Bargain Design.* She noticed the bright, yellow bedspread on the cover—it would look great in her bedroom.

He cleared his throat, bringing Grace back to the present. It never failed, when she was intimidated, her focus wandered. To stall for time to pull herself together, she took another sip of coffee. David Jenkins was looking at her as if she were an abandoned dog he needed to handle gently. His penetrating eyes seemed to see right into her mind. She fidgeted in her chair and searched for something to say. "So, what brings you here tonight?"

He didn't reply right away but took a drink of his coffee. He was tall, but not overly muscular. His long fingers curled around his coffee cup, and his left pinkie was crooked. Maybe it had been broken and hadn't healed properly.

"I had business here," he said, a small smile on his face. He set his coffee cup down suddenly, as if he had made a decision. "Grace, Brice Gallant has decided to go with abstract paintings rather than a mosaic design for his new office building. I'm sorry. He'll be letting you know on Monday."

Grace had known it, but hearing the words from this man was especially painful. She fought to keep her disappointment concealed with a question. "What do you do for Gallant? Mr. Gallant seemed to value your opinion greatly."

"My advice has been on target on a number of occasions, so he tends to value it."

Well, that's peachy. And were you the one to advise him to go abstract? "That's nice," she said, staring defiantly into his chameleon eyes. She would be damned if she let him intimidate her. She'd experienced enough male ego to last her a lifetime.

"Nice for me." He smiled, making him look years younger and catching her off-guard. "You see, contrary to what you might believe, I liked your design ideas. I have a proposition for you. Would you consider working for me?"

This time she barely kept her mouth from falling open. A job offer was the last thing she had expected tonight, especially from the Job Crusher. She thought of the dwindling funds in her checking account, her mortgage and car payment due at the end of the month.

Then quickly pulled herself together to talk business. "What do you have in mind?"

"I'm looking for artwork for my lake cottage. It's been in my family for generations and needs a bit of modernization. I think your beach glass mosaic designs may be the right touch. Are you interested?"

Nodding, she took another sip of her latte.

"It will require spending a bit of time at the cottage. I'll expect to be closely involved in the project, too. The cottage is important to me."

Discreetly she rubbed a sweaty palm on her skirt. The thought of spending a lot of time in this man's company sent unwelcome butterflies through her system.

"I've been considering this project for a while. A friend who owns a design magazine wants to follow my progress in the publication. If you take the job, I'll need you to work closely with the editors to provide them with photographs and updates as you go."

"What's the magazine?"

"*House Trendz.* Do you know it?"

Dear God, was he serious? It was a prestigious magazine, which had the reputation of discovering unique homes and showcasing them with beautiful *National Geographic* style photographs. Many of the residences pictured were of the rich and famous. She drew a shaky breath. “Yes. What’s the angle?”

“They want to showcase talented artists bringing new life to old cottages. After seeing your work this morning, I think you’re the right person for the job.”

Blood rushed to her cheeks, warming them. His flattery fed her ego, but she wasn’t sure she could trust it. He liked her work enough to hire her. This was praise indeed coming from the Job Crusher. Then again, maybe he expected to employ her for next to nothing. It wouldn’t be the first time.

“I liked your initial proposal and will give you a budget based on your time, the cost of supplies, and additional labor. I’m thinking fifty thousand dollars ought to do it. Is that acceptable?”

Grace nodded, dazed. Fifty thousand dollars was double what she had proposed for the Gallant project. It seemed her day was turning around after all.

“Will you be able to clear your calendar for the next several months? I have a busy work schedule, and the deadline is tight. I’ll need you to be on call, so to speak.”

Grace dug her nails into her palms so her excitement wouldn’t show. “Give me a second to check my calendar.” It didn’t have many entries, but he didn’t know that. Better to seem busy, than desperate.

Making a show of pulling out her fancy, new smartphone, which she was still trying to figure out, she opened her calendar. For a few seconds, she scrolled through the blank pages. Only a few entries were recorded. Her sister’s shower in two weeks, a dermatologist appointment on Tuesday, a reminder she needed to get fitted for her bridesmaid’s dress—if Claire’s wedding took place. “I have a few appointments, but for the most part, it looks doable."

He stood, scribbled something on a business card and handed it to her. Their fingers brushed for a moment, and a strange tingle, like static electricity, jumped from his hands to hers. The electrical charge raced up her arms and into the base of her skull, causing her head to pound. *A caffeine attack?* Dear God, she hoped so. She would need all her wits about her to pull off this job.

He gave her a brief smile. "I also have a residence—the address is on my card. If you'll meet me there tomorrow at nine, we can get started. I think the sooner I give you the particulars of the assignment, the better. You can develop a full design proposal once you get a feel for what's required."

She nodded, and he smiled again slightly. He shook her hand, which still held his card, and abruptly turned and left, his long legs making short work of his exit.

Grace couldn't help but stare after him. There was something strangely fascinating and, she hated to confess it even to herself, attractive about the man. Like when he had smiled at her and told her he liked her design ideas. But there was something else, too. *Hidden secrets.* Unbidden, his crooked pinkie came to mind.

Grace watched him open the door of the coffee shop and head out. She glanced down at the card in her hand. *C. David Jenkins, Economist and Consultant.*

Where was the girl who had been flirting with David when Grace had first arrived? She looked around for her, but the girl was nowhere in sight.

Grace turned his card over. On the back, he had written his home address, Shaker Heights. She sighed.

He lived on the east side of town. It would be a hike from her Lakewood home. Good thing he was generous with his design budget. She would need the extra dough to pay for gas.

Grace grabbed her purse and headed out the door. Time to get home and plan her strategy for tomorrow. She had a feeling she was going to need to be at her best to keep up with her new employer.

Chapter Three
Dating Games

"Pretty girl. Pretty girl." Harvey screeched as she came through the door.

"Now that's what I like to hear," Grace said. "How ya doing, Harvey honey? Did you miss me? Did you eat all your seed? You did, didn't you?" She refilled Harvey's food and water dish, chattering at the silky, gray parrot all the while. When she was through fussing with the bird, she shuffled to her office and turned on her computer, mentally composing a cryptic note to her failed date.

She opened her email and saw the familiar address almost instantly. *Mea Culpa,* read the subject line. Her lips curled with disdain and her eyes narrowed on the screen as if it were the offending date who had the nerve to stand her up. She clicked on the message, muttering. "You'd better have a darn good excuse."

"It's a wrap," Harvey chortled. Harvey had once belonged to her sister, a struggling actress. Claire had purchased him for five-hundred dollars when she was in between boyfriends and left him with Grace when she moved to California. Grace soon discovered Harvey came with a whole repertoire of theater words, such as *"break a leg," "stage right,"* and full lines from Shakespeare and other famous works. Sometimes his comedic timing was impeccable. Mostly he was downright annoying.

Grace ignored Harvey and read the email.

7:04 p.m.

Please forgive me. I know you are thinking I didn't show, but I did. You were talking to a man and didn't notice me. I didn't want to spoil anything, so I left.

Brains

Lame. She relaxed against the back of her chair, pushed the keyboard away, closed her eyes and contemplated her evening. Everything seemed like too much effort. She pulled the keyboard back and typed.

7:32 p.m.

You really should have said hello. The man you saw was a business acquaintance and not one I like all that much. This morning I lost out on a bid I was making because of him. He must have felt a twinge of conscience when he saw me, because he offered me a job. Gotta get to bed since I start tomorrow.

Gigi

She hit the send button with a satisfying click, flung off her heels and collapsed on the couch, tired from the stress of the day. She closed her eyes for a moment—the last thing she remembered before the sound of Cyndi Lauper, singing *"Girls Just Want to Have Fun,"* blared from her cell phone, jarring her awake. *Claire.*

"Hello, darling," squawked Harvey.

Grace blinked, disoriented, and struggled from the sofa to answer the phone, which was in her purse. She had to dig for it in the big bag, among all the clutter of receipts, makeup and assorted papers she was too busy to organize. Organization had never been her strong suit.

She found it before her voicemail kicked in. “Hello?”

“Grace, it’s me.” Her sister’s voice registered a full octave higher than normal.

Oh, Lord, not tonight. The thought was followed by a pang of remorse. She always tried to be supportive of her sister. “What’s up?” She forced a bright and cheerful tone.

“You’re never going to believe who came into the store.” Claire paused only a brief second before gushing on. “John Mayer! He had on blue jeans and a bright blue T-shirt, and he looked totally awesome. I asked him for his autograph, and he smiled and gave it to me. He said he liked my name.”

The last was said on a rush so that the word “name” ended as a high-pitched squeal. Grace held the phone away from her head. Impressive, but tonight wasn’t a good night to deal with her sister’s drama.

“Maybe he’ll use it in a song?” Claire giggled. “That would be so great.”

“Yeah, it would. Claire, what time is it out there?” She squinted at the clock on the microwave. *Midnight.*

“Yeah, I know it’s late, but I had to call and tell you. I also wanted to find out how your blind date went.” There was a slight pause while she waited for Grace to respond. “Grace, you did go on your date, didn’t you?”

“Yes, well, not really.” Grace sighed. “I mean, he never showed.”

“What? What an asshole. I hope you didn’t try to call him or anything.” Another pause. “Grace?”

“No, I didn’t call him. We haven’t exchanged numbers. I did respond to an email he sent.”

"He sent an email? What was his excuse? Somebody had better have died."

The comment made Grace want to laugh. Instead, she sighed. "No, nobody died. He saw me talking to one of my clients, assumed it was a date, and was scared off."

"What a wimp. I hope you put him in his place!" Pause. "Grace, you told him where to go, didn't you?"

"Sort of. I mean, I told him he was silly for not talking to me anyway."

"Oh, that will make him feel really bad." Grace could hear the sarcastic tone through the phone line. "You need to lose him. I can already tell he's a dick."

Grace laughed. Claire's bluntness was her most endearing quality. "I'm going to wait to see how he responds to my email first."

"Well, if you need any help telling him where to go, call me. Okay? I'm expert at that sort of thing."

Claire had been engaged three times but had yet to go through with it. She always got cold feet before the big day. The first time it was three months before the wedding. The second time, she made it to two weeks before. Now, she was engaged again, but they kept changing the wedding date. First, it was planned for April because spring weddings were so beautiful. Later, it was June because they needed more time to plan their honeymoon, and the latest was October because they got a good deal on a cruise.

Grace had yet to meet Tom Walters, Claire's fiancé. Theirs had been a whirlwind courtship, but from all accounts Tom had two things going for him: a good job and income. Lots of it. Grace wondered how long it would be before Claire drove him over the edge. Tom was a successful businessman, but to Grace—who knew her sister well—he seemed a little too stable for the flighty Claire.

"How are the wedding plans going?" she asked, almost fearfully. The wedding was a little over a month away. Based on prior engagements, this was when problems would develop.

"Great." Claire surprised her. "Tom agreed we'll spend our honeymoon cruising to the Greek islands. He bought our tickets."

"Sounds nice."

"There's one tiny problem."

Uh-oh. Here it is. Grace waited with bated breath. Claire had a way of dropping bombshells, which always started off as little problems.

"I can't find the right shoes to go with my gown."

"Oh, is that all?" Grace breathed a sigh of relief.

"What do you mean is that all? I must have searched every stinking department store in San Francisco, and I still haven't found what I am looking for. This wedding is only a month away. What am I going to do if I can't find the right pair? You saw the pics of Tom. I have to have the right heel, or he'll tower over me. I want to look graceful when the minister says kiss the bride. Not like a kitten kissing a giraffe."

"I'm sure it won't look like that," Grace said soothingly. Claire describing herself as a kitten was laughable. She was more like a lioness. Since Grace had never seen Tom in person, she didn't know how their height compared. Although she could use her imagination, knowing Tom was six foot four and her sister was five foot nine.

"Well, you know what I mean. The details are

important to me. Like Mom always told us, *'It pays to look good.'* Speaking of Mom, if you talk to her, don't tell her about the shoes, okay. Otherwise, she'll be giving me all kinds of advice I'd rather not hear right now. Well, I've got to run. And you need to get to bed, poor girl. I'll call you tomorrow. Nighty-nite. Love you. Bye."

"Love you, too. Night, Claire."

Grace groaned. Why did she have the sensation she was standing in quicksand and was slowly being pulled in over her head? She hauled herself off the couch and made for the kitchen to charge her cell phone. She was on her way to the bathroom to go through her nightly bedtime routine, when a ding from her computer indicated an incoming email. *Brains.* Grace hesitated. Should she ignore it until the morning? The man had stood her up. She refused to rush to read his message.

Still, five minutes later, she found herself at the computer holding her breath. In a flash, she clicked on the email.

12:22 a.m.

Dear Gigi—

Like I said, I'm sorry I didn't meet you as promised, but I was there. I'm new to the online dating scene, so forgive me. I really would like another chance. Can we try again? How does Friday look for you? We can meet at the same place and time. What do you say?

Brains

What did she have to lose? It wasn't like she had a lot of other options for a Friday night. She wrote back quickly and pressed the send button before she could change her mind.

12:38 a.m.

OK. It's a deal. But if it doesn't happen this time, that's it for dates. I don't like being stood up even in the virtual world.

G

Grace was proud of the firmness of her response. She had learned the hard way not to tolerate excuses from a man—especially from one she had yet to meet in person.

Chapter Four
Jenkins Doesn't Bite

Thursday morning looked to be another sunny day, but Grace tried to temper her optimism. Every time she was too enthusiastic, she ended up disappointed. Better to be cautious. It seemed to her most bad events in life were surprises. So it followed if she imagined all the bad things that could happen, they wouldn't happen because they wouldn't be a surprise. A bit convoluted, but it helped to ease her anxiety.

By the time she had dressed, eaten a quick breakfast and headed out the door, Grace had a mental list of nearly thirty disasters waiting to happen, including hitting David Jenkins's car in the drive or arriving on his doorstep with toilet paper sticking out of her pants. As she rang his doorbell and waited, Grace looked over her shoulder at her backside to be sure.

So far, so good.

His residence was one of those stately red brick homes with an under-stated charm on a well-maintained tree-lined street. The landscaping was meticulous, as was the entryway. No out of control daisies or peeling paint for David Jenkins. She pressed the doorbell again. Nothing. She pressed it a third time, annoyed.

On the first ring, a dog had barked furiously from somewhere inside the house. However, no dog was in sight when David Jenkins finally opened the door, so he must have put it in the basement or garage. She wondered if it was a dangerous dog like a pit bull or Doberman.

"Hello, Grace."

Jenkins was dressed casually in a green polo shirt and dark blue jeans, which fit his broad shoulders and long legs to perfection. Grace stared, her mind a blank. Her earlier indignation vanished, while her heartbeat sounded a loud thump in her ear. *Breathe, Grace.* "Hello."

He smiled. "C'mon in."

He ushered her into his home and an open kitchen. Gleaming granite countertops in a subdued shade of green contrasted nicely with white cabinets. From the looks of it, someone liked to cook. There were lots of new chrome appliances and a matching stove and refrigerator, which she eyed enviously.

"Would you like something to drink? A glass of water or cup of coffee or tea?"

"A cup of coffee would be great. With cream and a little sugar."

Grace glanced around the room curiously, as he pulled out a large mug from one of the cupboards and poured coffee into it from what appeared to be a freshly made pot. Everything was neat and orderly. He was either a clean freak or he had a housecleaning service that did a fabulous job. Or he didn't spend a lot of time at home.

She cast around for something to say. "You have a beautiful home. Have you lived here long?"

"About three years. Before that, I lived in New York. I grew up in Cleveland. I have family here."

She waited for him to elaborate, but he didn't.

"Follow me."

She trailed him through a large, open great room with shining wood floors. Grace spied strange antique objects, a flash of an ornate, gold lamp and a beautiful white fireplace, before David led her into another large room, which was his office. This room contained a mission style, antique desk and a collection of unusual fountain pens, which hung on the wall in a glass case. A sleek, chocolate leather couch covered one end of the room and there was a giant, flat-screened TV and bar, with an assortment of liquor bottles and glasses, on the other. The walls were tan, which might have darkened the room except for the oversized window that looked out upon a fenced-in backyard, which contained a large deck and lots of shrubs and flowers. A bird feeder hung near the window. Grace noticed a cardinal pecking at his breakfast.

David motioned to a leather armchair, and Grace took a seat, sipped her coffee, which was excellent, and waited for him to speak. He sat behind his desk in a matching leather chair, put on a pair of black reading glasses, opened a manila folder and pulled out a few papers. Still he did not say anything, which put her on edge.

"You have a lovely view from here. It must be nice to watch the birds at the feeder."

David nodded as he gazed at the papers in front of him, making a few notations in the margins.

"I own a bird." Grace tapped her fingers on the rim of her mug. "An African Gray parrot. His name is Harvey."

David nodded again as he perused his notes. His continued silence increased her nervousness. Were they going to get this meeting started or not?

"He was my sister's, but she couldn't take him when she moved to California, so I agreed to take him in. My sister is a wannabe actress, and Harvey has a flair for drama. He talks a lot and some of his language is colorful. Yesterday, he told me to go to hell. That was after I had cleaned his cage and fed him. Ungrateful bird."

David glanced her way with a warm smile. "I'd like to meet Harvey sometime. I have a dog. His name is Oliver. Perhaps you heard him barking earlier?"

"Why yes, I did."

"I put him in the basement so he wouldn't bother you. He can be aggressive with strangers. But he's loyal and friendly once you get to know him. Before you leave, I'll introduce you, that way you won't have to worry about him when you're here."

"All…all right." She wound a finger through her hair and twirled. "What kind of dog is he?"

He paused a moment, frowning at her fingers in her hair. Grace found herself dropping her hand into her lap. His eyes met hers. "A mutt. I brought him home from the pound a few years ago. He looks like he might be part Husky, part Shepherd, but I can't be sure." He paused again, then leaned back in his chair and studied her thoughtfully, a Mona Lisa smile on his face.

"You can call me David. My dog doesn't bite and neither do I. There's nothing for you to be nervous about."

How did he so easily read her emotions? She liked birds and cats, but was always a bit nervous around dogs the first time she met them. When she and her sister were young, a neighbor's St. Bernard had gotten loose and come to visit. It had knocked her over, and she had developed a healthy caution and respect for dogs after that.

"Now here's the deal." David changed the subject. "I'm thinking we can spend this morning discussing my thoughts for the design. You can ask any questions, if you want me to elaborate, and I can give you a tour of the cottage tomorrow. How long will it take you to pull together your initial proposal?"

Grace took a few moments to consider the question. "At least a week. What kind of timeline are you looking at?"

"*House Trendz* magazine would like to feature my cottage in their December issue, which gives us a few months." He dug an older copy of the magazine from the folder he had on his desk and handed it to her. A photo of Technoderm's Kyle Willard stared from the cover. The caption was titled *'Billionaire relaxes in style.'* The handsome blond CEO was dressed in a suit and sprawled on a couch in what looked to be a modern, loft-style New York City penthouse apartment. Willard was rumored to be one of the top ten wealthiest men in America. It was thrilling to think the man sitting across from her might appear in the December issue, and she would be the featured artist. She flipped through the magazine to gauge the style of the article. The photos were breathtaking. She pulled a notebook from her purse and did a quick sketch.

"I'll have a proposal to you as fast as I can." Maybe she could celebrate her new client tomorrow night with Brains.

David frowned suddenly, and Grace's heart pounded. She needed this job. She'd better quit thinking about Brains and worry about the man in front of her.

Magically, David's frown dissolved into a smile. "Okay. Let's get started."

They worked steadily for the next three hours. He outlined his ideas in a compelling way, and she found herself intrigued by his knowledge. He was bright. Grace had known it, but until now, she didn't realize exactly to what degree. Working together, their thoughts seemed to build, one upon another, effortlessly. Finally, he checked his watch. "It's past noon. Let's take a break."

Grace was surprised at how fast the time flew. Her head was buzzing with creative ideas.

"Are you hungry?"

Grace nodded. "I can run and get something and be back in an hour."

"No need. I'll make us lunch. How does an omelet sound?"

"Fine," she said, hiding her surprise.

Grace marveled at the incongruity of the situation. Yesterday, she would have never dared to imagine the man who prevented her from getting the Gallant job would be making her an omelet a day later. He did not look like the sort of man who was comfortable in an apron or liked omelets. But he looked fine in an apron, and he also made a mean omelet.

He brought out a bottle of wine from the office bar and poured them each a glass, which Grace sipped as she watched him work.

"So tell me about yourself." He opened a drawer, pulled out a knife and sliced peppers on a wood cutting board. "Where did you grow up?" He popped a piece of yellow pepper in his mouth.

"Parma, although my mother and stepdad now live in Strongsville."

He finished chopping the pepper and started on an onion. "Do you have other siblings besides the sister who left you with the parrot?"

"Oh, no. It's only Claire and I. How about yourself?"

He threw the vegetables into the pan and beat the eggs. "My sister Sophia and her husband, Brian, live a few streets over with their two children. And my mom and dad live in University Heights. They're still in great health but getting older, which is why I moved back to Cleveland. As a single guy, it wasn't hard to pick up and move."

Why was he still single? *Was he gay?*

David coughed violently, choking on the piece of pepper he was chewing. He grabbed the glass of water he had sitting on the counter, nearly knocking it over in his haste, and took a swig. The movement was the first clumsy one Grace had seen him make since she had met him.

"Are you all right?"

He nodded, set the glass in the sink, and went back to cooking. He poured the eggs in the pan, standing back to let them cook, and handed her two sturdy white plates and some silverware. "Since I'm doing all the cooking, you get to set the table."

"Of course," she said, taking the plates.

While she set the table, he poured her a glass of water and refilled her wine glass. He gestured for her to sit, dished out their lunch, and took the seat opposite.

"Who taught you to cook?" She stabbed into the fragrant omelet with gusto, and took a generous bite.

"My Grandma Jenkins. Her specialty and my favorite breakfast growing up was chocolate chip waffles and banana pancakes."

"Yum. Sounds like dessert for breakfast." Grace laughed.

"Ah, but that would be my grandma's banana crème pie. Nothing could ever top her pie."

"You haven't tried my grandma's German chocolate cake. Funny it's 'German' because my grandma was from England."

"Did she make scones and serve tea with milk?"

"Yes. How did you know?"

"Grandma Jenkins was also from England." He stared at her intently, and she found herself staring back a bit breathlessly. The kitchen, which had initially seemed large and sterile, felt cozy and intimate. Grace raised her hands to her heated cheeks. *Must be the wine.*

"Tell me more about your family. Any nieces or nephews?"

"Oh, no. Claire's not married…yet. She's engaged."

He looked at her with interest. "You say that like you're nervous she's making a mistake?"

He was perceptive. "Oh, not at all. It's…Claire's so impulsive. It's hard for her to follow through on anything. I remember when we were kids, she could never make a decision. She used to make me choose first, and in the end, she would do what I did. If I chose the red lollipop, she wanted it, too. Which was fine on the little things, but didn't go over well when we were in high school and dating. The day after I broke up with my steady boyfriend, Claire went out with him. I was so upset at the time. Lucky for both of us that relationship didn't last long."

"How about now? Does she still follow your advice?'

Grace frowned. "I guess so. Although it seems like she's been giving me the advice lately."

"Like what?"

The conversation had taken a deeply personal turn. Grace wasn't sure she should answer, but like a locomotive running at top speed, now she had started, it was difficult to stop. "She thinks I'm not assertive enough and easily intimidated."

"And are you?" His eyes drew her in. What was happening to her?

"I don't think so on the important things. But I do find myself giving in when I should be firm."

"Ah." He said, as if the single syllable explained everything.

She wondered what he meant, but he didn't elaborate. Instead, he collected her dishes, brought them to the sink, and proceeded to wash them by hand rather than stick them in the dishwasher.

"When's the wedding?"

"Oh, October 10, I guess. I mean if it happens. I do want it to happen. Claire needs a kind, stable man in her life. From what she tells me, Tom has a great job—he's a stockbroker—but unlike all her previous fiancés, he doesn't tolerate her shenanigans. I like that."

She plucked the tea towel from the counter and dried the dishes he set in the drainer. "I wish I knew whether Claire would go through with it this time. Every time she calls me, I cringe, waiting for her to drop the bomb that will tell me she's discovered a flaw, which will keep her from saying 'I do.'"

She shrugged, placing the plate she was drying carefully on the counter. “With Reed—her first fiancé—it was he couldn’t quit smoking. I admit it’s a nasty habit. Doubt I could marry a man who smoked, either. And Jacob, well, he wasn’t stable enough. We all liked Jacob, but he couldn’t hold down a job for long. Claire would have had to be the breadwinner in the marriage, and, well,” she paused, laughing, “you would understand why that wasn’t a good idea if you met her.”

David pulled the plug on the drain and squeezed out the dishcloth, folding it and setting it neatly over the side of the sink divider. As he turned to look at her fully, Grace noted again the handsome lines of his face. He checked his watch.

“It’s getting late. Let me get your stuff.”

David fetched her purse and briefcase from the office and handed them over.

“I don’t want to work you too hard on your first day.” He grinned, as he ushered her to the door. “Oh, I almost forgot,” he said, as they heard a bark from the basement door. “Why don’t we introduce you to Oliver?”

At Grace’s hesitant nod, David opened the basement door cautiously, grabbing the collar of a large black dog as he did so. With a tight grip, he brought Oliver to meet and sniff her over.

“Hi boy.” Grace held herself still to look less like a walking chew toy. Oliver’s tail wagged, so she took it as a friendly sign and bent cautiously to pet him. He responded by licking her hand, and they were friends. At least she hoped they were.

“Why don’t you work with what I’ve provided so

far and email me any additional questions."

"All right."

"I'll call you on Friday. Let's meet in the evening to go over your initial ideas. Come to the cottage at six. I can show you around."

Grace hesitated, thinking of her plans with Brains.

"As a bonus, I'll treat you to dinner afterward."

"Er…I kind of have plans for Friday evening. What about Saturday?"

"I'd like to get started as early as possible. We don't have much time. Can you make yourself available?"

His face had an uncompromising quality to it, and suddenly they were back to being client and employee. Grace sighed. She hated to move her date with Brains, but a client was a client and had to take precedence. If Jenkins was happy with her work, chances were good he would recommend her to some of his other business contacts. She assumed he had a lot of them. And she needed the money.

"Don't worry about it. I'll switch my plans."

"Great."

He opened the door, presenting Grace an enigmatic, charming smile, which was her clue to exit, and she did. Although she avoided looking over her shoulder, Grace could feel David's eyes on her back as she walked to her car. She checked the time on her cell phone—4:00 p.m. If she hurried, she could get her place cleaned and still have plenty of daylight at the beach. Her first meeting had gone well despite the change of plans. David Jenkins and his dog didn't bite after all.

Chapter Five
Life or Death

David closed the front door. He glanced out the small window, watching Grace Woznisky get into her ancient Honda Civic. What was it about her? From the moment he had spotted her on the beach outside his cottage six months ago, he'd paid attention. She made a pretty picture in her purple cover-up, her straw hat tilted to protect her face from the sun, and carrying her bright, yellow bucket she used to collect beach glass. But it was more than that.

Grace started the engine, pulling a pair of dark sunglasses from the car's visor and looking at her cell phone. Was she checking messages from that sister of hers who seemed to need her help at all hours of the day and night? As he watched her through the window, David couldn't resist sending out psychic feelers. The effort would make his ever-present headache worse, but he wanted to know.

Images flashed before him in quick succession, and David caught snippets of her thoughts. *Beach, messy condo, I can't go out like that.* His head throbbed in reaction, and he withdrew quickly. Grace was heading to the beach. Should he follow her?

His heart pounded, and he exercised his iron control to keep the beats steady and even. The reaction was instinctual from years of work in the field.

Emotions were deadly. David had learned long ago to regulate his heartbeat and breathing to lessen their interference with his energy waves.

Grace pulled onto his street, her car headed west toward her Lakewood condo. David turned and almost stepped on Oliver, who barked once, indicating he wanted out.

“You feel it, too. Don’t you buddy?”

He opened the doors, which led to the backyard, and the dog bounded out joyfully. The hot sunshine indicated another glorious Ohio summer day, reminding David of Grace’s smile.

David did not believe a match existed for him. Of course, he’d heard the stories. In his world, hackers and trainers melded together with frequent regularity. But it had not been true in his case. David and Meg had been off-the-chart oddities. After the accident, everyone assumed he’d link with Geneva—the strongest trainer known to the CMU. But he’d never felt the connection. So why did his energy waves so easily resonate with Grace?

Oliver barked happily at the bushes. A slight breeze brought some relief from the unrelenting heat. Great beach weather. Yes, he would follow Grace.

A strong protective instinct filled him. He knew from her thoughts she was fiercely loyal, and kind and giving to those she loved. But her giving nature also meant she could be manipulated. He did not want to see her hurt or frightened.

Unfortunately, he did not know about Grace’s connection with Gallant Enterprises until it was too late. Which was the trouble with his type of talent. Without a trainer, he could get some information, that which the person was willing to share readily or sometimes could not hold in because of the intensity of feeling. But David could not pinpoint the exact details he needed. She had fretted over her meeting at the coffee shop and her blind date. But in all his mind probes, she had never once contemplated Gallant Enterprises until the appointment had been made. There was no way he'd let her work for those crooked bastards. Unknown to Grace, Brice Gallant was currently being investigated for tax evasion.

His cell phone buzzed. After glancing at the number, he answered on the second ring. "Jenkins here."

"How are the headaches?"

David sighed. Peter never quit.

"Fine. No worse than normal."

"Good. We have another assignment for you."

"I'm not interested. You know that. I'm sorry."

"I know. I hate to bother you. But this one's life or death."

David's muscles clenched instinctively. "Whose life?"

"Yours," came the reply.

Chapter Six
Beach Glass

Grace flew around her condo, putting dirty dishes in the sink, stacking piles of papers she had left scattered on her desk, and periodically, doing a quick two-step. She couldn't pinpoint what was generating her happiness and excitement. Was it the new job and potential for steady income or something more?

She checked the time on her cell phone—half an hour down and a whole evening to go. Grace made herself a sandwich. She grabbed her beach bag and stuffed it with a water from the fridge, an apple from the fruit bowl, and her yellow "happy bucket," as she liked to call it, and was out the door.

Usually, she drove the short mile to Edgewater Beach, but today, Grace decided she would walk. Although she passed several of her neighbors on the way out, she couldn't shake the feeling someone was watching her. Glancing around, she failed to spot anyone. Grace was alone on the sidewalk. She hated the creepy sensation. She had noticed it often in recent months, but there was never any cause as far as she could tell.

Ignoring the goose bumps racing up her back, she continued walking until she arrived at Edgewater. Nothing was going to ruin her mood tonight. She had a new job, an interesting client, a potential boyfriend and a sister who might tie the knot. Plus, the sun was shining, and she had the rest of the evening free.

Grace strode up and down the shore, peering into the sand, hoping to spot a piece of beach glass or an odd stone, but the pickings were slim. Most of her collection lay on her workroom shelf at home—white, brown, or green fragments of glass bottles, an occasional piece of blue, yellow, or pink glass shining amidst their more common cousins. No red glass, however. Never red. She stared at the water whooshing around her ankles, hoping against hope for a scarlet gleam in the sand.

"Any luck?" The deep voice at her elbow startled her, and she nearly lost her balance. Grace turned to see a tall man in a blue shirt and bathing suit standing nearby.

"Oh, no," she said. "Not a good day for finding beach glass."

"It's a beautiful day, though, isn't it?" The stranger waved one large hand out to the deep blue water. A parasail floated over the lake. Grace took a closer look at her companion. Tall with a blond beard, he wore a Cleveland Cavaliers baseball cap and mirrored sunglasses, which along with the bright sunlight, made it difficult to see his features. Something about the beard and his nose was familiar, though. She gasped, recognition dawning. He looked like his picture on the dating site.

"You!"

"Yes, me. I couldn't wait until Friday."

"How'd you know where to find me?" Grace glanced around quickly to reassure herself they were not alone. Brains didn't look like a murderer but looks could be deceiving, and the fact he had tracked her on the beach was a bit alarming.

"It wasn't difficult. You said you come to this beach often. It's hot and sunny. Where else would you go after work on a day like this?"

He smiled at her, displaying an almost perfect row of white teeth. For some reason Grace was reminded of the big bad wolf.

"About Friday night. My new client scheduled a meeting. I was going to email you."

She turned and made her way to her favorite perch—an old rock jutting out toward the shore. He followed.

"All the better I didn't wait to meet you."

He held a hand out for her bucket and set it on the sand. Before Grace could guess at his intentions, Brains plucked her from the shore and seated her on the rock, his chest muscles barely moving at the effort. In a single swift movement, he sat next to her. Flustered, Grace busied herself retrieving her lip balm from her beach-bag and applying it liberally. She drew in a shaky breath. Her online man was gorgeous but a bit high-handed.

"So, am I what you had pictured?"

"Not exactly."

He chuckled. "Not handsome enough?"

"Oh, no, that's not…I meant…I mean, you weren't in a bathing suit in your photo."

Grace reached out a hand in protest and before she could withdraw it, he had captured it in his. She cleared her throat.

"What about me? Do I look like my photo?"

"Yes." He brought her hand to his lips and kissed

it, before letting her hand go. "You are everything I dreamed you would be."

Grace shivered. As a young woman, long before she had married Greg and had her romantic illusions dashed, she had dreamed of a man like this, one who would sweep her off her feet. So, why wasn't she more excited?

"I think, Gigi, you and I need to get to know one another better. Dinner tonight?"

"Where?"

"How about Dolce Promessa?"

"You remembered."

Dolce Promessa was the new Italian restaurant they had chatted about online. She had once written she was dying to go, but it was a little too expensive for her budget.

"Of course. I'll pick you up at seven. Where's your cell? I'll give you my number."

They exchanged numbers, and Brains jumped from his rocky perch in one easy movement. He looked up, grinning. Grace could see her startled reflection in his shades.

"I have to go. But I'll be looking forward to our date tonight. I have a feeling you and I are going to make a great pair."

He walked away, his long strides kicking up sand, before Grace realized she still didn't know his real name.

Her stomach rumbled, and Grace dug in her beach bag for the apple, rolling it in her shirt before taking a bite. Juice dribbled down her chin. As Grace bent her head slightly to wipe it, she spotted a flash of red hiding under a bit of sand. *Probably a piece of plastic.* But her curiosity was aroused so she scrambled down from her perch to check it out. She reached out a hand and let out an excited hop when she felt the smooth, hard surface. The perfect piece of glass!

She stood, rubbing her hands across the heart-shaped gem and bringing it to her face to take a closer look. How long it had been floating out at sea before making its way to the Great Lakes? Unbidden, David's face rose in her mind. Involuntarily, Grace glanced up and took a step back, flinching in surprise. He stared at her over the rock, like a phantom mirage, Oliver close beside him.

This must be her day for meeting handsome men on the beach. Had he been waiting for her? She had been with him a couple of short hours ago. What was he doing here?

He paused a few feet away, watching her as she recovered from her surprise. "Looks like you found quite a piece."

He took a couple of steps around the rock and toward her. "May I see?"

He smiled at her and held out his hand. "Sit, Oliver," he commanded. Oliver obeyed.

"I'm surprised to see you here." Grace handed him her discovery. She watched as he held it, peering closely. David did not immediately respond. As usual, Grace filled the silence. "Do you collect beach glass?"

He glanced at her and shook his head. "No, but I've always been interested in beach treasures."

David's eyes held hers. Grace could not look away. Did he mean she was a beach treasure?

"Who was that you were talking with?" He held out one hand to return the glass. She opened her palm, and he safely deposited it inside, all the while staring at her intently, waiting for an answer.

“Oh, a friend.”

“Your date from the other night?”

“Yes, how’d you know?”

“Call it intuition. What’s his name?”

“I…I don’t know.” Even to her own ears, the words sounded lame.

David studied her heated face thoughtfully. “Seems like an important bit of information.”

“Yes, well, we’re having dinner tonight, so he’ll tell me then.” Grace changed the subject. “So, what are you doing here?”

“My cottage is there.” He pointed up the shore a little way at a series of nice homes and a more private beach. “I come here often.”

“Oh.” Of course the cottage he had described earlier was one of the million dollar cottages at Edgewater. She should have guessed from his descriptions. But they had spent more time talking about its layout rather than its location. “What a strange coincidence. I spend a lot of time on this beach, too. I’m surprised I haven’t see you here before.”

He didn’t say anything, merely looked at her, expressionless. The pause stretched out between them. This time Grace was determined not to fill the silence. She looked toward the lake. The waters were a bit choppy with small white caps of foam. A few sailboats and a jet ski could be seen in the distance. It was mid-August and warm enough for swimmers. She and Greg had exchanged vows on the beach. A familiar gloom descended as she remembered the moment she learned Greg was cheating on her with a woman in his office.

Grace hadn't believed the gravelly voice on the phone. She should have. All the warning signs had been there.

Grace shook off her meandering thoughts and turned to David, hugging her arms across her chest, although she was not cold.

He was still looking at her, his expression serious. "Grace, I have to go away for longer than I expected, and I won't be able to meet you on Friday as planned."

"Okay." So she and Brains could have kept their Friday night plans.

"I'd still like you to check out the cottage while I am gone, though. My sister, Sophia, has agreed to give you the grand tour Friday evening. I asked her to contact you to make arrangements."

"Er…okay."

"Good, Sophia will be in touch."

He took a step closer, his inscrutable expression drawing her to him like a hummingbird to nectar. His strange eyes held hers and would not let go. "Don't you think you should at least know your date's name before you go out with him?"

David was right. Why hadn't Brains told her his name? Grace struggled to shake off the strange lethargy gripping her mind. She held up one hand, as if to ward off an unseen enemy. She shook her head, breaking eye contact. "I…I'm sorry. I think I'm going to be sick."

David grabbed her hands, otherwise she would have toppled backward into the sand. What was happening to her?

He led her back to her perch and like déjà vu, Grace experienced the familiar weightlessness of being lifted high into the air by a strong, handsome man. "Grace, sit for a minute. Go home and get some rest.

I'm sure your unnamed date will understand. Did you bring water?"

She nodded. "In my bag."

He rummaged around carefully until he found her water bottle and helped her drink it by holding it to her lips. What was wrong with her she needed to be fed like a baby?

David reached out a hand and smoothed her hair from her eyes. "Feel better?"

Amazingly, she did. His long, lean fingers seemed to make short work of her headache.

"I'm sorry, Grace."

She frowned. "For what?"

"For making you worry about your date tonight. It's not my place to question your decisions. If you want to keep your date, do it. But…be careful."

David brought his hands down and stepped back from the rock. Strangely, Grace wanted to follow him. Instead, she busied herself with her beach bag. She didn't trust herself to try and climb down from the rock on her own yet.

"Grace, are you okay?"

Dazed, Grace nodded.

"You have my private cell number. If you need anything, call me, okay? I know we haven't known each other long, but I hope you'll think of me as a…friend."

"David, you don't need to worry about me. I've been on my own for many years now."

"I know." He smiled, his austere features softening. His eyes glowed with an inner warmth, setting her heart racing. Slowly, as if worried he would frighten her, he reached one long arm out and gently ran a finger down her cheek. Grace could not look away. She shivered at the contact.

"It's…you remind me of someone…someone dear. I'm concerned about you all alone. Promise you'll call me if you're ever in trouble?"

"I'm sure I'll be fine."

David's cell phone went off, and he dropped his hand to reach into his pocket. His gaze never wavered from Grace's face as he answered. "Yes," he said. "I know. I'm on my way right now."

He pocketed the phone. Oliver barked and stood as if he had some unspoken communication with his master.

"Grace, I have to run. But, I'll call you when I return. I'll be anxious to find out what you think of the cottage."

He turned abruptly and strode up the beach toward the cottage he had pointed to earlier. Was it only moments ago? It felt like a lifetime. That's when she noticed the young girl waiting for him. The same one from the coffee shop. As he approached, she grabbed his hand and began talking seriously.

Grace stood frozen, her mind a blank. Who was the woman?

As she watched their earnest conversation, David glanced back. He shrugged, as if in apology, and waved. He turned his young companion toward his cottage and they walked briskly away, leaving Grace staring after them.

Chapter Seven
Dangerous Work

"Is that her?" Geneva asked. Like most trainers, she was nosy about his personal life.

David smiled. "Yes."

"Oh," she said with a sniff.

"She thinks you're my lover."

"Does she know about your…skills?"

"No, of course not."

Geneva stopped walking and placed her hands on her hips, indicating a lecture was forthcoming. She did not disappoint. "David, I swear. Sometimes I think all men are dense. You're interested in her, aren't you? She's a civilian. She's not one of us. She can't provide what you need. You'll grow bored and slip up. Or you'll end up controlling her. You know how it is. She'll freak and put us all in danger. And you know what you will be forced to do. Do you really want to tamper with her memories?"

David put both hands on Geneva's shoulders and pushed her forward. "When I want your advice, I'll ask for it."

They continued moving rapidly toward his cottage. It wasn't fair to take out his worry on Geneva. She was only trying to help. He sighed. As his trainer, she knew all about his fascination with Grace—had known for some time. Shielding his thoughts from her all the time wasn't possible.

David paused mid-step and tried again. "You're right. It's..." He shrugged helplessly. "I don't know what it is. There's just something about her. Her energy...it's...I can't quite put my finger on it. God, I'd almost think she's one of us if I didn't know any better."

"There is something odd about her, I'll give you that. I mean I haven't seen that particular shade of green light before. But we've checked the database. She's not in it."

He nodded and started to move forward, conversation over. But she gripped his arm again tightly, stopping him. "David, I know it's not my place. But we do need to talk about this. Her light...that color...she spells trouble. Don't ignore the warning. You don't want to hurt her. And for the record, I've shared this with your whole family and they agree with me—even Sophia. I know you're under a lot of pressure. But we think you need perspective. You aren't thinking rationally."

Taking a deep breath, Geneva ran a hand through her hair. He could tell the conversation was difficult for her. Close ties had knit their families together for decades. They may have guarded their privacy from outsiders, but there were few secrets among them. Being protective of each other was natural for them, and Geneva was stronger than most. She knew things the others didn't.

"I think it would be best to erase your memories of Grace. I could take care of it for you if you'd like."

David's entire body tensed. "Not without my cooperation." Steel edged his voice.

"Of course not. But you have to think about what you're doing. We need you right now. Your life is in grave danger, which means all of our lives are, too. Hell, that girl's also in danger. Did you even think of that?"

Fear gripped his guts with icy fingers. Geneva was right. Why had he not anticipated this? David's unknown enemy was ruthless. If David were being watched as Peter suspected, the enemy would pay attention to Grace—could even use her as a tool to wedge entrance into David's mind. He *should* keep his distance.

Of course, if it was as he and Peter theorized, no one could get through David's defenses. He was too strong. Besides it wasn't like he had linked with Grace. He'd merely stopped her from being used by Gallant. That was no reason for the enemy to target her, was it?

David sighed, rubbing a tired hand across the back of his neck. He wasn't certain he could stay away from Grace entirely, but he would try. "She's safe. But you're right. Grace could be in danger. I'll keep a close eye on her."

Geneva studied him with sympathetic eyes. She had been in his mind again. He would have to guard his thoughts more closely. She was far too strong for his liking.

"Well, good thing she doesn't know she has a psycho after her." Geneva grinned.

David laughed, which was undoubtedly her intention, and the mood lightened. He was grateful to be given a reprieve. Explaining his protective feelings toward Grace was difficult for even himself to understand, let alone Geneva.

They turned and made their way to Geneva's car. He preferred not to tunnel in from the cottage. Since it was nearby, they didn't need transportation to get to this particular destination, but they kept up appearances whenever they could. Besides, they had to drop off Oliver. David's type of travel could be dangerous for the body left behind. A safe location was required.

They drove the short distance to Geneva's apartment, parked the car in the garage, and saw Oliver safely stowed in her back bedroom. Soon they were in her office, door closed, shades drawn. The dark room helped them avoid distractions. David lay on the familiar blue chaise lounge and closed his eyes.

He felt the moment Geneva took control of the energy field in the room, creating the orange portal, which would carry him safely into their target's mind. It pulsed and beckoned to him like it always did. David watched the waves carefully, and when the sequence was exactly right, his mind reached out to snag the energy stream. There was a sensation, like entering a viscous fluid, and he felt the snap and crackle of the live stream zipping through his system. David slipped in undetected—a skill which had taken him many years to develop. He knew his cousins would be expecting him, but still he enjoyed the added edge he gained entering a target's mind on his own rather than being pulled in—an edge granting him a moment or two to study the scene and the players and to anticipate the action.

They were all there in front of him, Rolf, Kevin, and Jordan. He couldn't see his cousins in human shape. With the mind, there were no physical bodies, only energy waves. But since his brain still liked to manufacture a body, that's how he saw them. Rolf had placed himself in the center, like he always did, and it was he who recognized David's presence first.

Glad you could join us, cuz. Rolf didn't vocalize anything. He thought it. In this place, no words were necessary.

I wouldn't miss it.

We weren't sure you would be up to it, Kevin said. Kevin was the youngest and most easygoing one of the bunch. Whenever David looked at him, he remembered the little boy he had been, blond cowlicks sticking up every which way and a milk mustache. He was now twenty-three, having completed basic training after entering their hacker unit a year ago. David had a soft spot for Kevin and did not bother to hide it. He and Rolf kept a close eye on the younger cousin when they were all together. The kid showed promise, but was still so young.

David recognized the slight question in Kevin's energy, but he did nothing to dispel it. They should worry. It would put all of them on their guard. Even Rolf and Jordan were rookies in the field compared to him. Although they liked action, they did not fully understand the risk they took nor the deadly power of the energy fields they encountered. Not the way he did—especially now that the stakes were so much higher. Someone—some power hungry rogue hacker—wanted him dead. Since he had rejoined his unit, his job as the senior member of the unit was to keep them all safe. A familiar mantel of responsibility for the safety of the others settled around his shoulders like a lead cloak. Still, David was careful not to let a whisper disturb the energy field Geneva had created lest they be discovered before they even started.

Okay, we need to get a move on. He motioned toward the dark tunnel, which led to the memory center of the brain. *Let's go.*

They walked in formation, each of the three men taking an outside stance with David on the inside. Guarding him was critical, so he could track the information they were after, while concealing their presence. Their job was to help him navigate the energy fields and fight off the mind's natural defensive system, which operated similar to white blood cells attacking invading bacteria.

The portal dipped and swayed as they made their way toward the center of the target's mind. Dark blotches detached themselves from the sides of the cavern—an army of sorts—attacking his shield. He could feel the counter force of their energy waves, seeking to destroy the portal Geneva had created and put an end to his intrusion. Not only were the dark soldiers swift and lethal, they had been reinforced. For a moment, David registered surprise and nearly let the shield slip. Their presence had been anticipated.

Every mind had a natural defense—some stronger than others. This mind, the wife of Thung Yeh, the target they were sent to investigate, was incredibly strong. Although she had let them in initially, David had difficulty keeping their shield in place. He had to act quickly. If their target were to awaken while the shield was lifted, they would be discovered and the target's waking brain would take over and eject them—an event which could be painful, even deadly.

He wrenched his thoughts back to the work at hand. Control was essential. A tremendous amount of focus was required to create and hold on to the neutralizing waves disguising their presence.

They worked their way quickly past the cerebrum and the basil ganglia and into the hypothalamus, which was at the center of the brain and processed memories. While his men penetrated and destroyed the black energy shards, he slipped into the center, searching her thoughts until he was satisfied. He could find no memories leading to Thung Yeh's mission except for one—a short thought, as if someone had been interrupted during the elimination process. He examined the image carefully. The target was at what appeared to be a sales convention. She was looking for someone; spotted a man in the distance. From the back, he appeared to be tall and broad-shouldered. He wore a dark navy suit. A young, beautiful woman clung to his arm.

David felt a sudden disturbance, as though someone skipped a rock along the surface of a pond. A tell-tale buzz and hiss signaled the approaching mind blast. His heart raced, knowing they were in terrible danger. What he did within the next few seconds would determine their survival. David signaled the others urgently to prepare themselves. He scrambled to produce the energy force necessary to wipe the mind of their presence and eject them each back through their respective portals.

Power rippled through him. One of his cousins screamed in agony. *Kevin.* Deadly waves erupted. He hurtled sharply through blackness and into blinding light as the portal winked out of existence. The return was jarring, and he panted at the sharp pain in his head.

"Arrggh."

Someone was groaning loudly. It was a minute or two before he realized the voice he heard was his own.

"Hush now." Cool hands gripped his.

David squinted his eyes open cautiously. He was in the familiar office, Geneva beside him. Although it was still daylight, he knew from experience they had been under for some time.

"What is it?" Geneva demanded, suddenly alarmed. "Was it…?"

"Not Rolf." He ground out. Geneva and Rolf were an on-again, off-again romance. He privately believed Geneva would have been a much better match as a trainer for Rolf. But Peter had paired David with Geneva.

His eyelids were heavy but he managed to open them briefly to see her bending over him, her expression anxious. He was breathing too fast. He closed his eyes.

Geneva began the process of eliminating the dead energy waves, which was crucial to restore his normal levels. But David could sense her unanswered questions, so he spoke again as soon as he could manage.

"Kevin." He gasped, a thousand drill bits driving into his skull. He took another deep breath. "I believe he made it back but I don't think…. not in one piece." The pain caused him to speak more harshly than he intended. He sucked in air and spat out, "I can't be certain."

He tried to calm his breathing, but the mission had taken its toll. As the usual after effects gripped him, David summoned all his strength to force his worries to the back of his mind, enabling him to recover.

Geneva closed her eyes. Was it relief Rolf had survived? Or was it fear for Kevin, who would be in tremendous pain even if he had survived? Perhaps, it was a bit of both. Whenever a soldier died in a mind battle, his energy was absorbed into the target's mind. Lucky for Kevin, David had managed to penetrate the field and destroy the counter-waves. But a part of Kevin's life-force had been trapped in the field and absorbed before it could enter the portal. Whether Kevin could survive without the portion was questionable.

His breathing grew unsteady with his worry, and he sensed Geneva's silent reprimand. He must remain calm so that he could recover. They would not know immediately. Kevin would have to be watched carefully for the next forty-eight hours. No doubt their Cleveland headquarters would be in a state of pandemonium.

"It was a hit at least." Geneva didn't ask. As his trainer, she knew David was seldom unsuccessful in finding the required information and wiping the minds of his targets. He was incredibly good at what he did.

Twenty years ago when he had joined the unit, he had been eager for adventure. He'd had his share, too. Most of his comrades had long since left the force. They'd married, had children and kept themselves and their families away from the watchful eye of the government. He had chosen a different path. Right from the beginning, David had been stronger than the others—better equipped to navigate the dangerous energy fields. So he had kept on, erecting powerful defenses for important world figures or wiping the minds of those who wished to do them harm. Until the accident that claimed Meg's life.

He should have retired three years ago when he had the chance. He forced his breathing into a calming pattern, as he had been trained, and tried to stop his legs and arms from shaking. *Deep breath in the stomach, fill lungs, slowly breathe out.* The day his employer discovered a plot by the Chinese government was the day he should have turned in his badge. He hadn't though. At the time, he was the only one capable of preventing the Chinese from stealing information from one of the brightest scientists in the United States, Basil DuMar. DuMar had been working on artificial intelligence. Robots. He had achieved a breakthrough, which would have significant positive impact on the American economy when it was brought to development. Someone had to protect DuMar. All eyes turned to David. And like a big sap, he agreed to one last mission.

To be fair, the task had seemed simple in the early days. He had tracked those in on the plot, jumping from mind to mind as he discovered new details, leading to more targets. Stealthily entering their minds, he wiped all memories of their attack plans and replaced them with new memories—all without revealing his presence or alerting the public. If the Chinese were unaware of Basil DuMar's discoveries, they wouldn't know there was anything worth stealing. The method was cost effective and non-violent, which is why the government liked it so much. It had worked, too. Until the last mission.

David gripped the arms of the couch where he lay. Geneva immediately grasped his hands, the warm contact and flow of neutralizing waves soothing. *Deep breath in...breathe out.* Still, he couldn't stem the tide of memories.

They had encountered a deadly new energy source: someone or something capable of magnifying and inflicting potent levels and not afraid to kill, rather than wiping the minds of their victims. The hacker appeared to have powerful backing—perhaps another country—but no one could figure out which one. The only certainty was some other powerful hacker also wanted the secrets in Basil DuMar's brain, too. Only David and his team stood between them.

David opened his eyes to see Geneva watching him. How much did she know? Had she explored his more painful memories when he was unaware or his defenses were low?

He tried to stop the bitter memories from surfacing, but it was too late. They flooded his mind, washing in from the dark corners where he had buried them deep.

The mission had been like countless others he had endured. They had been in the mind of Chinese diplomat Thung Yeh, who was suspected of masterminding the plot to steal DuMar's technology. The procedure should have been a simple in and out. Instead, they were attacked by someone who hijacked and channeled David's own immense energy waves.

A low moaning sound seemed to echo the hollowness inside him. He had been lucky, that day. The stranger was not prepared for the power David generated, and his aim was slightly off. Acting on instinct, David used the seconds gained to escape through the portal, his mind intact. The rest of his team, along with Thung Yeh, were not so lucky. David's rapid exit left the stranger in control, and he left no one inside alive. Thung Yeh never woke from a coma.

Worst of all, David's former trainer, who had felt the strange tremors and knew he was in jeopardy, had ignored protocol and had attempted to rescue him—a mistake, which cost her life. His fault.

The moaning continued. Geneva hummed softly, passing gentle hands over his forehead. Her ministrations offered some relief to the debilitating headache that had him in its grip. The headaches had started shortly after the failed mission. David quit the case, even though his attacker had remained unknown and on the loose. Someone else took on the lead role. He chose to remain in seclusion and keep a low profile. David was content with the isolation until today, when he learned his life, and possibly the lives of those he loved, was in danger. Now, the tables had taken a sudden turn.

If Peter's suspicions were correct, the stranger was tracking him—had found a trail leading directly into David's brain. David had built an incredibly strong mind defense over the years, which was necessary in his line of work. But Peter feared David had left a small energy shard behind in Thung Yeh's mind, which the stranger had found and was using against him. The shard was large enough to create a temporary portal, but whoever had entered was not strong enough to get past David's natural defenses.

He should have figured this out long ago. But he had been distracted by the woman on the beach. Which explained why the headaches had only grown worse and had not receded once he was away from the deadly energy waves. The stranger would not stop, which meant David would have to come out of seclusion to find, track, and erase his enemy before his enemy figured out how to penetrate his barriers and put an end to David's existence and the rest of his team. He would not allow another member of his crew to be killed on his watch.

"Hush, now." Geneva continued to croon softly.

David realized the moans issued from his own mouth. He struggled to stem the flow of anxious thoughts.

Their expedition today had targeted Thung Yeh's wife, Li Su Yeh, who was staying in Cleveland, while attending a scientific convention hosted by the local university. Her mind had contained knowledge of Thung Yeh's plot to steal DuMar's secrets. Thoughts that would have led straight to his enemy. *Damn.*

The rogue hacker had beat them to it. He had strengthened Li Su's mind and wiped it clean of the information David and his men were after and set a trap that triggered her mind to awaken prematurely. David was uncertain how useful the one shortened memory that remained would prove.

He grimaced, imagining Kevin's injuries, possibly fatal. They should have left at the first sign of disturbance. They were losing people quickly. Who would be next? The question hung in his mind, a cold reminder of his failure once again to protect those he loved.

"David, don't torment, yourself." Geneva whispered above him. "Meg wouldn't want that."

So she did know. He had feared as much. He fought carefully to contain his sudden emotion, which would only slow his recovery.

Geneva passed her hands over his forehead, and a deep lethargy swamped his senses. Her job was to neutralize and calm his mind force while he was incapacitated. Left unattended, his energy waves would continue to destabilize, until eventually, he reached the point of a mental breakdown. David had witnessed a similar tragedy in a former colleague.

Geneva continued to massage his temples, shaking off the discordant waves. To distract and calm his brain, David made a mental grab for a soothing image. *Grace.* What was it about her? When he had seen her talking to another man on the beach, for a moment he had been unable to control odd feelings of rage. Thankfully, he had been too far away to interfere or he might have broken a few government rules.

Even after the stranger departed, and David had joined Grace on the beach, he struggled to suppress the confusing thrum of anger in his system. Was that why he had pushed her so hard? He had not meant to manipulate her. It had been instinctive, the slight mental push. His protective instincts taking over. *Strange though.* Grace had resisted the attempt. Or had he imagined that? But her nausea afterward could not be imagined.

He yearned to see her again…to reassure himself she was safe, of course. But that would have to wait until he was well rested. While Geneva finished her ministrations, David finally drifted into a deep and healing sleep.

Chapter Eight
Mad Dreams

David Jenkins was attracted to her. She couldn't have mistaken the signs, could she? He had told her to call him if she needed anything. And he'd caressed her forehead like he couldn't resist touching her.

And then he disappeared with another woman.

Grace's skin itched…the heat. She swatted at a non-existent mosquito. Her instincts shouted at her. What was she missing? She could still feel the touch of his hand on her face. And those green eyes…

And then there was Brains. Strong, confident and good-looking. The perfect romantic image of her inner fantasies brought to life. So why wasn't she more excited about Brains?

She dug for her cell phone, which was vibrating. She had silenced it earlier and stuffed it in her bag so as not to interrupt her meeting with David. Grace had seven new texts. She scrolled through them quickly. There was one from Brains, but most were from Claire.

6:02 p.m. I've got news. Call me.

6:03 p.m. Call me, okay? I need to talk to you.

6:04 p.m. Why aren't you texting back? It's important.

6:05 p.m. WHERE ARE YOU!!

6:06 p.m. Ok. Now I am worried about you. I need to talk to you. I'm going crazy.

6:07 p.m. You must not have your phone on. Call

me…please.

It was finally happening. Claire had cold feet and was calling off the wedding. Grace found her sister's name in her favorites. While she waited for her to answer, she opened the final text from Brains. Grace had texted Brains on her way home to tell him she didn't feel well and wasn't going to make dinner. They would have to shoot for Saturday.

6:34 p.m. So your new employer is working you that hard already? Unfortunately, I have a business event Saturday. Can we try for Sunday, noonish?

"Grace! Where have you been?" Claire bypassed the usual greeting.

Grace sat and flipped off her sandals. "What's going on?"

"Oh, I don't know. Stupid stuff. Tom doesn't understand why our credit card bill was so high this month. He thinks I'm a big spender, and I need to learn how to economize. He doesn't realize how much it costs to put on a wedding in San Francisco. I mean, Mom's helping but there're so many things we're paying for ourselves. He's driving me crazy. I don't need this nitpicking right now."

"Claire, it's okay. Calm down. That's normal stuff. It's natural for Tom to be worried about money. He's a successful stockbroker. He invests other people's money. I think it would be surprising if he wasn't looking at your expenses." Grace was careful to keep her tone reasonable.

"You don't think he's trying to control me? I mean, I don't want to make the same mistake Mom did with Burt."

Control was a big issue for both Claire and Grace.

Burt had been their stepdad for a short, but important, part of their childhood, when they lived in the small apartment in Parma. Their real dad had been hit by a drunk-driver when they were still toddlers. Burt had tried to be a good dad in his way. He would take them sled riding or to the movies. One time he built a circus for Grace with a real trapeze and monkeys with movable arms. She still had pieces of it somewhere. He was, however, extremely fastidious, always pushing the women in the family to keep a clean house. Since their mother would never win any awards for her housekeeping, Grace could recall many heated arguments ending with Burt leaving the house, slamming the door behind him. Usually he came back the next day, shamefaced and willing to try again. Until one day, he didn't. When they finally saw him again, he was living in a rented apartment downtown.

"I don't think Tom is anything like Burt. Mom was as bad as Burt was, don't you remember? Neither one was willing to compromise. That was part of their problem."

Claire took a deep breath. Before she could argue, Grace hurriedly tried a different tack. "Tom loves you. Didn't you tell me he agreed to go to Greece because that's a place you always wanted to see, even though he had been there before? And didn't he agree to a wedding on the beach even though he wanted an inside wedding?"

"Yes." Claire's voice wobbled.

"And remember that time you had way too much to drink and barfed all over his expensive car? You told me he never got upset at all with you."

"Yeah, I remember." Claire's voice had softened.

"And how about that time he paid your rent when you were behind on your bills?"

"That was Reed," Claire said dryly.

"Oh, well, the point is still the same. Tom wouldn't do all those things for you unless he truly loved you. That's what true love's all about."

"I guess." Claire sounded almost back to normal. Grace crossed her fingers. She checked her watch. Eight o'clock…five o'clock in San Francisco.

"Tell you what. I think you should pour yourself a nice glass of wine, run yourself a hot bath, light some candles and chill. You and Tom are stressed because your wedding is around the corner. You need to spend some quality time together where you are not thinking wedding. I'm sure you'll feel better tomorrow."

"Yeah, you're right. A bath sounds good right now." There was a pause. "I need to ask you something and don't be mad. But I wanna know. When you and Greg were getting married—did you have any doubts about him? I mean he was sleeping with another woman right under your nose. Didn't you have any inkling?"

Leave it to her sister to point out her failings. But did she? It was a question she often asked herself. Was she that blind? Or was Greg an incredible actor.

The truth was she had believed Greg was who he had portrayed himself to be. Or maybe she couldn't bring herself to believe anything different, even though Claire had warned her. Regardless, there was no one more surprised than Grace when she found out Greg was with another woman. But she couldn't tell her sister or else Claire would never marry Tom. And Tom was a good guy, wasn't he?

"When its true love, there's a special vibe." The words came from some deep and wise part of herself, as she recalled the caress from David Jenkins. "I never felt that vibe with Greg. I should have known something was wrong."

"Really? Do you think Tom and I have that vibe?"

Grace weighed Tom's steady income with Claire's flightiness. "Yes, I do."

"Yeah, I think so, too. Okay. Thanks sis. I feel better."

"Do me a favor. Call Tom and talk to him, okay? Kiss and make up. Tell him you love him."

"Okay. I will. Thanks for the pep talk. See you in a few weeks! Love you."

The shower...Yikes. This wedding was around the corner. She had to make sure Claire was at the altar. "I wouldn't miss it. Love you too, Claire. Bye."

Grace ended the phone call and breathed a giant sigh of relief. Where had all the talk of vibes come from? She visualized herself on the beach with David Jenkins. She should be picturing Brains, but the image of David as she had last seen him haunted her. What was it about her new client? She and Greg had not kissed until their fifth date, and it hadn't set off any fireworks. David Jenkins had simply caressed her cheek, and she shivered with excitement and anticipation. The mental image was only ruined by the girl he held hands with afterward. Grace winced. The vibes she felt were all on her side.

Thinking about David made her remember the design proposal due Friday. She needed to get busy if she were to have something to discuss with his sister. She put on her coziest pajamas, made herself a cup of coffee with plenty of cream and sugar and started her laptop. She grabbed her phone to reply to Brains.

8:23 p.m. Sunday works. C U then ☺

Grace hit send on her message with a firm finger and then sat at her kitchen table, spreading out her notes and sketchpad. Three hours later, she stretched tiredly and decided it was time for bed. She had drafted a basic design. She would rest her brain tonight and finesse the design tomorrow.

Within minutes of her head hitting the pillow, Grace was dreaming. She knew she was dreaming, but it was so real. She was back on the beach looking for glass. She had spied a speck of color and was reaching to grab it when someone else was there before her. There was a flash of white skin and she gazed into a pair of penetrating blue eyes. The stranger stared at her intently, willing her to look him in the eyes. The man before her had long black hair and a sinister beauty. But within seconds, fear pulsed through her body. The man was controlling her, generating a powerful pull. Grace resisted.

Her heart beat hard in her chest as she recognized the danger. Instinctively, she made the sign of the cross, praying frantically. "Our Father who art in heaven, hallowed be thy name."

The stranger continued to stare at her closely, pulling her in slowly with his eyes, taking her over. "Thy kingdom come, thy will be done, on earth as it is in heaven."

Although he did not touch her in the nightmare, invisible arms held her still, while he penetrated her mind. He would not yield. She continued to make the sign of the cross, waging an intense mental battle as they stared one another down. Grace would not give in without a fight.

"Give us this day, our daily bread and forgive us our trespasses. As we forgive those who trespass against us. And lead us not into temptation but deliver us from evil."

Suddenly, the stranger broke eye contact, and Grace awoke gasping for air and breathing rapidly. She was in her bedroom. It was still dark. She checked the clock…4:00 a.m. Grace reached over and turned on the light. She peered around the room, searching each corner thoroughly for an intruder. When she was sure no one was there, she rose and made her way to the bathroom. She gazed at her reflection in the bathroom mirror. Her eyes looked lost and dark, the skin around them swollen and puffy. Her head hurt.

Feeling threatened, Grace imagined someone was in the room with her. She kept checking over her shoulder to be certain. Was an invisible spirit trying to possess her? She would not be going back to sleep any time soon. Grace doubted she would ever be able to sleep again. If she did, whatever it was would try again, and this time, maybe it would succeed.

And she would never wake up.

Chapter Nine
The Key

For an untapped talent, Grace Woznisky's mind had been stronger than he anticipated. So strong in fact, she had nearly ejected him. Excitement coursed through his body, giving him an erection. He would claim her for his own. The only thing standing in his way was Jenkins.

He gritted his teeth. Jenkins was a dead man. He almost had the key now. It was nearly in his grasp. A few more twists and turns and he would be in, he was sure. Once Jenkins was out of the picture, there would be nothing to stop him from having Grace Woznisky—or anyone else he wanted for that matter. As far as he knew, he was the most powerful mind hacker alive outside of Jenkins. And the beautiful part was the government was completely unaware of him. He was outside their catalog so to speak—a branch of the genetic tree they did not know existed.

He tossed a hand through his thick, blond hair. Grace hadn't been able to keep him out—few people could—but she did fight him, which had caught him off-guard, yet was strangely exciting. He had not been able to stay under for long from this distance. Only long enough for him to satisfy his curiosity and assess the situation. David Jenkins had not established a link. Grace Woznisky was up for grabs. All he had to do was win her trust. And eliminate the competition.

He sat up suddenly, brushing Kaitlyn away. What he needed was the key—one small bit of new information that would help him break down the final barrier in Jenkin's mind. He should have found it by now.

"What did you find?" As twins, they shared a special mental bond.

"He hasn't linked with her," he said, his tone short. She knew well not to disturb him while he was thinking. He got up, walked to the kitchen and grabbed a glass from the cupboard. *Damn.* Every mind had a way in—some sacred memory that it guarded. Even a mind as strong as Jenkins' mind had a weakness. He gritted his teeth. It could not elude him forever. He would find it.

He poured himself a ginger ale, walked back to the couch and sat, stretching out his long legs on the nearby coffee table and neatly missing his cell phone. He yawned and stretched. It was not easy working during the day and flying across the country to track his targets. No one must suspect him, which meant that except for his sister, Kaitlyn, he worked alone and usually at night. The energy waves in a sleeping mind were slower and shorter, making them easier to manipulate.

He and Kaitlyn had been working this way for as long as he could remember. They knew exactly how to share energy. That's what made them such a brilliant team.

No one had ever understood this—especially his mother. It was this ability that had kept them from eviction time and again from the slum house where they had lived the first eight years of his life. The landlord would show up, eviction papers in hand, and feel compelled to give them more time, scratching his head all the while.

He was only sorry he did not understand more before the accident. He could have done so much more for her if he had. He had not meant to harm his mother that fateful day. If he had realized how powerful they were at such a young age, he would never have pushed her. Instead, he would have protected her. A familiar anguish and rage took root, like a dead tree, inside him. He blamed them all. His father for leaving them alone without knowledge of their abilities. The social worker who supervised their case for placing them with Mr. Whitley. And his poor, innocent mother for being too ignorant to understand.

Kaitlyn had taken the worst of it from the dirty, old man. He had been far too busy trying to fit in with the kids in school to take note of her silence. He supposed he had wanted to be like them—had wanted them to like him. That excuse seemed paltry now, but he was honest in admitting the truth—at least in the dark recesses of his mind in which no one but Kaitlyn traversed. He knew now that he could never be one of them. He no longer cared to try. He was far too powerful. He had spent a lifetime showing the world how powerful he was, and he'd be damned if he would let one lone hacker, no matter how resistant, stand in his way.

He set his drink down, a slight tremor in his hand, and picked up his cell. Grace Woznisky would be the mother of his future children. Though he would need to tread carefully until he killed Jenkins.

Chapter Ten
A Real Date

David's sister was a surprise. She was dark, like David, but there the resemblance ended. Where he was controlled and deliberate, she was quick to laugh, answering the door with a welcoming warmth and smile.

"C'mon in. I'll show you around." Grace clutched her tape measure and notebook and looked around for Oliver, but he was nowhere to be seen. She could only assume he was with David on his travels. Sophia led Grace into the front room where a bank of windows faced the lake.

"Wow! What a view." The evening sun dazzled, reflecting off the water like a thousand candles.

"It's fantastic, isn't it? I've always loved it. It's been in our family for ages. Can I offer you something to drink…water or an ice tea perhaps?"

"Oh, no. I'm good."

"Well, let me show you around."

Sophia led her into an open, farmhouse kitchen with a large, rustic table, which took center stage. A glittering lantern style ceiling lamp shone brightly above. Sophia noticed her eyeing it curiously.

"That light has quite a legend behind it. As the story goes, our great, great grandfather brought it home from Ireland in honor of his bride, who had taken a liking to it."

"I can see why. It's lovely." Grace marveled at how the light cast a golden shadow on the centerpiece below, adding to the rustic charm of the table.

"Yeah, well, the Jenkins men are known to do anything to please their women. The whole cottage was purchased for our great, great grandmother. She was homesick for Ireland, so he built it for her. Of course, the original cottage was much smaller than it is today. Each generation has expanded on the structure. By the time my father inherited it, the cottage was a bit chopped up and none of us used it much. David bought my share and hired an architect, who did a wonderful job of opening up the space, don't you think?"

Grace nodded, marveling at the design, which blended the old with the new effortlessly. "Do you work full-time for David or are you just on call, so to speak," she asked, as she busied herself taking measurements.

"You mean David didn't tell you?"

"Tell me what?"

"We…we have a sort of family business—a security business. The whole family is part of it. Even my husband, Brian."

"Oh, well, I haven't really known David long. We met a few days ago."

"Well, David speaks highly of you. He told me you're a really talented artist."

"He did?" Grace couldn't hide her surprise.

"He did. I know David isn't good at giving compliments. But he would never hire you to work for him, especially on his precious cottage, unless he thought you were top-notch."

Grace's pride swelled. "Thank you. I enjoy what I do."

Sophia's cell phone rang, and she picked it up and looked at it. She grinned. "Speak of the devil. Hi, David. Everything okay?"

Grace thought she sounded anxious.

"Are you sure? Yes, okay. She's here now." Pause. "No you're not interrupting. We only started. Uh-huh she's good just like you said. No, I wouldn't say that. No, she seems fine. Okay. Here she is."

Sophia held the phone out to Grace. "Brothers." She shook her head in mock despair. "He wants to talk to you."

Grace took the phone, while Sophia busied herself with some sort of panel on the wall. Soft jazz filled the room.

"Hi."

"Everything going well? Sophia says you're feeling okay?"

David's voice sounded rough, conjuring memories of the last time she had seen him and his concern for her. Grace wondered what he was wearing and where he was sitting. Was he in a power suit and tie in some high rise building? Or maybe since it was Friday evening he was back at his hotel. She could picture him stretched across a king size bed, his tie loosened, shoes kicked off and five o'clock shadow on his chin. She dragged her thoughts back to the conversation with some effort. "Yes, I'm much better. When will you be back in town?"

"Why? Are you eager to see me?"

His bluntness caught her off guard. She let out a nervous laugh. Was she eager to see him? She thought she was. David Jenkins was growing on her. Her lips turned up in an involuntary smile. “Well, I’m anxious to discuss some ideas for the cottage with you.”

“Good.” His deep voice sent a shiver up her spine. “I’ll be back tomorrow night. I’ll pick you up at six. We can grab a bite to eat.”

“Er…okay? Do you normally take those you hire to dinner?” She couldn’t stop herself from asking and waited with some anxiety for his answer. He chuckled, a sound she was fast becoming familiar with.

“Only when I want to. Dress nice. We’re going to Club 32.”

She opened her mouth to argue but shut it. *Club 32? The private millionaire’s club?* He clearly moved in a different social circle. Was this a date? She was being asked on a date by the playboy David Jenkins.

“Grace?”

“Yes?”

“So there’s no doubt in your mind, this is real a date I am asking you on. I plan to pick up where we left off on the beach.”

It was as if he plucked that thought right out of her head. She was speechless for a moment. He was chuckling again.

“Night, Grace.”

“Good night,” she said, a bit breathlessly.

*****

David ended the call and checked the time. 6:00 p.m. Grace would be heading home shortly and so would he. He had awakened from a deep sleep barely thirty minutes earlier. Geneva had given him his privacy as she usually did. She would be somewhere close, though, in case he needed her.

He rubbed his temples wearily—the persistent headache was worse than normal. He really should keep his distance. But the longer he stayed away from her, the more he found himself anticipating their next encounter. He longed to sit face-to-face and reassure himself she was not the target of the rogue hacker.

His cell phone buzzed, alerting him to a new call. *Peter.* "Any news on Kevin?"

"He's stable. We'll know more in the next few days. Are you recovered?"

"Yes."

"Headache?"

"Yep."

"Good. That means the hacker still can't get in. We have new info, and it's not good."

"Is it ever?"

"We don't believe the attack originated from outside the US. We think this might be an inside job."

"A traitor?"

"Negative. Although the possibility exists, we don't think it's someone on our team. But it is someone who knows about us and has a lot of influence and power. "

"Any leads?"

"Not yet. We're working on it. We suspect it's someone who's heavily invested in the tech industry. Someone you know—maybe a business partner or acquaintance. We think they have an idea of what you're doing—perhaps they know where you live or where you travel. They may even be a friend of your family."

David's stomach rolled. It would be unbearable if one of his family members were in on the plot. He thought of his cousin Percy who lived in Tennessee. David hadn't seen Percy in a while, but he had heard talk about his temper and lack of control—two traits that could be deadly in the field. He wasn't fooled at Peter's tone either. Peter was much more worried than he was pretending to be. "Maybe they have infiltrated one of our people?"

"Not likely." Peter denied. "They've all been reinforced like you—but it is always a possibility, yes. We need to run some tests tonight. Be prepared."

"Certainly."

"And David. This goes without saying but be very careful what you reveal to anyone not involved in the project. As long as they don't know your secrets, your close friends would be unlikely to be in any danger. But I suspect our rogue mind hacker will be ruthless in extracting information from an unguarded mind."

He didn't need to read minds to know what Peter was thinking. He didn't have close friends outside his family. Peter was worried that Grace might be in danger. A cold chill ran up his spine. The hacker must be found and stopped as soon as possible.

Chapter Eleven
A Warning

Grace awoke to a familiar sound. “Curtain call, curtain call.” Harvey squawked.

She rolled over and peered sleepily at the alarm clock—8:00 a.m. She stretched her legs and lay there for a moment, her mind alert and refreshed. She was having dinner with David Jenkins tonight. A surge of adrenaline had Grace flinging off the covers.

She was halfway to the bathroom before she remembered she had forgotten to feed Harvey. No wonder he was squawking. Grace refilled his food and water dish and was closing the cage door when the doorbell rang. She peered through the peephole. A woman was holding a bunch of flowers. Grace unlocked the door and opened it.

“Are you Grace Woznisky?” The women held an extremely large and fancy bouquet.

“Yeah, that’s me.”

“These are for you. Aren’t you a lucky girl. What’s the occasion?”

The florist handed her the arrangement and held out a pad for Grace to scratch her name electronically. She did so, blushing. “I’m…I’m not sure.”

“Well, I’d say you have an admirer.” The woman gave her a friendly smile. Grace smiled back, handed the lady her pad, and took the flowers inside. She stuck her nose in the bouquet, a mix of yellow Gerber daisies, purple roses, white baby's breath and other greenery, and breathed deeply. Their light, floral scent was pleasing. Setting them on the kitchen counter, she quickly found the card and read: *Beautiful flowers for a beautiful lady. Looking forward to dinner. I'll pick you up at 6. David.*

A bubble of happiness broke free inside her, threatening to overflow into tears. It had been a long time since a man had sent flowers. Purple roses were one of her favorites, too. She remembered from a class she once took they meant the sender was enchanted with the receiver. Greg hadn't been much for flowers—he usually went for nighties.

She rummaged around in her cupboards until she found a vase and cut the stems at an angle under warm water as she had been taught. She arranged them artistically and placed the vase in the center of the table. On impulse, she pulled out her phone, snapped a photo and sent it to Claire.

*****

Across town, David cracked his eyes open, groaned and stretched. He had not slept well. He had spent most of the night battling Peter's "tests." His thoughts turned to Grace. Had she fared better?

An image of Grace as David had last seen her at Edgewater popped into his head, followed quickly by the mystery man, who had scurried off at David's arrival. He was going to have to take stronger measures, but he refused to draw on his talent for that. He did have some skills in his arsenal that had nothing to do with mind hacking. He hoped they did the trick.

Oliver was by the door, patiently waiting for his

daily walk. David found the dog's leash, put on his jacket, and headed out. They had gotten about half way around the block when his cell buzzed. He checked the number and answered. "Awfully early to be calling on a Saturday."

"The tests were all negative." Peter reassured, his voice calm. "Your mind is still intact from what we can tell."

"Don't sound so surprised."

"I'm not. Rest this weekend. We need you for another mission on Monday, and this is a biggie. You'll be investigating several targets, all heads of large corporations. This is a scouting mission, but we're sending in a full crew because if one of these turns out to be our man, you could be in for the battle of a lifetime. Which reminds me, Kevin sends his regards."

David closed his eyes. Those simple words cut into a giant chunk of metal remorse around his heart. "Thank God."

"He suffered some slight memory loss but otherwise, seems to be intact. Of course, it's going to be a little time before we determine whether he's fit to go under again."

"Understood."

"Well, I won't keep you." Peter hesitated.

"What now?"

"Yes, well, some of your teammates are questioning your…competence."

"They think I can't perform."

"I wouldn't exactly say that. They know you still have talent. They don't think you're at the top of your game. They think you should be benched. There's talk of bringing in your southern cousins."

"You aren't serious?" David was angry, but as always, kept it well-leashed.

"I told them you're still the most senior and powerful hacker we have on the force, but all these numbskulls can see are your recent disasters. They think you should have remained in seclusion. I didn't want to tell you this because I think you have enough to worry about. But you need to know, because if anyone else gets hurt on your watch, there may not be much I can do. Adam has been on me to make changes."

Adam Ortiz was senior officer in charge of all the Special Forces. He'd never been a big fan of the CMU. He preferred more traditional methods. "So why haven't you brought in Percy to relieve me?"

"David, you know damn well why. Percy Withers wouldn't last two damn seconds. That branch of the family tree has never been strong. Your team needs you, even though they are too thick-brained to know it. Without you, we don't stand a chance."

David could picture Peter running his hands through his iron gray hair, his forehead wrinkled with concern.

"Look, I only told you because you need to know. But you can rest assured as long as I'm in charge, it's not happening. Be ready Monday. We need you at full strength and at the helm."

"I'll be there."

Chapter Twelve
Date Night

"Did you miss me?" He was sitting across from Grace at Club 32 in downtown Cleveland, cleanly shaven, not a hair out of place and looking hot. She knew she appeared outwardly calm, but her thoughts were a jumble. He'd collected her exactly at 6:00 p.m. as promised and whisked her to their destination. They had ordered drinks—him a water and she a glass of wine. Grace peered at David over her menu and caught him studying her, his mouth quirked in a small smile.

A familiar blush took root, her cheeks warm. David's grin widened. He reached out and tucked a stray bit of her hair behind her ear. The romantic gesture made Grace blush some more. She found it hard to think and gave herself a mental scolding. *Grow up Grace. You're not sixteen.* She reached for her wineglass and forced herself to take a tiny sip and set it down carefully. How to answer? If Grace said she missed him, she would seem too eager. If she said she didn't miss him, then David would think she didn't like him, and perhaps he would be turned off.

He laughed suddenly. "Cat got your tongue?"

Grace settled for honesty but with a wry touch. "Of course I missed you—all of a few days." That seemed to satisfy him. He smiled again and raised his menu. How had she ever believed him stern?

"Their pasta is good and so is their walleye."

"So what were you doing on your trip?"

"The usual. I'm working with a team of researchers on a project."

"Sophia said you have a family business?"

"That's true."

God, getting him to talk about himself was like prying open a treasure chest—she knew something good was inside if she could only break the lock. She tried again. "Are you all economists?"

He set his menu aside, giving her his full attention. The impact of his stare traveled straight to her nether regions. "No, some of us in the family have more exciting jobs. How's the design coming along?"

She gave up, doomed to date a mystery man. "Great. I drew up a rough draft last night and brought a copy with me for your review. I shared my ideas with Sophia yesterday, and she thought you'd like them. I think you'll be pleased."

"What did you think of the cottage?"

"David, it's beautiful. The original structure and architecture are fantastic. And all the improvements you made are perfect. It's a thrill to be allowed to showcase my art in the place."

"Great, because if I like your work, I have some other projects in mind. If you're up for it, that is?"

Grace took a sip of her wine to give herself time to think. "Sure," she heard herself say, while another part of her mind was screaming at her to stop and reconsider. *Take the money and run far, far away to a distant land. And don't look back.* His eyes drew her, and she struggled to break the connection.

"Good," he said with some satisfaction. He looked

like he was about to say more, but the waiter arrived to take their order. She decided to try the chicken and risotto, and he went with the walleye. The waiter departed, leaving them in silence, David's gaze once again dissecting her. She threaded a hand through her hair absently and searched her brain for something to say.

"How's Oliver?"

"He's safe at home enjoying a dog biscuit. He would like you to come visit him after dinner. He's at the cottage."

Was David inviting her to go home with him? Would she accept? "I'd like that."

He nodded in acknowledgement, and she could tell her answer pleased him because he smiled at her with genuine warmth. Getting a smile from David Jenkins was fast becoming necessary to her peace of mind—she wasn't sure why that was so.

He snagged the wine bottle and refilled her empty glass. "How's your sister?"

"Still engaged." She grinned. "At least when I talked to her Thursday. She and Tom had gotten into a spat, but I reminded her of some of his better qualities, which seemed to do the trick. Barely a few months away now. I'm looking forward to the wedding—and not only to see her happily married. This will be the first real vacation I've had in three years."

"Workaholic." He raised his glass in toast.

"My boss is a slave driver." She tapped her wine glass against his water glass before taking a swallow. "How often do you travel?"

"It depends. When I'm working on an assignment, like now, it can be frequently. Other times, maybe once every few months."

"Do you enjoy what you do?"

"Usually. But lately, not as much. I'm thinking of retiring."

"You're too young to retire. What would you do with yourself?"

"I can think of a lot of things. Maybe settle down and start a family."

Not for the first time, she wondered why such an attractive and intelligent man had never married. *Closet drug addict? Gambler?*

David quirked one eyebrow at her. "What about you?"

"I'd like to be more settled."

Grace thought of Brains as she had last seen him on the beach. Across from her, David's face took on a strange, almost hard expression. Although she'd known him for less than a week, she was beginning to recognize the look. There was something he wasn't telling her. All her fears and doubts rose inside her. This situation was not what it seemed. They were advancing into unexpected territory.

"Did you ever learn the identity of your beach admirer?" He poured the last of the wine into her glass.

"No, not yet. Who was that girl you were with on the beach? She was also with you in *Coffersations*."

"Her name is Geneva. She's…my business partner."

"Oh, I see."

"What do you see?"

David was smiling at her again. What was so damn amusing? "She works with you? Right?"

"That's right." He was still smiling.

"What's with the smirk?"

"You're jealous."

"What…how…I'm not jealous. I barely know you."

David reached out, and before Grace could guess his intentions, grabbed her hand. She tugged, but he would not let go. "Whatever you say. Let's go."

David paid their bill, and they left the restaurant, his hand firmly grasping hers to lead her to his convertible. They spent some of the ride home in companionable silence as she took in the stars. She spotted the summer triangle high in the night sky, as a breeze off Lake Erie cooled her flushed cheeks. By the time she remembered his cottage, they were already there. He parked the car, took the key from the ignition, and turned to face her. "I neglected to tell you how beautiful you look tonight."

"Flatterer. You don't look so bad yourself." He smiled, or at least she thought he did. It was dark in the car, so it was hard to tell. He removed his seat belt and leaned across the seat and undid hers as well. But he made no move to get out of the car.

"Grace, I need to tell you something." He reached over and grasped her hand. He paused, deliberating. She waited patiently for him to continue. "I have to go away again on Monday and won't be back until Wednesday or Thursday."

"Okay." Privately she wondered if the young girl would be traveling with him.

"I'm telling you because I don't want you to be concerned when you don't hear from me."

"Oh, I don't expect you to have to call me." Grace reassured him. "Because we went out on one date doesn't mean you owe me anything…although I do appreciate you telling me, of course."

"I would like to see you again…tomorrow."

She grimaced. "I have plans for tomorrow. I'm sorry."

"Change them."

"David, I'm sorry. It's something I have to do. I can't."

Grace knew the moment he planned to kiss her. He bent forward, his breath warm on her face and the rich scent of his aftershave enveloping her. David wanted her. There was no mistaking it now. All the cells in her body seemed to want him, too, and she closed her eyes and parted her lips in expectation of a kiss that never came. When she opened her eyes, he was staring at her, like the cat who got the canary, but all he said was, "Change them please. For me."

If she changed them would he kiss her? There was only one way to find out. Her date with Brains was more curiosity than anything at this point. She could reschedule, right? If they had waited this long, there was no reason they couldn't wait a little longer.

"All right. I'll change them."

He let out a slow breath, as if he had been holding it in, anticipating her refusal. But instead of kissing her, he opened his car door and said, "Great. Let's go say hi to Oliver."

Grace didn't know whether to be relieved or frustrated.

Oliver was waiting for them, tail wagging, as soon as David opened the front door. Grace eyed the large dog as he went from David to Grace and back again in excitement. Eventually, he settled with a rawhide David dug out from a cupboard. As David rummaged in the kitchen, Grace took the opportunity to look around again. She couldn't help but be impressed with the cottage. It was not overly elaborate, but quaint and well-constructed. Rustic wood floors covered by a deep, plush cream piled rug gleamed. A slip-covered, green sofa faced the giant pane of glass overlooking the lake. She could spend hours staring out the window. It was a beautiful view even in the dark with moonlight shining off the water.

David brought her a cup of coffee with plenty of cream and sugar as she liked it. She was impressed he remembered and told him so.

"I remember everything about you."

She was flattered, although she guessed he was not being entirely truthful. "Oh, yeah? What's my bird's name?"

"Harvey," he said instantly.

"Pretty impressive. Let me see." She tried to think of the most obscure thing she might have told him. "What's my favorite dessert?"

"German Chocolate Cake. You won't win. I told you I remember everything."

She laughed. "I wouldn't be so sure. How about Claire's fiancé?"

"Tom." He grinned. "Give up?"

"When's the wedding?" He couldn't possibly know everything there was to know about her.

He waggled his eyebrows. "October 10."

He did remember everything. She tried again. "What's my mother's name?"

"Elaine."

She frowned. "But I didn't tell you my mother's

name. How did you know that?"

He tried to brush it off. "You must have mentioned it when we were talking about our families."

She had? She eyed him suspiciously. "What's the name of my ex?"

"I don't believe you ever talked about him. But Brice Gallant did during your presentation at Gallant. His name is Gregory. Last name…Tilko. Which means you were once Mrs. Tilko."

She was suitably impressed, but he was finally wrong about one thing. "Wrong. I kept my maiden name."

"Ah, you got me," he said smoothly, turning her to face him.

Her eyes immediately dropped to his warm, sensual lips. What would it feel like to experience those lips on her? Grace raised her eyes to his and drew in a sharp breath at what she saw there. He wanted her. He wasn't hiding his desire. So, why didn't he kiss her?

Suddenly the answer was there in her mind. How Grace knew what David was thinking was beyond her. But she knew. The same way she knew how a piece of glass would fit perfectly in one of her designs. David wanted it to be her choice. If anything were to happen between them, she would need to make the first move.

Before she could think more about what she was doing or why, Grace placed her lips on his. David did not pull away, but he did not respond immediately either. So, she did what she had secretly imagined doing since their first meeting and ran her hands through his dark locks and down his back. The silky texture followed by the taut muscles started an ache deep inside.

For a brief moment, David remained unmoving. Grace reveled in the freedom to touch his body, while her lips teased his. But he did not allow her to remain in charge for long. As she continued her exploration, shaping the hard muscles in his shoulders and running her hands inside his shirt, David deepened the kiss, wrapping his arms around her and dropping to the couch with Grace in one swift motion. His tongue moved into her mouth, scraping her teeth. The rich smell of his cologne had Grace wanting a whole lot more than he was offering. The odd tingling sensation, which she had experienced once before on the beach, formed at the base of her skull and spread throughout her body. What was happening? Her heart beat hard, tapping out a fast rhythm. Oliver barked once, as if sensing her emotion. Grace took a calming breath and instead of resisting, gave herself up to the electrical current that seemed to run between them.

David pulled away from her. “Grace, look at me.”

Dazed, she obeyed, but it was difficult to focus on his lips, when all she wanted to do was kiss them. She forced herself to look into his green eyes and found them dark with desire. Grace shivered.

“I want you, Grace. More than you can possibly know. But you need to…understand something about me first.”

“What?” she asked, breathless, surprised to hear the trembling passion in her own voice.

“I don’t share. And contrary to what you may think, I don’t sleep around. If we are…intimate…then I’ll want more than a one-night stand.”

In all her life, Grace had never known a man’s desire like this. He was staking his territory. Despite his air of mystery, David's arms offered a safe harbor. Grace never wanted to leave them. Which was plain stupid. She just met the man.

"Grace." He drew her name out on a ragged sigh, laying his forehead on hers. "I don't want to rush you. If this is too soon, say so."

The tingling sensation seemed to pierce her temples. She struggled to clear her mind, but it was like walking through cotton. It seemed impossible they had only met this this week. It felt like forever.

David started to pull away. Panic raced through her system. "It's not too soon."

David lifted his face to hers. "You can't mean that." His green eyes seemed to search her soul.

Grace nodded. "But I do." She did mean it. She didn't know how or why she trusted David, but she found she did with a surprising certainty.

He stared at her, his always perfect hair messy and green eyes glowing with a dark passion. Slowly, as if he thought she might change her mind, David placed both of his palms on either side of her cheeks. "Don't be afraid," he whispered, then proceeded to trace the outline of her lips with his tongue. Grace could smell the rich scent of aftershave mixed with the lake breeze. The electrical charge spread into her face and down her back.

David pulled her from the couch and carried her to his bedroom. Soon they were lying on his soft mattress. Overhead, moonlight streamed through the window making geometric patterns on the opposite wall.

She should put a stop to this. Common sense dictated she reconsider. But under the onslaught of his skillful hands and embrace, Grace could not find the strength she needed to haul herself off the bed and out the door. Her last logical thought was her mother would be expecting a phone call. But it soon vanished under the powerful passion that sprang between them.

Chapter Thirteen
Pumpkin Pie

Grace awoke to the sound of the lake and seagulls crying for their morning breakfast. For a moment, she lay there trying to piece together where she was. It didn't take her long to remember her passionate evening, especially when the object of her passion was staring at her, a pleased look on his face. She couldn't stop the blush that started in her chest and spread to her face.

"You have nothing to be embarrassed about." He ran one long finger along the side of her cheek.

"I know," she said, a bit defensively. "I don't know why I blush like that. I'm not embarrassed."

David studied Grace for a moment. As if he were satisfied with what he saw, he kissed her softly on the lips, taking his time. After a few minutes, he moved away slightly to look her in the eyes. "Good. Let's have a repeat."

It was some time before Grace had another coherent thought. When she did, it was that she had to use the bathroom. She rose naked and walked across the plush carpet. She knew David watched her but shrugged it off. When you had to go bad enough and after a night and morning of shared passion, there wasn't much more to be embarrassed about.

By the time she came out of the bathroom, David

was nowhere to be seen, but she heard the sounds of dishes rattling in the kitchen. She needed her cell phone, which was in her purse in the other room. Grace looked at the pile of clothes at her feet. She didn't want to wander around naked, but she didn't have it in her to put on her fancy dress from last night. She spied a dresser across the room and rummaged in it. After the third drawer, she found a stack of sweatpants and tops, all neatly folded. She pulled one from each stack. The blue sweatshirt had Chief Wahoo on the front, and the pants were gray. She put them on. They were way too big but would do for her purposes.

Grace rolled the sleeves and ankles and wandered out to the main room to look for her purse. She could hear David humming in the kitchen as she felt for her cell phone in the bottomless cavern that was her handbag. That was unusual. He never hummed. How she knew that about David was beyond her, but Grace found the knowledge was hers. She selected Brains' cell number and texted him.

9:02 a.m. I'm sorry. Something's come up. I'm going to have to cancel.

David was studying her, a glass of juice in his hand. "Canceling your plans?"

"Yes." Guilt made her cheeks bright, like she had been caught with her hand in the cookie jar. Despite his confidence last night, David didn't know *everything* about her, Grace reminded herself. Still, she quickly deposited her cell phone back in her purse.

"Good, because I've got plans for us today. Those look good on you." He pointed casually to her outfit.

"I'm sorry…I snooped in your dresser. I needed something to wear."

He smiled. "I don't mind. I like you wearing my clothes. Come and eat. Breakfast is ready."

David fed her scrambled eggs and toast. She tried to get out of him what they had planned for the day, but he said it was a surprise. "I'll need to go back to my place and pick up some clothes."

"No you won't." He smiled playfully. "You look good in my sweats."

Grace liked him this way—happy. David needed to smile and laugh more. But she did require her own clothes and clean underwear.

Paramour, singing the chorus about crying for your mama, blared from the other room. Her mother. Grace had forgotten all about calling her. She ran for her phone. By the time she found it in her bag, it had stopped ringing. She'd better call her back right away, or her mother would have the police searching for her. She pressed the callback button. She could hear David humming again, while he cleaned the dishes. "Hi, Mom."

"Oh, thank goodness you're all right. I was starting to worry about you. You were supposed to call me last night."

"I know. I'm so sorry. We got home late, and I was tired and forgot." The excuse was lame. It was not like her to forget. Her mother sounded suspicious.

"How was your date?"

"Great. We went to Club 32—you know the private restaurant? Fancy."

"Good. How'd you like him? Do you plan to see him again?"

"I think so…yes." She didn't dare tell her mother that their first date wasn't technically over and had already morphed into a second. David came into the room and sat on the couch. He wrapped his arm around her and pulled her to the cushion with him as she was talking.

"Did you kiss him?"

"Oh, Mom, do we have to?"

"What do you mean do we have to? I'm asking a simple question. I'm your mother. I'm entitled."

Grace sighed audibly into the phone. "Yes, I did."

"Now was that so hard? So, was he a good kisser?"

Behind her David stifled a chuckle and buried his face in her hair. "Mother! Can we move on?" He nuzzled the back of her neck. She was never a great multi-tasker and was worried that this combination might be more than she could manage. That didn't stop her mother or David from putting her skills to the challenge.

"What about the other one? Are you still planning to meet him?"

"No…at least not today. I'm trying to reschedule that." She gasped and pulled away as David bit a particularly sensitive spot on her neck.

"Everything ok there?" Her mother had uncanny hearing.

"Yes, I got a paper cut."

"What do you have planned the rest of the day? Do you want to come for dinner? You can invite the new beau if you'd like."

"Oh, Mom, I don't think…"

David straightened suddenly, turned her to face him and nodded.

"Mom, hold on a second. I think I'm getting another call." She put the phone on mute. "What?"

"Your new beau would like to meet your mother."

"Are you serious?"

"Of course."

"Be careful in making up your mind. My mother is wonderful, but she worries about me and will grill you with twenty questions. Are you completely, totally sure you want to subject yourself to that?"

"Absolutely." He winked and then got up, kissed her on the lips and disappeared into his bedroom. She took the phone off mute.

"Sorry, Mom. That was David calling. I asked him if he'd like to join us for dinner, and he said yes."

"That's wonderful. Do you think he'll eat pot roast? Or I could make a lasagna. What does he like?"

"For God's sake Mom, I only met the man. Make the pot roast."

"Pot roast is good." His voice called from the other room. "I'm English, remember?" She winced, wanting to shush him. She wasn't ready for her mother to know they were together.

"Who was that?" her mother asked.

"Oh, some program on the TV." Grace lied quickly. "Make the pot roast Mom. He's English."

"What's his being English got to do with pot roast?"

"I don't know. I think it sounds like an English dish." She could hear David laughing in the other room and then the shower running. She would kill him.

"Okay, I'll make the pot roast. Is pumpkin pie English?" She sounded anxious.

"I don't know Mom but don't worry about it. I'm sure he'll eat pumpkin pie. Who doesn't? What time do you want us there?"

“Six o’clock and don’t be late. And don’t worry about bringing anything either. I’ll have everything ready.”

“Okay, Mom. We’ll be there. Love you.”

“Grace?”

“Yeah?”

“Ask your friend if he likes pumpkin pie. I know he’s there with you.”

“Mom.” She groaned. Her mother was way too perceptive.

“Well, I don’t want to serve it if he doesn’t like it.”

“Okay, okay. I’ll text you. Bye, Mom.”

“Bye, honey. See you tonight.”

Grace disconnected. She was going to kill David as soon as he got out of the shower. She sat on the couch for a moment contemplating her options. She could go back to bed and wait it out, or turn on the TV she saw on the wall—if she could find the remote. She looked around but it was nowhere in sight. Or—the thought seemed to come out of nowhere—she could join David in the shower. That sounded like the best plan of all. After all, she needed a shower, too.

She planned to surprise him, but he heard her coming, because he opened the door and beckoned her in when she got to the bathroom.

The next hour was filled with splashes and giggles but eventually she was clean and dry and back in his sweats. David had put on a pair of new jeans and a dark green shirt that brought out the green in his eyes. It was a good color choice. He looked fantastic. It wasn’t fair. She was a mess. No makeup and her short hair got all curly when it dried naturally. She would have to redo it when she got home.

"You look fine." He watched, as she smoothed her hair with her hands for the bazillionth time. "Are you ready?"

"I'm not sure. You haven't told me where we're going?"

"Yes, I know." He reached out to tweak her nose. "C'mon."

"Wait a minute. Do you like pumpkin pie?"

"Who doesn't?" He laughed and opened the front door. She grabbed her purse, slipped on her sandals from the night before, and they headed out. Oliver whined behind them, but David told him firmly that he must stay home, and he settled obediently.

David took her out on the lake on the speedboat he kept docked there. It was still summer, but the smell of a discarded campfire on the beach reminded her that fall and Claire's wedding were around the corner. They spent some time speeding around the lake, shouting over the sounds of the waves and the boat. Eventually, they headed back to shore, and he showed her his favorite spot. It was much higher than the beach where she would gather glass. The perfect perch to check out the beachcombers without their knowledge. Explained why she never noticed him.

As they walked, he kept reaching out to hold her hand or drape an arm around her. She felt strangely like they had been doing this forever and not just since Tuesday.

Later, he drove her to the nearest department store where he insisted she buy a new set of lingerie, a sundress, a sweater, a new pair of sandals and some makeup.

"Can't we make a pit stop at my place? I have

plenty of clothes there. I don't need new stuff."

"I don't think so. That will take too long. Don't worry about it, sweetheart. I've got it covered."

"David, no way are you buying me new clothes." Grace calculated the dent the purchase would make to her checking account and realized she couldn't afford it. If he wouldn't take her home for her clothes, she'd have to spend the remainder of the day in his T-shirt and sweatpants.

"Yes way," he said, his tone firm. "This one's on me."

She reached for the bill, snatching it out of his hands. "David, I mean it. I don't need new clothes."

He made no move to grab the bill out of her hands but studied Grace carefully, mischief in his eyes. "Then I'd like my sweats back," he said quietly.

"Oh," she said. Out of all the things he possibly could have said, those five simple words made her question her rationale. "Oh, all right." She thrust the bill in his face.

For lunch, they ate at a waterside restaurant. She used a tactic of her mother's and drilled him with twenty questions. Although later she would think that she hadn't learned much of anything, for now it felt intimate and revealing.

"So, what's the C for on your business card?"

"It's Carl. I'm named after my dad, Carl senior. My mom didn't want to call me junior, so everyone's always called me David."

Grace nodded encouragingly. "So, how long has your family been in business?"

"For many years now. It all started with my great, great grandfather, who incidentally was also a Carl.

And my great, great grandmother, whose name was…Meg."

"And who are your clients? Anyone I would know?"

"Well, that depends on how well you know Uncle Sam. Our biggest contract is with the government."

Grace laughed. "Oh, Uncle Sam and I are good buddies, especially at tax time. But I think he's one of those friends who takes and takes and never gives, if you know what I mean."

David smiled, reaching out to snag her hand across the table, encouraging Grace to continue her line of questioning.

"What were you like in high school?"

"Competitive. I was on the swim team."

"I bet your mother liked that—less chance of injury than football."

"Oh, I don't know about that. I broke my finger, and it has never looked the same since." He wiggled his crooked pinky finger, putting to rest the burning question that had been nagging Grace since their meeting at *Coffersations*.

"Were you a good student?"

"Yes. In math, especially. I won a full scholarship to New York University and eventually to the University of California, Berkeley. That's where I completed my Masters and a PhD in economics."

Grace received her communications degree from Cleveland State, which she had finally finished paying the loans on a few years ago. What the heck was she doing dating a man with a PhD from Berkeley?

They finished lunch and went back to the cottage. He disappeared into what she suspected was an office or spare bedroom to make some phone calls. She decided to use the time to check in with Claire. When she grabbed her cell, the first thing she noticed was a text from Brains.

3:09 p.m. Can we reschedule? Let's try Wednesday night, 8:00 p.m., same place. A little late, but I do have a day job remember.

3:10 p.m. Or we could meet in our dreams.

Chapter Fourteen
Declaration

"Before we go in there, you need to know something about my mother." They were sitting in David's car outside her Mom and Glenn's house, a white ranch in a middle-class neighborhood. Grace swallowed nervously. What the hell had prompted her to introduce David to her mother of all people? This was so unlike her. She was having major misgivings now that they were moments away from the big meeting.

"Grace, I'm not worried." David reassured her with a slight smile. "I think I can handle your mother."

"You don't know my mother. She's a bit overprotective. She also worries about me. Those two details can make for drama."

He reached out and stroked her cheek. "Don't worry about it. Your mother will like me."

Strangely, Grace believed him. An hour later and with three glasses of wine in her, he was right. David and her Mom were talking like old friends. Even Glenn had un-bended and shown David his collection of vintage pens. David seemed to know the exact right thing to say to charm both of them. With her mother, he talked about how much he admired Grace and thought she was a talented artist. He mentioned that he was a Democrat (her mother was staunch) and that he liked to cook. They talked for some time about favorite recipes. She could tell her mother had warmed to him.

After he and Glenn spent some time looking at the pen collection, David mentioned he had a few old fountain pens himself that might be worth something, including a silver Waterman. That led to a discussion of antiques—turned out, David had a rare book collection, too.

His charm and class impressed Grace, although she was having a hard time staying focused on the conversation. They were sitting next to one another at the table, and he had his hand on her knee. Periodically, he would caress her leg. It was difficult to control her reaction whenever he did that.

Her mother was drilling David about his family. Grace tried to stay alert, but by now, she was tipsy.

"What exactly do you do, David?"

"I'm an economist, which means I pay attention to economic trends and get paid to consult with businesses and offer advice. In fact, that's how I met Grace. She came in to meet with one of my clients, and I recognized her as the beautiful lady I kept seeing on the beach. I couldn't believe my luck."

He gently rubbed her knee. Her mother laughed like a young girl. "That is so romantic. Glenn, isn't that romantic?" Glenn grunted, which was a typical response that meant he agreed or at least wanted her mother to think he agreed.

"I'll get the pie," her mother said now. She headed into the kitchen. "Glenn, come and help." Glenn dutifully tagged along.

"So tell me." David leaned over to whisper in Grace's ear. "Do you think your mother likes me?"

She laughed. "You win. I don't know how you managed to win her over so soon, but you did. Did you spike her drink?" She took another swallow of wine. It was fruity, her favorite kind. She was not a big wine connoisseur, but this wine seemed particularly good tonight.

He waggled his eyebrows at her. "What, you don't think I'm romantic?"

Grace had a sudden vision of the flowers he had sent her the morning before and had to fight back a rush of tears. It had been so long since she had gotten flowers from a man. She blinked to disguise the hot liquid, but as she was quickly learning about David, nothing made it past him. He grasped her hand and turned her to face him. "If I would have known they meant that much to you, I would have sent you a room full of flowers." He brought her hand to his lips and kissed it.

At that moment, Glenn and her Mom returned from the kitchen, large plates of pumpkin pie and ice-cream in their hands. "You do like pumpkin pie, don't you?" Her mother asked.

"Of course. Who doesn't?" He gave Grace an innocent look. She giggled.

Noticing the exchange her mother said, "You and Grace have gotten mighty close, mighty fast." It was a statement and not a question. *Uh-oh.* Her mother was on the attack. Grace could kick herself for letting the wine make her complacent. She knew it was too much to hope that David would come away from the encounter unscathed.

Next to her, David stilled. He did not fidget or get upset. If anything he seemed calmer and more in control. “Sometimes, you know a good thing when you find it.”

“How do I know you won’t hurt her? Grace has been through enough.”

“Mother. Let’s not talk about this now. Please.” Both her mother and David ignored her. Glenn kept his head down and went on eating his pie. He knew better than to interfere when his wife was on a mission about one of her daughters.

“I would never hurt her.”

“Easy to say, hard not to do.” Glenn was still silent but looked up from his pie with interest. “Grace needs a man who will shower her with the affection she so richly deserves. She wasn’t treated well by her ex-husband. But she likes you. I can tell. And once she gives her heart, she’s intensely loyal.”

“Mom, please. I don’t need me to speak for you—I mean you to speak for me.”

David raised his glass to her mother. “To Grace.”

“To Grace.” Her mother raised her wineglass, nudging Glenn to do the same. That’s how Grace found herself, wine glass in hand, toasting herself. The next thing she knew, they were back outside, a to-go carton of her mother’s pot roast with them.

“Goodbye, David.” Her mother hugged him, while Glenn shook his hand. “Take good care of our Gracie. She’s going to have a headache in the morning.” Her mother only used Gracie when she was feeling particularly fond of her.

“Of course. Goodbye Mr. and Mrs. Ellis. It was nice to meet you both.”

Her mother turned to Grace, kissing her cheek and whispering in her ear. “Hang on to this one. He’s a keeper."

Soon, they were back in his car, speeding toward her condo. They were silent for a short time.

"Like I told you yesterday, I don't sleep around." David finally said. "I may even be falling for you." He flashed her a playful wink.

"But you hardly know me."

"I know all the essentials. And what's more, I'm pretty certain you feel the same."

Somewhere in Grace's mind, a door slammed shut. Why would David think she was falling for him? Was she? She couldn't stop the panic racing through her system. Why had she had that third glass of wine?

Grace didn't remember asking him any questions, but David answered as if she had, his deep voice sounding calm and determined. "You can choose not to believe me. I won't stop you. But I'm not going anyplace, Grace. And I won't let you shut me out."

David parked outside her condo, collected the bag of her clothes and leftover pot roast from the trunk and walked her to the door. He waited patiently while she dug for her keys. It took a few minutes as she searched through her purse. Grace tried to fit the key in the lock but had a little trouble. David carefully took them from her, fitted them in the lock, opened the door and walked her through, shutting it behind them.

She fumbled for the lights, found them and turned them on. "Romeo, Romeo." Harvey squawked from his cage.

"Smart bird." David spoke over her shoulder. "So, we finally meet."

Grace turned around to find him studying Harvey with his usual intense focus.

"He can be a bit annoying at times, but we get along okay. Would you like something to drink?" Grace offered, although the evening had drained her energy.

"How about you sit, and I'll make us some coffee. Decaf."

"You don't know where I keep my stuff."

"I'll find it." A few minutes later, he brought them both steaming cups of coffee and set them on the table in front of her. He sat next to her, and they sipped them in companionable silence. She struggled to keep her eyes open and must have dozed on his shoulder for a while, because he shook her gently and suggested she go to bed.

Alone?

Again, he anticipated her thoughts. "I have to get some rest tonight. I have a big day tomorrow with the trip I have scheduled. I will call you, though. And I'd like to see you on Wednesday. Walk me to the door?" He smiled at her.

She nodded, feeling bereft. Silly, considering how long Grace had known David and how many years she had been on her own. How could she possibly have such strong feelings after only a week? Why did it seem like a lifetime?

David pulled Grace with him, half carrying her to the door. When they got there, he kissed her goodnight, his whiskers rough against her cheek. Could she be falling in love?

He stepped back abruptly, an odd glitter in his eyes. "Grace, when I come back we need to talk."

She nodded. How did she ever think his eyes were cold? They glowed with warmth and acceptance.

"You can trust me, Grace. I won't let you down."

David seemed sincere. But Greg had seemed sincere too. He told her all kinds of beautiful, romantic things. But in the end, they were only words. It was his actions that had had the final say.

David was frowning. Whatever he was thinking caused him to lean in suddenly and kiss her, hard, his hands winding through her short hair. His lips ground against hers until she opened them and his tongue swept inside, as if he could banish all resistance with a kiss. Long minutes passed, while she lost herself in his embrace. Could fate have handed her a charming, good-looking, rich man that loved her in a matter of days?

It was only much later, while she lay in bed, remembering their passionate weekend together, that she recalled her upcoming date with Brains. She had promised David they would see each other on Wednesday. It seemed she and Brains were fated not to meet. And that was her last thought before drifting into a deep, but restless, sleep.

The first thing Grace saw was the stranger with the magnetic eyes. His long, dark hair was drawn back in a ponytail and he was shirtless, revealing sculpted muscles. They were in what she could only suppose was his bedroom, given the masculine furniture and clothes. He beckoned to her from where she stood in the doorway, and Grace found herself walking steadily toward him as if pulled along on a string.

The stranger shook his head at her, glaring. "You've been a bad little girl, Grace. Why have you been leading me on? I think I will make you pay."

"No." Her heart beat out a loud rhythm as if in time with the Lord's Prayer that she recited feverishly. Faster and faster the words spun out, her hands making criss-cross patterns across her chest in the sign of a cross.

He laughed, the grotesque sound echoing all around her. "I don't care if you've linked to him. You're mine, Grace. God can't save you. Only I can. And if you want to live, you must listen carefully."

Grace tried to listen, she did, but when he opened his mouth, the screeching sound that came out was like a thousand bagpipes scraping across her brain. She was not sure how long it went on. In her dream state, it seemed forever.

As suddenly as it began, the pain vanished, and Grace could breathe again. A tender touch on her face had her opening her eyes to see David in front of her. He looked angry, but Grace knew it was directed elsewhere and not at her. "Are you okay?"

"I am now." She noticed she was no longer in the cruel man's bedroom but at the window of David's cottage, gazing at the night sky.

"See that star?" He pointed to a luminous star in the distance. "When you're frightened, think hard of that star, and I'll come. He can't hurt you when I am near. Think of that star. It will summon me to help you. Can you remember that, Grace?"

"Yes." She was weightless, falling down, down, faster and faster, like she had jumped from a tall building. David's hand no longer held hers. Grace suspected that when she reached the bottom she would die. But she never learned her fate, because right before she hit the ground, she awakened to a dark room and the sound of her own voice, screaming.

Grace lay there, panting, and tried to catch her breath. Her mouth tasted like cotton balls, while the relentless throbbing in her head battered her skull. *Too much to drink. The nightmare stemmed from that. It's my punishment for over indulging on all that wine and beef.*

"It was a dream." Grace said the words aloud to calm herself, the sound of her own voice hoarse and eerie in the quiet room. *A bad dream.* She looked at the clock—6:00 a.m. Time to get up anyway. It was Monday. Claire's shower was on Saturday. Grace would meet her at the airport Friday. *All normal. Only a dream. A scary and bad dream. It's not real.* She had to keep reminding herself. Otherwise, Grace didn't know if she would be able to make it through the day ahead.

Chapter Fifteen
Strange Memories

David, what's wrong? Stay focused. Now's not the time to be distracted.

Geneva's warning came right on time as their protective shield wavered, and he narrowly missed the dark soldier in front of him. He was having difficulty keeping his hands and his mind to himself. But his vigilance last night had saved Grace's life…and had nearly gotten her killed. David and his crew were in the mind of Stu Littleton, the CEO of Panda Enterprises—one of the largest technology research organizations on the planet. They had already done a general sweep but had not found any evidence leading to their hacker. Stu appeared to be exactly what he was, a CEO of a large corporation. David did not believe he was or knew their rogue hacker.

He signaled his men, drawing from Geneva's endless energy supply to zap their connection and return them to their respective portals. Since they would hit several targets in quick succession, they had tunneled in as a group from their headquarters.

David lay in the recovery room, battling his emotions. Dark anger festered like a bad blister, threatening to burst and destroy his sanity. He had nearly lost Grace. A few minutes more and the rogue hacker would have taken it too far. He struggled to draw in air, his shallow breaths not generating near enough oxygen for recovery.

"She's fine. Better off than you. Your anxiety is slowing your recovery." Geneva advised calmly, her familiar voice acting as a beacon to guide him to safety. David fought hard to dampen his rage, which burned inside him—a furnace fueled by the knowledge *he* was responsible for her being the target of the hacker.

"Rest now, David." Geneva commanded, dispelling the erratic waves, so that he could slow his heartbeat and breathing. He and his crew would enjoy a brief respite before entering the mind of their next target, Jason Langley. Langley held patents on numerous inventions, as well as a large number of shares in several corporations that specialized in solar-powered devices. More importantly, Langley was a former mind hacker who had retired from the CMU ten years earlier due to a minor infraction. He could be their rogue hacker and if he was, would be expecting them. David determined to do a better job controlling his emotions.

"When were you going to tell me?"

He forced his eyes open in time to catch Geneva's brooding stare. "There wasn't time. I learned myself last night."

"So the hacker is after her now, too? You can't go on like this. Your mind needs recovery time. Your infatuation is going to get you both killed."

Anger rushed to the surface, and he sat up abruptly. "You know what they say about eavesdroppers."

"I wasn't eavesdropping. You were broadcasting your fear so loudly, I couldn't help but get the message. You're losing your edge, David. And she's the reason.

You need to cut her loose."

"It's too late for that." Fear skated across the surface of his mind as David recalled the moment he had entered her dream and realized someone else was present. All of his training had called for him to strike immediately, but he knew Grace would be hurt in the crossfire. At a minimum, she would suffer memory loss. More likely, her mind would be wiped clean. He couldn't take the chance. So he focused on bringing Grace to consciousness, allowing the enemy to escape.

"Why, David? Why is it too late?"

Geneva turned and walked back to his bedside, leaning over him like some avenging angel, the dark jacket she wore resembling wings. "Just erase her memories, and she'll be fine."

He didn't say anything.

"What have you done? And don't give me any bullshit. You've been accessing her mind at a distance when I'm not present. We both know there's only one way to do that."

"We are linked." He admitted, running a weary hand through his hair.

"And she doesn't know? When were you going to tell her? When's she's dead?"

Geneva's anger and the explosion of energy in the room lit a fuse of guilt through the core of him. David stood suddenly, towering over her. "I never intended to link with Grace. It just kind of happened between us. Her energy, it's…well, I've never felt anything like it. I'm stronger when I'm around her."

Geneva was looking at him strangely, almost disbelievingly. "You slept with her. Oh, for Pete's sake." She threw up her hands in disgust. "What happened to keeping your distance? No, don't answer that." Geneva scraped one hand roughly over her forehead.

"I'm going to tell her. Everything."

"Great. Just great. The hacker's stalking her now, isn't he? Last night's episode was not the first time he's been in her mind. She's a target."

David had to hand it to her, Geneva had pulled the relevant facts from his mind and put the pieces together quickly.

"Yes." He admitted, and plopped back on the bed.

"Does Peter know?"

"Not yet. I'll tell him after we hack Langley."

Geneva paused, turning her back on him and walking to the window to gaze out at the scene below. After some minutes, she strode back to his bedside. "There's nothing to be done now. You rest. I'll get us some dinner. Let's get Langley over with, and we'll both see what Peter has to say."

Despite her orders, David could not sleep until he checked on Grace again. He found her in conversation with what appeared to be a new client. Grace needed the money, he read in her mind. He'd need to do something about that. David didn't want her worrying about paying bills, especially when it was a simple matter for him to remedy. He would have Sophia offer Grace a large advance on their next assignment.

*****

Across town, Grace wasn't sure how she got through the day, but she did. Something strange was happening. A hangover? But hangovers didn't cause unusual memories did they?

Over lunch, she did a quick Google search on

hangover symptoms, but all she discovered were what sounded like bad lyrics to country western songs.

Grace saw a recurring image of a girl with dark hair. She was someone dear to her—but Grace didn't recognize her. The girl had pale skin, and she liked to read—a lot. Grace saw her sitting on her bed reading, while their mother called from downstairs. Except it was not Grace's mother. This mother was tall and slim and liked to play the piano.

Later, while she walking home from a client meeting, Grace caught a whiff of tobacco and pictured her grandpa, pipe dangling from his lips as he made smoke rings for her. Strange. Both sets of grandparents died before she was born. Grace had no idea if either grandfather had ever smoked a pipe. She called her mom to find out.

"Mom, I know this is going to sound strange, but I need to know. Did Grandpa O'Neill or Grandpa Woznisky ever smoke a pipe?"

"Not that I recall. Why do you need to know?"

"Oh, for some genealogical research I'm doing." Grace lied, hoping her mother didn't ask too many questions, because she had no idea how she would connect the two. Thankfully, her mother was distracted.

"Your sister is driving me crazy," she said now. "Do you know what that girl did? She asked Damian Ross to her wedding, and Damian said yes. So now we will have a celebrity at your sister's wedding!"

"Mom, who's Damian Ross?"

"I don't know. Your sister said he was a local talk show host. You mean you don't know who he is? I thought he was famous."

"I never heard of him. If he's a celebrity, I don't

think he’s a famous celebrity.”

“He’s not?” Her mother sounded deflated. “Well, I’m not sure why Claire would mention he was coming if he wasn’t famous. Are you sure?”

“Yes. I’m certain. Don’t worry about it. Damian Ross, if he does come to the wedding, will be fine. Listen, Mom. I have to go. Thanks for answering my question.”

“All right. Make sure you’re on time to pick your sister up from the airport on Friday. Her plane gets in at 5:30.”

“I’ll be there. Don’t worry.”

“That’s what you always say, but it’s my job to worry. Speaking of which, Grace, have you asked that nice David to be your date for the wedding?”

“No, I haven’t. I wasn’t planning on it.”

“Why ever not? Has he done something? Are you still seeing him?”

“Yes, of course. David has been completely kind to me. I don’t know if I want him underfoot at the wedding, that’s all.”

“Grace, ask David. You meet a nice man like that. It’s the perfect opportunity to introduce him to the rest of the family. Especially Aunt Peggy. You know how she’s always on you about getting married again.”

“All right, Mom, maybe. I’ll think about it. I gotta run. Love you.”

“What’s wrong with you girls? You’re both so afraid of commitment.”

“I’m sorry, Mom, I’m getting another call. Bye.” Grace disconnected before her mother could guilt her into asking David to the wedding. She was not going to rush things this time around.

Grace checked her watch. It was 3:00 p.m. in Cleveland. That meant it was noon in California. She quickly dialed her sister's number but got her voicemail. "Claire, call me. I need to talk to you."

A few hours later, it happened again. While ordering her favorite Chinese takeout, Grace heard herself request the cashew chicken. What was wrong with her? She preferred sweet and sour, didn't she? It was as if someone had gotten a hold of part of her brain and compelled her to think about the cashew chicken. Maybe she should see a doctor.

Her cell phone rang. *Claire.* Grace grabbed the phone like a lifeline.

"What's going on?" Claire asked.

"I'm not sure. Have you ever ordered cashew chicken when all you wanted was sweet and sour?"

"Huh? You aren't making sense. Did you get bad takeout?"

Grace tried again. "Have you ever dreamt about total strangers?"

"Sure all the time." Claire spoke matter-of-factly. "Last night, I dreamt a new director was in town. He gave me a choice part, too. I got to perform on stage in front of tons of people. Everything was going great until I looked down and noticed I was naked." Claire giggled and Grace couldn't help but join her. "I was kind of bummed when I woke up. That dream director was hot."

"It didn't bother you that you were naked?" Grace found herself asking, curiously.

"No, that part was kind of cool. So what's with the dreams you've been having? Are they hot-looking strangers?" Claire was clearly not taking their conversation seriously.

"Mine aren't so fun. More like nightmares. Although there's an attractive man in them. Except he's not nice. He commands me to come to him, and I have to do what he says. When I don't, he punishes me by making my brain hurt."

Claire laughed. "It's a dream. It's not real. Why are you getting so worked up?"

"Because afterward, my head hurts. It's not just in my dream."

"Oh. Right. That is weird. Maybe you'd better get yourself checked out. What if you are having a mini-stroke or something? I've heard of people our age getting those. Call Doctor J." Doctor J was their childhood doctor, but they both still relied on him for advice.

"Well, that's reassuring," Grace said wryly. "All right, I'll call him right after I get off the phone. But something else weird is happening, too."

"What's that?"

"I…I keep having these strange memories. They feel like my memories, but I know they're not."

"Like what?"

"Well, I'm pretty sure you and I don't have another sister."

Claire laughed. "You mean Mom had a child and gave her up for adoption? Good one."

"Of course not. That's what's so weird about this. I keep remembering a sister and another mother. And yesterday I smelled tobacco smoke—like from a pipe—and I remembered that Grandpa smoked a pipe. But I had no clue how I could know that. So I called Mom, and she said none of our grandpas smoked. It's like I'm believing my dreams are reality or something."

"That's too cool. Think about all the sexy men you could dream about. You could get all kinky in your dreams, and it would turn into reality. Which reminds me, how did your date with Brains work out? Those were some knock-out flowers he sent."

"Oh, those didn't come from Brains. In fact, we didn't have a date."

"So who sent the flowers?"

"Well, I'm sort of seeing someone else. We had dinner at Mom and Glenn's."

"What! This is huge! This is monumental! I can't believe you didn't call and tell me. And Mom didn't mention it. Who is he?"

"Well, it kind of happened. I didn't plan on bringing him to Mom's for dinner. It's…he wanted to go, and Mom wanted to meet him, and I said yes. His name is David Jenkins. He's one of my clients. We were working on a project, and he asked me out."

"So did Mom drill him with twenty questions? Did she like him? It's killing me that I wasn't a fly on the wall for this."

"Mom grilled him. But the weird thing is she likes him. She wants me to invite him to your wedding." Grace took a deep breath and continued. "To tell you the truth, Claire, I think I'm falling for him. He sends flowers. He's romantic. He's sensitive. He seems to be sincere. But I'm not such a good judge of men. And I have only known him a short time, so I refuse to let this happen too fast."

"God, I'm jealous."

"Claire, you have Tom! He's good looking, he treats you well, and he loves you. Plus, you're getting married. What do you have to be jealous about?"

"I love that stage of falling in love when everything is new, you know. It's the best." Claire sounded wistful.

"But no one can stay in that stage forever. And it's not real. Early on, we're just in love with being in love. It feels good. But what happens when they discover you slurp your soup and don't wear underwear? True love needs to stand the test of time."

"Yeah, yeah. Easy for you to say. You're falling in love. So, will I get to meet this sweet romantic man at the shower?"

"Showers are for women."

"Don't you want me to check him out for you?"

"Sure—as long as you keep your hands off."

"Well, if your new man flirts with me, like Greg used to do, that's a sign he may not be such a good guy. I'm helping you."

"I suppose." Grace acknowledged reluctantly. Her sister had been blessed with the looks in the family, and she knew it. Every man that she came in contact with couldn't help but do a double-take, including any men that were supposed to be with Grace. Greg used to tell Grace all the time that if he wasn't with her, he would go after her sister. It was inevitable that David would be wowed as well. But all that attention could and did go to Claire's head. It was no wonder she kept getting cold feet at the altar. There were so many men to choose from—how could Claire possibly figure out which was the right one?

Grace's phone buzzed. It was David. "Claire, I swear David knows whenever I'm talking about him. That's him on the line. Gotta run."

"Okay, call me later. I want to hear more about

him." Claire hung up.

"David, hello."

"Grace, I don't have long to talk. I have to get back. I miss you and have been thinking about you off and on all day. How are you feeling?"

"Better. I had a headache this morning, but it's not so bad now. Um…David, can I ask you something?

"What's the matter?"

"Oh, nothing's wrong. I mean…nothing really." She took a deep breath and forced a normal tone. "David…is there someone else? I mean you would tell me if there were, wouldn't you?"

Long pause. Why did Grace have the impression he was taking his time to formulate an acceptable response? "Of course not, Grace. I told you that's not my style. Why do you ask?"

"I don't know…I just got the impression that perhaps you had another…someone you've known for a while. Someone you care about."

Crickets. "David?"

"Grace, you have nothing to worry about. I promise. Are we still on for Wednesday?"

He hadn't answered her question. "Um…yeah, of course."

"I thought we could hang out at your place."

"All right." Grace had a sudden vision of herself and David in her bed. Her face grew warm. Not for the first time, she was glad he couldn't read her thoughts.

"Grace." David sounded suddenly chipper. "I asked Sophia to stop by with a check for your work on the initial design."

"Great." She had been wondering when she was going to get paid but hated to mention it after the weekend they'd had together.

"I also asked her to give you an advance for the materials you'll be purchasing. She can give you a few thoughts I had on the design, and we can talk more about it on Wednesday."

A deep wave of insecurity battered at the gates of her heart. Had fate handed her a man who was obviously well-to-do, well respected, good-looking and smart without a catch? Who was the girl she saw?

"Still there?"

"Yes, I'm sorry. Okay. I'll look for Sophia to stop by. Is that tomorrow?"

"Yes, she'll be over in the morning after she gets the kids on the bus."

"Okay."

"Grace."

"Yeah?"

"I miss you." There was an awkward pause, while doubts assailed her, and Grace thought of what to say. David did not wait for her reply. "I can't wait to see you on Wednesday."

Chapter Sixteen
Rescued

8:30 p.m. So, because you're dating someone you can't talk to me anymore?

Grace stared at the text.

8:35 p.m. Don't be silly, she thumbed. *We can still talk, but I feel uncomfortable dating two men at once. I'm sorry. I would hope you could respect this and would give me the same courtesy if you were in my shoes.*

8:36 p.m. I'd still like to get together. Just as friends. No pressure. We could meet at the coffee shop tonight.

8:37 p.m. I don't think that's wise. If things don't work out, I'll get in touch. Let's leave it at that.

8:38 p.m. I'm not much good at that.

Grace sighed. How could she go from being celibate for two years with no good men in sight, and now she had two men in the space of a couple of months?

I'm sorry, she texted back. She didn't wait for a reply but tossed her cell phone aside. She plopped her head back on the couch. Almost immediately, the attractive man was there in her mind, as if he had been waiting for her to fall asleep. As usual, she fought to keep from looking at him, but he pulled her in slowly with his eyes.

"You are mine." He told her in his commanding voice. "It does no good to fight. I've been waiting for you all day."

"Why do you want me?"

"You don't even know your own talents, do you?"

He started walking toward her, and she noticed they were on the beach. The sun was not shining. The sky looked overcast. A bad storm was coming. She struggled to disguise her fear.

"You have something I want," the stranger told her. He stood in front of Grace now. "If you don't give it to me, I will take it from you. I could take it slowly and painfully. Or I could take it quickly, and you'll feel nothing. Which is it to be?"

"It depends on what it is you want."

"Ah, Grace." He reached out and grasped her chin almost painfully. "These are not games we play. Although I would like to play them with you. I don't need to ask your permission for what I want. I can take it. Let me see."

A strange sensation, like a flutter in her mind, assailed her.

"Ah, yes," he said. "You're holding his memories. So clever of you. I think I will take these though."

Pain tore at her, unearthing a memory. *The star. Imagine the star,* David had told her, *and I will come.* Grace fought hard to bring the star into focus. A sharp jolt had her gasping for breath. She struggled to scan the night sky. There it was…a soft pinprick of light, glimmering in the dark.

"David please come," she begged, although she did not know if he could hear her.

*****

Inside the mind of Jason Langley, David snapped to attention. Grace was in trouble. He needed to go to her immediately. He signaled Roland, who was closest. They had not finished their review of Jason Langley, but it didn't matter. David would make an immediate exit. The others would have to depart with him. What he was about to do would tax his talents to the max, but he had no option. He fought hard to stay calm and in control. Quickly and efficiently, David summoned the energy he needed and zapped the connection, sending them all back at once. He suspected Langley knew what they were about and had let them enter without resistance. Which most likely meant he had nothing to hide. He hadn't been waiting to attack them as they had feared.

David did not bother to talk to Geneva but immediately transferred his energy to match Grace's waves and found himself flying through the portal in her mind, adrenaline pumping. Would he be too late? Her brain immediately welcomed him, as if sensing relief was near.

David searched for the pinpoint of light Grace had created, zeroed in. He was with her in her mind, seeing through her eyes. He spotted his enemy immediately, catching a glimpse of his energy as he ejected himself back through a temporary portal. David fought the urge to comfort Grace and immediately searched for any remnant left behind that might help him track the rogue hacker. As usual, the man had covered his tracks well. Disappointment flooded his system. He turned to Grace. The hacker had stolen some of her memories. He could see the missing spots, like empty file folders in a drawer. Memories she held of him. David hoped vehemently the hacker did not find what he was looking for in the stolen moments.

Cautiously, David brought Grace into sleep. He calmed her erratic pattern and watched as her energy waves fell into a normal rhythm. She would not survive the attack unscathed, but Grace would survive.

David could not stay with her longer. He needed to return to his body immediately. His energy was waning, and he would be trapped. David had already been out much longer than the rules allowed. Wearily, he focused his mind on the portal, but it was difficult to create the amount of energy needed to pull himself through. His first two tries were not sufficient. He wasn't going to make it. He summoned all of his reserves, gave one last mighty effort, and barely slipped through. *Thank God.*

Geneva was working frantically over him. She called his name, but it was impossible to respond. He strained to open his eyes and finally managed it, although his eyelids were like iron flaps.

"Oh, dear God, you're alive!" Geneva's hands were shaky as they worked to eliminate the deadheads, their name for the terminal energy waves. He nodded but did not have the strength to reply.

Much later, David awoke, disoriented, to the buzzing of his cell phone. *Sophia.* The call went to voicemail before he could answer. He checked the time. *One o'clock in the afternoon.* He had slept nearly twenty-four hours. Was Grace okay? He focused on her mind and immediately the portal beckoned, warm and inviting. David breathed a sigh of relief.

Geneva must have sensed he was awake because she joined him. "How are you feeling?"

"I've been better."

"Headache?"

David nodded. He avoided telling her it was worse than normal. His enemy had wasted no time in trying to use whatever information he had gathered to probe his mind. The headache, as well as the fact that he was awake, told him that the bastard had not succeeded yet. Which meant he would be back to steal from Grace again soon. This time, David was determined he would be ready. Grace might not survive another mind assault. The hacker had not been gentle with her. David fought an internal battle, suppressing the anger coursing through his system. There was nothing more deadly than an out-of-control hacker.

"Grab a seat at the table. I'll get you something to eat."

David nodded, grateful Geneva spared him one of her lectures, although he knew that would come. His batteries badly needed a recharge. David followed Geneva to the table.

A few hours later, after a shower and a hearty lunch, Geneva shared the news. "Peter was here earlier, but you were sleeping. He needs to talk to you."

Tension settled in his gut. "I'm off the force."

Geneva grabbed his hand, squeezing gently. "I'm sorry, David. I really am. Peter fought for you. I did, too, for what it's worth, even though I agree your relationship with Grace is detrimental to our success. But the rest of the men don't feel safe with you at the helm. You aborted a critical mission. You've linked with a civilian. They've asked for a replacement, and Adam has agreed. Peter had no say in the matter. They're bringing in Percy as your replacement."

David had known when he left to rescue Grace the ramifications would be severe. The manuals were clear on that point. Section two, item ten was drilled into every new mind hacker's head from day one of training. Never leave a mind before the end of a mission unless your life or the life of your crew is in jeopardy. Since Grace was not part of his crew, saving her life should not have distracted him from their mission. "I'll call him."

David found Peter's number in his favorites and hit send. Peter picked up immediately. "Did you save her?"

"Yes, but only in the nick of time. Our rogue hacker was not gentle. I'm puzzled why he has not wiped her mind completely. The only thing I can think of is he wants her alive for some reason."

"David, I know you did what was necessary. I want you to know I don't blame you. But I very much fear our operation is in trouble with Percy at the helm."

"You think our friend will be successful." It was not a question. "What about Brian? He would do it if you asked."

"Negative. Adam will not release him from his current case. He wants Percy. David, you need to erase Grace's memories of you. You know it as well as I do. It's the only thing that might save you and her."

"I won't do that."

"Our hacker will most assuredly succeed. He's looking for something that will weaken your mind. I don't need to tell you of all people what that takes—a deep-rooted emotion of some sort. Do you think he might find that?"

David did not speak. He didn't need to. Both he and Peter knew what the hacker sought was most assuredly in Grace's mind.

Inside his chest, his heart thundered. David

imagined it cracking in two. He must do what was necessary to protect Grace. He could not let Grace or himself become a puppet to be used at will by a madman. There would be time enough after they caught the hacker to get to know her all over again. Maybe he would even do it better the second time around. If David acted now, they would have a chance to fall in love properly later.

"I'll take care of it," he said, and ended the call.

Chapter Seventeen
Truth Revealed

Grace awoke to a knock on the door and the sound of Harvey squawking in his cage. She blinked and tried to remember where she was. Her condo. She had fallen asleep on the couch. She still had on her clothes from yesterday. Grace lifted her head and groaned. Had someone punched her?

The knock on the door continued, a bit more urgently. “Just a minute.”

She called out to buy herself some time, but the effort sent a sharp stab of pain through her forehead. She made her way into the bathroom and glanced at herself in the mirror. There were large dark circles under her eyes. She was not fit for company. She hurriedly brushed her teeth and finger-combed her hair. She would walk over and look out through the peephole. But unless there was another load of fresh flowers from David, Grace wasn’t opening the door.

She changed her mind, though, when she spotted Sophia standing patiently, an envelope in her hand. *Maybe a message from David?* She opened the door to find out. “Hi. C’mon in. I’m sorry it took me a while. Rough night. What brings you my way?”

“Didn’t David mention I would be stopping by?”

“Not that I recall.” Grace said blankly.

“Oh, that brother of mine. He was supposed to tell

you I was coming to drop off a check for your work on the design and for the materials you'll need to purchase. He's also drawn out a few suggestions he has for the layout."

"What design?"

"You know, on his cottage." Sophia gave her a puzzled look. "He told me to give you an advance on that. I was under the impression he had approved your design."

"No, I don't think so." Grace was fairly certain she wouldn't forget that conversation. She was anxious to get started.

"Well, I'm going to give you the checks anyway because David asked me to. It's your call whether you want to cash them or tear them up." Sophia held out an envelope with Grace's name on it.

"Okay." Grace agreed, taking the envelope from her. She would sort it out with David later.

Sophia made no move to leave. Automatically, basic politeness went into play. "Would you like something to drink—a cup of coffee or tea?"

"Sure, coffee would be great."

"Have a seat." Grace offered her a spot on the couch and went into the kitchen to prepare the drinks. She came back a few minutes later with two mugs and handed one to Sophia. Grace's head still hurt, but at least she was capable of moving around.

"I won't stay long. Is everything okay?"

"Gee, do I look that bad?"

Sophia smiled. "Let's say you looked better the last time I saw you. What's the matter? Are you ill?"

Grace took a sip of her coffee. It wasn't the best cup of instant coffee she had ever tasted, but after the nightmare she had endured, was a great pick-me-up. Sophia was patiently waiting for Grace to answer, a concerned look on her face. She deliberated. Should she lie? How embarrassing to admit that she was having such horrendous night terrors. Sophia would know she was having a nervous breakdown. "I've been having a few bad dreams."

"What sort of dreams?" Sophia's voice took on an odd tone, and she sat straighter on the couch.

"Well, I know this is going to sound weird. But I keep dreaming of a strange man. He was good-looking the first time I saw him. Now I want to run the other direction." Grace laughed.

"And do you?" Sophia peered at her intently over her coffee cup.

"I try to, but I can't. In the dream, he controls me. I have to do what he tells me to do no matter how frightened I am."

Sophia's face took on a stern expression. She set her coffee cup on the table and pulled out her cell phone.

Grace continued. "The weirdest part is, when I wake, I don't feel well. I usually have a headache. It's gotten so I dread going to sleep at night because I know he'll be waiting. I don't suppose you've ever experienced anything like this, have you?"

"It's familiar," Sophia told her.

Grace nearly dropped her coffee cup. She had expected Sophia to laugh her off or say something lighthearted to make her feel better. Grace had not expected her to identify with her. "How long has this been going on Grace?"

"Nearly a week, I think."

"Does David know?"

"No, I haven't told him. I didn't take it seriously the first couple of times it happened. I sometimes see David in the dreams, too. I'm always so grateful. Whenever he comes, the nasty man disappears." She gave a shaky laugh. The whole thing was crazy. "I've made an appointment for a physical. I'm concerned I may be having a mini-stroke…or something." The something was the nervous breakdown coming on, but she avoided acknowledging the possibility in front of Sophia.

"How is this familiar to you? Do you think there's some medical explanation?"

Sophia rose and walked to the couch. She put her coffee cup on the table and sat next to Grace, grasping both her hands. "Grace, what I'm about to tell you is going to come as a shock. I warned David he should have told you a long time ago—we all did."

"Warned me about what?" Grace put a hand on her aching head. She was having a hard time following the conversation.

"Do you want to know why you're having these dreams?"

"Yes, I do," Grace said. Maybe Sophia would tell her she was going crazy, and this was the first sign of it, or Grace had some bizarre illness.

"The man you encountered is real. He's not a dream man or a figment of your imagination."

Grace stared at her blankly. She was losing her mind because nothing Sophia was saying was making any sense. She tried for levity. "So, you're saying I need to get out more?"

"No, I'm saying you aren't crazy. The man in your

dreams is a real person. That's why it seems so real to you."

"You're kidding me, right?" Grace tried again. "This is a joke? Did David put you up to this?" Insane laughter rose inside her, dangerously near the surface.

"No, this isn't a joke," Sophia said calmly. "He's a real person who's able to get inside your mind. That's why he's able to control you and make you do things you don't want to. Men like this work for the government. Think of them as highly trained and paid military men who, instead of being trained with guns or knives, have been taught to use their minds as weapons."

"So this dream man is a real person who's able to get into my mind?" Grace heard herself asking, her tone slightly hysterical, while some other part of her brain was sorting through the facts. "You expect me to believe there are people in the world who can read minds?"

"Yes, because there are," Sophia said simply. "But they don't generally bother with everyday civilians, so it's strange he's targeted you." Sophia paused, while Grace struggled to understand what she was being told.

"The only exception is when they need information. In those cases, they may investigate a civilian target. But they're sensitive to that and never show themselves or inflict harm. Their goal is to make a quick hit, get the information they want and exit without the target being aware or anyone being hurt. The government doesn't want people to know about the mind hackers—that's what they call them—which is why they go to great lengths to make sure no one gets hurt. There are only a few families with the skill, and they're closely watched."

Grace struggled to grasp the conversation and make logical sense of it. "Let's say I believe there's some maniac out there who has chosen to read my mind." She spoke slowly. "What could I possibly know that could do him any good?"

"I don't think it's what you know. I think it's who you know."

Grace frowned. "David?"

Sophia nodded.

"What does David have to do with a power-hungry maniac who haunts my dreams? Are you telling me that's David?"

"Oh, no, Grace. David isn't the bad guy. He's exactly what he portrays himself to be. You told me yourself he comes to rescue you."

"David's a mind hacker." The truth settled on her like static cling. She kept remembering their first encounter on the beach, and the way he seemed to know where she would be. Had he read her mind? A wave of dizziness hit her like a wave crashing into shore. It had finally happened. She had lost her marbles. On that thought, she slipped into unconsciousness.

When Grace awoke, she was lying on the couch, an anxious Sophia bending over her. "Oh, thank God. Don't try to sit up."

Grace couldn't have even if she wanted to. She lay there, groggy, and tried to remember how she got there. She struggled once again to process what Sophia had told her. There were people who could read minds that worked for the government. *Okay. Sounds far-fetched.* But Grace guessed she could believe it. What was harder for her to process was her new boyfriend and client was one of them. Every time she thought of it, Grace grew cold with anger and a deep, empty fear. David had been in her mind. He had been controlling her. That's why she had let him make love to her. It was why she'd invited him home to meet her mother even though that was so unlike her. He had manipulated her all along. Nausea rose inside her, threatening her sanity. Once again, she had let herself fall for a dishonest man.

"I'm so sorry, Grace. Are you okay?"

"No, I'm not."

"I didn't want to have to be the one to tell you. I warned David." Sophia sounded angry. "But he has feelings for you. You have to understand, having this ability can make you crazy. It's hard to find a suitable partner. And David is stronger than most. He's not used to having feelings he can't control. That's why he tried to handle it by himself and didn't tell you. He wanted you to have a chance to get to know him the traditional way. But you have a right to understand the danger of your situation and who you're dating."

Grace focused on her breathing, in, out, in, out. Sophia was still talking.

"When we knew for sure you were the one he wanted, we warned him he needed to tell you the truth and let you decide for yourself. But would he listen? No. He insisted you would fall for him naturally if you were given the time."

Grace's nausea receded a little. The yoga breathing was working. In, out, in, out.

"We told him your life could be in danger. That the hacker after him could come after you, as well, to try and get to him. Did he listen? No. He said he would handle it."

Grace narrowed in on Sophia's words. A hacker—the man in her dream—was after David. She sat up slowly, her head clearer. She focused on Sophia. "What do you mean the hacker's after David?"

"He is. He's been after him all this year. We've been working around the clock to track him, but no one seems to know who he is. All we know is he's extremely powerful and influential, and he wants David. He also doesn't follow any code of honor. This guy doesn't hesitate to kill. If we can't find him, the whole mind hacker program is in jeopardy. We all are."

"How has David eluded the hacker this long?"

"He's powerful, but so is David. David's the strongest mind hacker the government has ever had in the program. They're not even sure the full extent of his ability as his energy is off the charts and, well, David has always been a little more unique than the rest of us. He cannot control or kill David unless he's able to break into his mind."

"How can the hacker possibly use me to get to David?"

"David has strong feelings for you. Where there are strong emotions, there's energy. It's difficult to explain to a lay person, but the hacker can use that energy in the right combination to get past David's defenses."

"How come you know so much about this? I would think the government wouldn't want David sharing all this with his family. Unless...are you part of the program?"

Sophia nodded. "I didn't lie to you earlier. Our whole family is in the business. We have no choice. We're born into it."

"So you're a mind hacker, too?" *Dear God.*

"Not exactly. I can't read minds. I'm what is known in the trade as a trainer. It's my job to help transport my husband, Brian, safely into and out of a target's mind. I have the ability to absorb and target energy. Without me along, Brian would not be able to get into most people's heads."

"So, Brian's a mind hacker?"

Sophia nodded.

"What about the kids?"

"The kids are too young to be involved, but they'll need to know their legacy one day."

"Your parents?"

"Yes, them too. But they both retired some time ago." Sophia's phone let out a chirp, and she looked down to collect her messages. Whatever she read caused her forehead to crease.

"I need to head home. Brian needs me. I hate to leave you. Are you going to be okay? I know I've given you a lot to think about. But I've had enough of this. You should know the truth. I texted David earlier and told him what I was doing. He'll get here as soon as he can."

Grace nodded. "I'm glad you told me. It explains a lot."

"Obviously, you cannot talk to anyone about this—not your mother, sister, anyone. If you need to talk, talk to me or David. We'll do what we can to keep you safe. The government doesn't take kindly to those who can't keep its secrets."

"What will they do to me if I make a mistake?"

"They're easily capable of erasing your memory and those of your family and friends. If you don't want that happening, I'd advise you to stay silent."

Chapter Eighteen
Confrontation

Grace didn't know what she would say to David when she saw him. After Sophia left, she had spent the better part of the day thinking about the strange predicament she found herself in. She knew her feelings for David were most likely a pretense, forced on her by his mind-controlling abilities. But that didn't stop her from feeling them. It pained her to realize everything about their relationship had been a lie. Were any of their conversations authentic?

Grace recalled their encounter on the beach when David had caressed her face. How perfect the moment had been—both sexy and precious at the same time. Had it all been an illusion? Had David planted the memory in her mind? Sophia had indicated David was powerful. But what exactly was he capable of?

Underneath her anger, there was deep-seated fear of him and his abilities. Was David capable of making her love him despite her anger? Grace shivered.

For most of the day she sat on her couch counting the hours and minutes until David would arrive at her doorstep. But when he did show, Grace was woefully unprepared. Before she could invite him in, he moved forward and pulled her to him in a fierce hug and used his feet to close the door behind him.

When David finally released her, and Grace looked

into his eyes, he didn't look like the smoothly confident and controlled man she knew. His hair was disheveled, and his eyes were bloodshot. "How are you feeling?"

"Okay, considering. I know what you are."

David nodded. "Sophia told me."

Grace pulled away from him in an effort to put some distance between them, giving him her backside.

David followed her. "It's not how you think."

She turned on him. "What would you know about it?" Grace tried but could not keep the bitterness from her words. "Oh, that's right. You can read my mind. Read this." She poured her anger and fear into a mental message, shouting at him in her mind. *You fucking jerk. How could you involve me in this mess? You lied to me, and I hate you for it.*

David flinched but immediately regained control, which would have been impressive if he cared for her like he said he did. But she was sure he only liked how he could control her.

His face took on a pained expression. "That isn't true. I never tried to control you."

"You can mess with people's minds." Grace threw the words at him, sputtering in her anger. "You can make them think they're falling for you, when they're not. You can act sweet and tender when all you are is…" Grace gulped and tried desperately to stem the hot flood of tears. "A big, fat liar."

"Grace. I never meant to hurt you."

Grace turned away.

"Please, Grace. Look at me."

"Why, so you can control me again?" Grace shot back. "Is it easier when I look in your eyes? Is that how it's done?"

David was silent.

"Okay, fine. Control me." She looked him in the eyes. "But remember, whatever you make me do, it's all a lie."

Her words would make any other man angry. But David's expression didn't change. He reached out and grasped her hands. His eyes seemed to look right into her soul. Grace found herself drowning in their depths.

"I cannot help what I am. I can read minds. I can change thoughts. But I would never hurt you. Think, Grace. If I were controlling you, why wouldn't I have made you speak your feelings for me?"

"Because you read my thoughts." Grace sniffed.

David smiled. "And they made me want to shout for joy. You don't know how long I've waited for you to feel something positive for me. But that's not the point. The fact is, I didn't make you admit it, did I? I gave you the time you needed. If we were to fall in love—together—not any one-sided kind of love, I would want you to love me for me. Not because I can make you think you love me. That's not real love."

She pulled her hands from his. "How do I know you aren't controlling me now?"

David shrugged. "I don't suppose you do. But I need you to trust me. If I wanted someone to control, I wouldn't need to go after you. There are any number of people I could choose. Hell, the whole world for that matter."

His eyes glittered wildly and for a moment Grace was afraid of what he might do. But as quickly, the look vanished. David grasped her hands in his again. "You're special, Grace. I'm not sure what it is exactly, but I've searched for someone like you my whole life.

Now that I've found you, I refuse to let the fact I can read minds separate us. If you can look at me and tell me you don't care for me, and it's the truth, I'll know. As much as it pains me, I'll let you go. But I don't think you can tell me that, can you?"

Grace wanted to deny it. She didn't want to care for him. But the truth was when Sophia had told her a hacker was after him, Grace had experienced a deep worry for his safety. She cared. But was it love? Doubts assailed her. Was David making her feel these emotions? Could she trust him?

David watched her, and Grace knew he was in her mind, reading her thoughts. He shook his head. "I can't make you feel things. I can only make you have certain thoughts that might lead to those feelings."

What was it like to read minds? As if someone had grabbed her brain and took control, Grace looked through David's eyes, felt as he felt. For the first time in her life, she saw herself as desirable. Memories and emotions flooded her mind. David watching her on the beach, while she gathered glass. David jealous after seeing her talking to Brains. David concerned when she became nauseous, worried he was the cause. David wanting her but needing her trust first. David making love to her… *Too much!* As suddenly as the foreign thoughts and visions appeared, they dissolved, and Grace was back inside her own head.

"Now do you understand?"

"Was I—did I read your mind?"

He nodded.

"I think I need to sit." She walked to the couch on shaky legs and sat. David followed her.

"It works both ways. I don't expect you to share all

your thoughts with me and never know mine. I'll freely share my mind with you."

David sat on the couch facing her and held her hands. Foreign thoughts formed as David opened the doors to his mind again. With each came a rush of emotion. Grace saw herself as she had appeared to David in his home. He fought a mix of curiosity and desire. He did not want to hurt her. He wanted her to have time to get to know him and hopefully return the attraction. It was all there for Grace to see in pictures.

With one hand David reached up and gently rubbed her scalp. Slowly, the headache Grace had been battling all day lessoned. Was this what it was like to be David? To know what someone was thinking all the time like this would drive her mad.

"It did when I was younger," he told her slowly.

Grace did not have to read his mind to know it was difficult for him to share this side of himself. She was being offered a rare and priceless possession. Grace let her breath out carefully lest she interrupt the flow of information.

"It was especially hard knowing when someone didn't like me or had bad intentions. That happened a lot," David said softly, stroking her hair. "I had to learn how to block it out. In my family, we're told early on we're gifted, but I've always viewed it as the family curse. You wouldn't believe some of the lies told by the most angelic people. That was one of the things that attracted me to you from the first." He smiled at her. "You're honest and trustworthy."

"Uh…maybe you're not as strong as you think. I told a lie the first time we met. Wait a minute. That's what you were doing that day, weren't you? You were reading my mind! You knew I lied about the budget, didn't you?"

David chuckled, the sound reminiscent of their first encounter. How cold he had seemed that day. But even then, she had not been able to keep her eyes off him.

David reached out and touched her chin, turning her face to gaze into her eyes. "Okay, so maybe you're not entirely perfect. But that little lie bothered you a great deal, didn't it?"

Before she could respond, his lips grazed hers, the stubble of his day old beard rough on her sensitive skin. David must have been in a hurry to get to her if he hadn't taken the time to shave. Grace's earlier hurt and anger slipped away under the gentle onslaught of his lips on hers. A familiar desire pooled in her belly, but she fought the rising tide of passion. There was something she needed to ask. Next to her, David stilled, anticipating her question even as she formed it.

"David, I was…I mean would you…" Why was this so hard? She tried again. "I was wondering if you would come to San Francisco with me for Claire's wedding. I mean—"

David didn't let her finish, cutting her off with a short, sharp kiss. He brushed his thumb across her forehead to pull the hair out of her eyes, smiling tenderly. "I would be honored to attend your sister's wedding with you and meet the rest of your family."

*****

A deep sense of triumph coursed through his system. Despite what he was, Grace had accepted him. Slowly, she'd settled against him on the couch, and they'd spent several moments in silence. Peace. A truce. Companionable bliss.

It would make his next actions all the more painful.

What irony. After finally gaining her acceptance, he must erase the precious memory. They must return to being strangers.

He caressed her face lovingly, enjoying the feel of her soft skin beneath his fingers and fighting an inner demon. Her eyes fluttered shut, and her breaths became even as she dozed. The last time they had made love, she had stretched her body across his bed naked, and he had feasted greedily. Little did he know that would be their last time. They would not be intimate again…not for a long while…perhaps never.

Even as he comforted her, he knew he would have to work hard to keep his promise. If he couldn't track the hacker, he couldn't risk being at the wedding. Not for the first time, David was glad Grace didn't read minds. She needed her sleep, and it would be easier for him—and her—if she did not know what was happening.

He sucked in a sharp breath and gently extricated himself from holding her. His next actions would end their relationship. It went against the essence of his genetic makeup to let her go. He had to remind himself over and over her life was in danger if he did not act tonight.

David stood slowly, making sure not to wake her. Tenderly, he adjusted the pillow under her head and the afghan covering her. He strolled over to the cabinet where he saw in her mind she stored her beach glass. He was curious to see the collection she had built all those months he had watched her on the beach and the special piece of glass David had left for her. He reached in and pulled out the red heart—David needed a memory, and this was not one he wanted to forget. Taking a deep breath, he entered Grace's mind. What he was about to do was dangerous for both of them. He must maintain complete control at all times. David sent her into a deeper sleep. Grace obeyed the command easily.

Delicately, he sifted through her thoughts, removing all memories of him, and duplicating others. Time seemed to drag slowly. Sweat beaded on his forehead, the drops dripping into his eyes as David worked carefully to extract her thoughts in chronological order. One mistake could create irreparable damage.

When David was positive he had captured all Grace's memories of him, he gently backed through the portal. He closed his eyes, clutching the ruby red glass in his hand until it seemed to glow with an inner radiance. Satisfied, David opened his eyes. *Success!*

His love was breathing gently. David couldn't help but smile, pocketing the glass. Harvey was squawking in his cage. "To be or not to be, to be or not to be."

David gave the bird a mental stare down. "Shut up."

Harvey fell silent. David shot him a satisfied smirk. Sometimes his abilities came in handy.

For a moment he watched her sleeping and could not resist stroking her cheek. It might be a long time before he could physically meet her again. Automatically, his mind reached for hers, and he had to exert great control not to enter.

After a few minutes, he walked to the table, and took the envelope with Grace's name scribbled on the outside and the bouquet of flowers sitting in the vase on the table, and left. He would take care of that shortly. He had a few more minds to tamper with tonight and a hacker to pursue.

Chapter Nineteen
Opportunity Knocks

The clock ticked the seconds away endlessly but did not disturb the woman on the couch, who might have slept the day away if not for the pretty gray bird in the gold cage. "Out, out, out."

Harvey's screeching finally broke into Grace's dream, and she awoke disoriented. She spent some minutes trying to figure out what she was doing on the couch in her clothes. For the life of her, she could not remember how she got there. She must have slept well because she felt rested. Harvey continued squawking in his cage. "Romeo, Romeo."

"I wish." Grace sighed. "No Romeo here. Just little old Juliet."

She yawned and stretched, arching her back like a cat after a good nap. She looked at the clock. *Noon!* She counted the hours on her fingers until she reached fifteen. Could she have slept that long? By the rumblings in her belly, she must have. Grace was hungry.

She went to the fridge, but all she could find was a left-over container of pot roast. She took it out and sniffed it over. It looked okay, but since Grace couldn't recall where it came from or how long it had been sitting around, she pitched it. The only other option was a carton of yogurt or a ham sandwich, neither of which sounded filling. She needed much heartier fare. Grace would go to *Coffersations*. They offered egg and cheese bagel, plus she could get good coffee to clear the cobwebs in her brain.

"Hello, David." Harvey called as she passed by his cage. Grace gave him a puzzled look. When she thought she'd heard them all, Harvey demonstrated that his vocabulary was boundless. *An old boyfriend of Claire's?*

As she grabbed her jacket to head out, she noticed the pile of bills on the kitchen table. She needed to get cracking on her next job, or she was not going to make her condo payment. The usual anxiety kicked in as she worried over how to make ends meet. She took her notebook with her. That's where she recorded all her ideas and possible clients.

Yesterday, her mother's neighbor, Nancy Gordon, expressed an interest in having Grace design a small mosaic piece for her patio. Nancy was eighty-five and still kicking. She was a sweet lady but talked a lot and was opinionated. It was hard to get a word in edgewise. Grace did not relish having to listen to all her stories and hints on how to design the piece. But unless she could find a better offer, she was going to have to work with Nancy. She was paying Grace three hundred dollars in advance to do the job and another eight hundred when it was completed.

When she left her condo, it was raining. It was a light mist, and she had her umbrella, so she decided to walk the short block to the coffee shop. The bell on the door rang its familiar greeting as Grace entered, causing déjà vu and an adrenaline rush. Of course, she came to the coffee shop a lot, so the déjà vu part wasn't surprising. *But why the excitement?* She shrugged off the strange feeling.

Grace made her way to the counter and ordered brunch. The shop was not crowded, so she was able to get her food quickly. She took it to a corner table and tried hard not to ravish it. For a few minutes, she enjoyed her meal in silence, but soon enough, she opened her notebook and considered her options. Grace was contemplating getting in touch with a college friend who was a marketing manager for a local steel company, when a dark shadow fell across her notebook.

"Hello Grace." Without waiting for her to respond, the man pulled the chair out across from her and sat. "How've you been?"

"Greg! What…how…what are you doing here?"

"Would you believe me if I said I happened to be in the neighborhood?"

"No." *What the hell?* Grace studied him. His face looked flushed. Whatever Greg was here to tell her, she wasn't going to like it. "What's wrong?"

"Nothing. This is about you. Brice told me you contacted him to make a pitch."

"Yes, I did. But he wasn't interested."

"Did he tell you why?"

"No."

"You don't need to look so suspicious. He had a good reason. He has another project he thinks you will like better. It's great. You'll be working with one of his best customers."

"So why not tell me himself? Why send my cheating ex-husband to tell me?"

"He didn't send me. He has no idea I'm even here. Look, he mentioned you'd been in to see him. He was in a pickle. He needs an artist right away to consult with one of his top clients. I suggested you might be perfect for this new assignment. I know you're hurting for cash. It's the least I can do."

"And how would you know I'm hurting for cash. I haven't talked to you since you told me about the first assignment." She watched him closely. He looked at his hands, a clear sign there was something he didn't want her to know. "You've talked to Claire, haven't you?"

"Well, I was concerned about you." His tone was defensive. "And I knew you wouldn't talk to me. It was the only way I knew to find out how you were and what you were up to."

"Claire should not have talked to you. My finances are none of your business anymore."

"Look, regardless of what you think of me, do you want the job or not? I talked to Brice, and he's willing to commission you."

Grace wanted so badly to tell him where to go. But she kept thinking about the pile of bills at home and her empty bank account. "When would I start?" she asked reluctantly.

He smiled. "I knew you'd come around. You can start Monday. They're having a meeting with the client. Brice said if you wanted the job you're to meet them at the office at 8:30 a.m. sharp. I'll let them know that you'll be there."

"Wait a minute. What are they willing to pay?"

"That's the great part—this client is loaded. He'll meet your hourly rate for consultation as long as the project takes. I took the liberty of telling him you charge seventy-five dollars an hour."

It did not sit well with her to feel beholden to Greg.

And she didn't trust him. There must be something more than an appeased conscience in this for him. But for the life of her, she couldn't think what. Grace forced herself to say the right thing. She pushed the words through her clenched mouth. "Greg, thank you for suggesting me. I do need the work."

He reached across the table and tried to grab her hand, but she snatched it away. "I'm appreciative," she said. "But don't touch me."

"Fine, fine." He shrugged, rose, and pushed his chair in. He leaned, placing his hands on the table. "Grace, I don't know if you can ever forgive me, but I want you to know I'm sorry. Really." He turned his back, and she watched him walk out of the coffee shop.

The whole conversation made her skin crawl. The slime had neatly turned the tables. Not only was she beholden to him for a job, but she was also the unforgiving and resentful one. How did he always do that to her? He'd cheated on her. With a coworker! One he was no doubt still with! Grace had a right to be angry.

She stood, grabbed her notebook, and left the shop, stewing on Greg's audacity all the while. It didn't matter how many jobs he got her, Grace would never forget his treachery. She had given him her heart and rather than cherish it, he had stepped on it. She pictured it in her chest, bruised and bleeding. Seeing Greg made her realize it still hurt.

Thankfully, it had stopped raining, so she pulled out her phone to call Claire. Her sister answered on the first ring and was talking before Grace could say hello. "So you know how you've been having all those weird dreams lately? You must have rubbed off on me because I had a weird one last night, too."

"What weird dreams?" Grace asked.

"Don't act all mysterious. You know those weird dreams where a handsome man makes you do things. Well, I had one last night. I dreamt I was in our old house—the one in Parma. At first I was complaining to Burt and in walks this gorgeous guy. He tells Burt to get lost and he looks at me."

"And?"

"And he tells me to do something, but I don't remember what it was. I don't remember anything else. The dream kind of ended. Now I wish he would have at least kissed me or something. We could have had kinky dream sex."

"Oh, Lord. Speaking of weird, I had the strangest thing happen. I saw Greg, and he offered me a job."

"Really? That's fabulous. When do you start?"

"Don't you 'oh really' me. You knew I would run into him, didn't you? You told him I was broke!"

"I'll kill him! Greg wasn't supposed to say anything! Grace, I'm sorry. Truly. He promised me he only wanted to do you a good turn. He feels guilty and wanted to make it up to you. I knew you were short on cash so I kind of hinted getting you a job might be a way to ask forgiveness."

"I admit I do need the work. But I'm not happy he knows about my financial picture. You shouldn't have told him that. And you shouldn't have told him where to find me. I would prefer you gave him my email. He caught me so off-guard."

"But I didn't tell him where to find you. All I told him was you needed a job. I swear." Claire's tone had a note of sincerity in it.

"Yeah…well…I still don't like that he knows my financial situation. And now I feel like I owe him. Which I hate." She spat the last word into the phone.

"I'm sorry. I knew you were bummed about not getting the Gallant job. And I knew you would never ask Greg yourself. I thought it was a little thing I could do for you."

"Please tell me you did not call him!"

"It was a quick call. I asked him if he knew you had interviewed with Gallant. He had. I asked him if he could influence Brice, and he said he would. That's it. I swear."

Grace sighed. Getting mad at Claire wouldn't change a thing. And she knew her heart was in the right place. But it galled her to know Claire and Greg had been talking about her behind her back. Greg had cheated on her for crying out loud. Her family should be angry on her behalf, not consorting with the enemy.

"So are you mad at me?"

"Yes! I don't like you talking to Greg about me. Oh, I'll get over it, I'm sure. I do need the money. But don't call him again, okay? I don't want to owe him any more favors."

"Of course. I won't. I promise. Cross my heart. Grace, I have to go. Tom's sister is calling. She's driving me nuts. I'll see you Friday at the airport."

"Wait…what did you mean about me having weird dreams? Oh, never mind. I know you have to run. See you Friday."

Grace disconnected, slightly less annoyed than before the call. It was nice she and her sister had the kind of relationship where they could clear the air right away. It was hard to stay mad at Claire for long. Her ex-husband—now that was a different story. She could cheerfully wring his neck and Brittany's, too.

Grace let herself into her condo. The first thing she needed to do was to call the bank and see what she could do about her mortgage payment. She was hoping they would give her a slight extension, although she guessed it might cost her, since this was not the first time she hadn't made a payment on time.

She rang the branch and asked to speak to the manager. They put her through. "Hello, Mel? It's me, Grace Woznisky." They had been on a first-name basis since the last time she couldn't meet her mortgage payment. Grace hoped Mel would be as understanding.

"Well, hello, Grace. How are you today?"

"Fine. Well, not really. The reason for my call is I'm afraid I'm going to be late on my October mortgage payment. I was wondering if there was anything you could do to help me out again. Business has not been good lately, although I did land a new opportunity that is expected to pay well. I start Monday, and I'm going to ask for an advance so I'm fairly sure I should be able to make payment relatively quickly after the first of the month."

"Let me look up your account. What was that number?"

Grace gave it to him.

"Let's see now. Hmmm. Well, now. You say you won't be able to make payment because of lack of funds in your account?"

"Yes, that's right. I won't have enough funds to cover that payment along with all my other expenses this month."

"Strange. Your account indicates you have a

current balance of eleven thousand two hundred thirty three dollars and twenty-nine cents."

"I…What!? That can't be right. Of course, I wish it was right. But there must have been some mistake."

"Ummm…hmmm. Well, I see there was a deposit into your account on August 18 of ten thousand dollars."

"There was? How can that be? I mean…I haven't had work for several weeks now. Where did the funds come from? Much as I'd love to claim the money, I'm pretty sure it's not mine."

"It looks like you received a wire from a credit union. It appears to be a legitimate deposit. You don't know why someone would have deposited this money into your account?"

"I wish I did. But honestly, I don't think that's my money."

"Well, I'll certainly check into this for you. Let me do that, and I'll call you back."

They hung up. Grace couldn't believe it. It had to be a mistake. Some poor old lady was scratching her head trying to figure out where her retirement income had gone. Grace had done the honest thing in letting them know it wasn't hers.

Her cell phone rang. The bank. She answered.

"Hello, Grace?"

"Yes?"

"It's Mel. Everything appears to be right and tight. That money was wired from a source that prefers to remain anonymous. They refuse to be identified but have confirmed you're entitled to the cash. It's yours free and clear."

Grace nearly dropped the phone. She was lucky

there was a couch behind her because her legs collapsed from under her, and she practically fell onto it. "Grace, are you still there?"

"Yes, I'm having a hard time believing this isn't a dream."

"It's not a dream I can assure you. Looks like you don't have to worry about your mortgage payment or any other bills this month. Congratulations."

"Thank you. Thank you for all your help. But why would someone donate ten thousand dollars to me? It doesn't make any sense."

"I assure you the donor is legitimate. The funds are yours free and clear."

"Okay, well, thank you. Thank you so much."

"You're quite welcome. Anything else I can do for you?"

"No, that is all I needed. Thanks again, Mel. Goodbye."

Grace flung her phone aside a bit breathlessly. *Ten thousand dollars. In my checking account.* That was enough to pay all her bills this month and some. For the life of her, Grace could not imagine who her anonymous donor was and how she could have possibly deserved it. Claire and her mom did not have this kind of money. Greg did, but she had seen the way he had been during the divorce. She had had to fight him for half of what they owned, which was hard because at the time, she had been so angry she didn't want anything from him except her dignity. But she'd needed the money to afford a place to live. She thought hard. There was no one else that might know her financial situation that would care enough to try and gift her with cash. She was stumped.

Chapter Twenty
Back to Business

David was getting closer. The rogue hacker was starting to get nervous. He could tell because for the first time David had found a trace of his presence in a mind that wasn't Grace's. Unfortunately, the mind happened to be her sister's. The hacker must have been in a hurry because he had left behind a telltale wisp of energy—not enough for David to track to its source but an important clue as to his state of mind. The hacker was having trouble containing all of his energy during his mind probes. Controlling energy was a vital part of the job. A hacker that could not control every energy wave put themselves and all who depended on them in jeopardy. David imprinted the foreign energy on his mind.

He had spent the afternoon doing what was necessary to ensure Grace's safety and that meant removing her mother and sister's memories of him. The hacker would not find any reason to harm Grace when he returned tonight as David was sure he would do. And when he returned, David would be ready for him.

*****

Two thousand miles away, the hacker smiled ruthlessly. He knew he was smarter and stronger than all the rest. He was in control of his destiny, no one else. He frowned. It had not always been this way. A long time ago, they had tried to break him. It still made him angry when he recalled the names they used to label him. A little boy who had lost his mother.

I showed them all, didn't I? He was so much smarter and stronger than any of them realized. Not one of them had made it out of the slums, where they had all got their start. He and Kaitlyn had seen to that.

And women loved him. He read it in their minds. They thought he was so handsome. *Dazzled by his dimples.* He liked the alliteration. They could not respond fast enough to his requests. He let out a deep chuckle. The irony was not lost on him. He had come a long way from the slums of Detroit. He had indeed shown them all.

He frowned. Except Grace. She was not dazzled like the others. *Jenkins's fault.* Grace had fallen for the weakling. Allowed him to place a portal in her mind. Well, they would all be jumping to his tune in the end. Especially Jenkins. When this game was done, Jenkins would be a puppet on a string, and he would hold the string. The thought made him gleeful. He would never be made to feel worthless again. He would call all the shots. With some effort, he reined in his emotions. The closer he came to success, the harder they became to contain.

Grace was meant to be the mother of his children. Her genes would effectively carry his talent to the next generation. He had stolen a few memories to keep Jenkins off the scent, and it had worked. But those memories were mostly useless to him. What he needed was all of Grace.

She was the key to cracking Jenkins's mind. Once he had Grace under his belt (he smiled at the analogy),

Jenkins would be like a docile kitten. The first step was accomplished. Jenkins had removed Grace's memories. But he needed to find a way to eliminate Jenkins's portal.

He puzzled over that for a while. He could hire a hit man. But with his high profile, if anyone got suspicious, he and Kaitlyn would have their hands full trying to cover their tracks. They had been successful this long because they worked alone. He did not relish bringing someone else into the fold. No, the easiest solution was Grace herself. He needed to convince her mind Jenkins was not safe. To do that, she would need to believe *he* was her protector.

He smiled.

There was a certain thrill with Grace. He enjoyed bending her to his will. The fact she always fought, even when she knew he was in charge, was exciting. He liked a little spirit in a mate. Liked the feeling it gave him to assert his superiority.

He smoothed has hands over the fine crease in his pants and looked at himself critically in the mirror. Yes, Grace would be lucky to have him. Best of all, their children would inherit the talent from both sides without the government having a clue.

God, the sister was a beauty, too. Disappointing the talent had not manifested in her. No matter. He could have her, too, if he wanted. That would come later. For now, he could not afford to be distracted. Once Jenkins was out of the way, he could have anyone he wanted. There would be no one strong enough to challenge him. No single person would ever dare to cross him again.

His phone rang and he answered absently. "You have everything set for Monday? Well done, my friend.

You'll be rewarded as promised."

*****

Grace was dreaming. It must be a dream because she was back in her childhood home in Parma. The house seemed bigger and bolder than she remembered with many rooms and hidden treasures if only she could find them. She kept opening doors to look inside each room, but they were all deserted. Where was her beach glass? Why was her family not at home? Frightened, Grace opened her mouth to call out to her mother and stopped. An intruder had entered the house, no, a man—someone familiar. Had she invited him? Grace didn't remember doing so. She walked toward him, but the closer she walked, the farther away the man got.

*****

David had been so sure the rogue hacker would return tonight. But he had not. Apparently, the enemy had known what David planned and had moved on. That could be the only explanation. He suppressed his frustration. At least Grace was now safe.

He ducked, narrowly missing the detecting energy beam that whizzed past his face. David quickly threw up a shield. *Short waves.* Grace was awakening. Her subconscious mind no longer had her previous memories to associate with his energy and was struggling to determine if he posed a threat. Thank God the portal was still intact. David was not at all certain he could protect her without it. He needed to get out before she detected his presence.

He stayed with Grace until dawn when her conscious mind assumed control, and he knew she would be safe. The minute he slipped back into his body, his phone vibrated. It took him a little while to shake off his lethargy and answer. But the caller was persistent.

"Jenkins."

"Well?" Peter asked.

"He wasn't there. I thought for sure he would be. He obviously expected me."

"Well, I've got good news and bad news. Which do you want to hear?"

"I'll take the bad news first."

"Percy wiped out on his first mission."

"He survived, I take it?"

"Correct."

"I'd say that's good news. But I'll humor you, what's the good news?"

"Alex wants you back on the force as soon as possible."

Chapter Twenty-One
Wedding Shower

"Tom sounds like a lovely man. Does he have any brothers?" Aunt Peggy winked at Grace.

"Not that I know of." Grace shook her head.

"Such a shame."

Aunt Peggy was looking at Grace with concern. Grace prepared herself for the usual inquisition.

The shower was winding down. She had collected Claire, who was staying with her through Sunday, at the airport yesterday. Tom couldn't get the time off to come to the shower, since they were taking so much time for the honeymoon. But her sister, in true Claire fashion, had arrived with a male companion, which she introduced as James. Claire and James were in a production together, and so she had bribed him to come along to keep her company. Tom, she was told, knew James well and had not minded.

"Are you seeing anyone new, Grace dear?" Aunt Peggy was not her mother's sister for nothing.

"No, I'm not. I've been way too busy with work lately."

"Your mother told me you were meeting men on the Internet. You know that's dangerous, don't you? They say sexual predators use the Internet to lure their victims. It makes me nervous to think of you finding men that way."

Yep, definitely related. "Well, really there's no need to worry. I decided not to meet him. He never showed for any of our in-person meetings anyway."

"I'm relieved to hear you say that. Your cousin Lena has a boyfriend now, did your mom tell you?"

Grace looked across the room at Lena, talking to Claire and James. "No, she didn't mention it. How'd she meet him?"

"He's an attorney at her law firm. They took one look at each other, and it was love at first sight."

Lena was a lawyer and good at it. She had helped Grace out when she divorced Greg. It was one of the reasons Grace had money to purchase her condo. She could feel nothing but gratitude to Lena as she had been in no state to negotiate on her own. It did not surprise her to hear Lena was dating a coworker. From what Grace saw of Lena's life, there wasn't much free time to meet someone any other way.

"I'm glad she's found someone. I'm sure they have a lot in common."

"Grace!" Claire shouted from across the room. All eyes turned to stare at her. "Come talk to me and James."

In a rare instance, Grace found herself grateful for Claire's loud mouth. "Excuse me Aunt Peggy."

Grace strode toward her sister and James, greeting them warmly. "Nice to meet you." She shook James's hand.

"I've been looking forward to meeting you for some time, Grace. Claire talks about you a lot."

"Oh, yeah?" Grace eyed her sister, who was smiling at her, a satisfied expression on her face. So, her little sis was playing matchmaker. "What does she say?"

"You're a phenomenal artist."

"Phenomenal is a bit of a stretch, but thank you."

"Don't thank me, thank your sister. She has nothing but great things to say about you."

Claire laughed, and James eyed her appreciatively. So that was the way the wind blew. Claire had herself another admirer. Grace should have expected it. She wondered if Tom had an inkling. "What do you say we make a threesome tonight…go out to eat, maybe some bowling." Claire suggested.

"Sure." Grace shrugged.

"Sounds good to me," James agreed.

That was how she found herself sitting next to James in a seafood bar with him trying to feed her oysters. The bar featured a local band, who happened to play Claire's favorite song, which led to her springing up and heading to the dance floor. All the males in the bar, including James, turned to stare. Eventually, he turned back, pushing the oysters. Grace had never tried oysters. They looked slimy. But James was persistent, so to shut him up, she tried one.

"So, do you have a boyfriend?"

Grace choked on the oyster. James reached over a big hand and slapped her on the back, and she finally felt the oyster slip down her throat. She guessed that was one way to swallow an oyster. "No, I don't," she said, when she was able to speak again. "Do you? Have a girlfriend I mean?"

"I did up until two months ago."

She quirked an eyebrow at him in question.

"Shelley decided she liked women. One in particular—Claire."

Grace nearly choked all over again, this time on her water. It was some thirty seconds before she could speak again. "Does she realize that Claire is heterosexual and getting married in a few weeks?"

"She does, but I think she was tired of hiding her affection."

"Does Claire know?"

"She does now. I walked in on Shelley making the moves on Claire. I'm pretty certain your sister was as blown away as I was."

"James, I'm so sorry. That must have been devastating."

"Honestly, I understand why she's attracted to Claire. Your sister is something special."

Grace couldn't help but laugh. "You didn't have to grow up with her."

James smiled back.

*****

David did not like where the conversation was headed. It was pure torture for him to have to watch the action and not be able to intervene. He was supposed to be resting for their next mission. Instead he had chosen to spy on his love. He had checked on Grace to make sure she was safe. He figured with her sister's shower, Grace would be exhausted and getting ready for bed. The last thing he expected was to catch her on a date with a man who looked like a pro wrestler. Not that he could see her date—he saw the image in her mind. She hadn't wasted any time finding another boyfriend.

Only years of training helped David control the jealousy racing through his system like a lit fuse. He could not stay with her. But damned if he would let her date a pro-wrestler. He withdrew temporarily. Ten minutes later, he had talked Sophia into helping him. The pro-wrestler had been busy. He was holding Grace's hand and doing his best to plead his case.

"I thought there was something special about you from the moment I saw you."

This time David caught the echo of his unvoiced thoughts: *Your sister is mighty special, too. It's a shame she's getting hitched.*

*****

"I'd like to see you again before the wedding. What do you say we do this again?"

Grace was nodding her head, when James added, "Baby, you have mighty big tits."

She froze and all that came out of her mouth was "gaah." James looked like he was as surprised as Grace.

"I don't know why I said that. I didn't mean it. Of course, I don't mean you don't have nice…ahh…you know what I mean. But I wasn't thinking about that. It kind of came from nowhere."

His face was as bright as a red balloon. Grace didn't wait around for explanations. She was already headed across the dance floor to find Claire. "I'm going home." She called back over her shoulder.

"Grace wait, please. I…I don't know why I said that. I mean you look great but…"

Grace ignored his plea and kept walking until she reached Claire. "Time to go. I'll be outside."

Claire took one look at her face and didn't ask any questions. She collected her things and was soon outside, where she found Grace patiently waiting by their car. "What happened?"

"James paid homage to my boobs."

"Really? Are you sure? That doesn't sound like

James."

Grace looked at her. "Yes, I'm sure. He told me he liked my tits. Not to mention he called me baby. I hate men that do that."

"Okay. Well, calm down. Maybe he had too much to drink. Listen, you drive, I'll ride shotgun and James, the bad boy, can ride in back."

Grace nodded and dug out the keys as James rushed out of the bar, continuing to apologize. Thankfully, Claire was good at filling the awkward silence, and the ride home wasn't as uncomfortable as Grace had dreaded. She was also grateful James was staying at a hotel. They dropped him off and were at her condo within twenty minutes. She was relieved when she could close her front door on the disastrous evening and sag against it.

*****

David laughed. He had not lost his touch. Grace was uncomfortable, and he was tired, but that was a small price to pay for peace of mind. He could now rest easy knowing she was back in her condo, no harm done. Hopefully, the pro-wrestler was too embarrassed to spend any more time chasing after Grace. If not, David had plenty more ammunition up his sleeve.

Chapter Twenty-Two
New Client

Monday morning, Grace fought a rising tide of new job nerves, as she carefully considered what to wear to her meeting with Gallant's star client. She chose a navy blue pant suit and pink blouse with a pair of short heels.

Grace arrived about ten minutes early and was asked to wait in the lobby. Eventually, Brice's assistant appeared to take her to the twentieth floor, where he had his office. When she got there, he was talking to another gentleman who turned to greet her when she entered the room. Grace barely managed to keep her gasp of surprise in check when she saw who it was. He looked even more handsome in person than he did in the newspaper and on television, dressed in a charcoal suit and light blue shirt, his blond hair slicked back. Something about his stance was familiar for other reasons, too. Brice made the introductions.

"Grace Woznisky, this is Kyle Willard. Kyle, Grace has been hired to assist you with your pet project."

She was still in shock but managed to reach her hand out in response to his outstretched hand.

"Hello, Grace. It's nice to meet you. Again."

So they had met before. Where? When? His voice was deep and melodic and sent shivers up her spine. Where had she heard it before? His eyes were an odd shade of blue—an angel's eyes. Except Grace was pretty certain he wasn't an angel. He pulled a padded chair out from a round, wood table and gestured his hand out for her to take a seat. She did so. He walked around and took the seat opposite her. Again, something about his gait and manner was familiar.

Surprisingly, Brice did not sit. Instead he walked to the door. "I'll leave you two to get acquainted."

"I believe the last time we met we neglected to exchange names."

That's when it hit her. "Brains? You're Kyle Willard, techno genius?" Wait until she told Claire. She would never believe her. Her online man was Kyle Willard! This was as good if not better than John Mayer. *Silly.* Still, the fact she had nearly dated a billionaire wasn't lost on her. Claire would be impressed. Grace imagined herself pulling out her cell phone to take his picture. As usual, her thoughts were running away with her. She wrenched them back to the present. Kyle was watching her, a small smile on his face. Her stomach churned.

"I'm sorry if I've taken you by surprise. I like to go incognito at times. It makes it easier to meet new people—know who I can trust and such. Do you forgive me?" He smiled again, his blue eyes seeming to peer inside her mind.

"Yes, of course. I mean, we only chatted online a bit, and you looked so different on the beach. I had no idea you were him. I mean Kyle Willard."

"No need to be nervous. This is strictly professional. At least at the moment." Another blinding smile came Grace's way.

"Are you curious to learn about my pet project?"

"Yes, I am."

"My company is on the verge of a technological breakthrough in the field of bionics. We have spent many years researching and designing artificial body parts. Our newest prototype is unique in that it most perfectly emulates the movement of the human body. When fitted with this bionic limb, those who were formerly disabled can do all the activities those without artificial limbs can do—only better."

Willard paused to give her time to take in the magnitude of the advancement. Grace was suitably awed.

"This year, I'm opening a museum to showcase the company's innovations. I would like to intersperse some of the displays with artwork. Gallant tells me you have talent. What do you think?"

Grace found herself blushing. It was the way Willard looked at her, like he undressed her and liked what he saw.

"I think I have good ideas. But what exactly would you be wanting?"

"I'm not ready to reveal the details. First, I need a bit more information."

He leaned back in his chair and crossed his long legs. His blond hair made a sort of halo around his head with the sunlight streaming in through the window behind him. She pictured the Archangel Michael she used to have over her bed as a child. Did he have any idea of the impact he was having on her? From the way he was looking at her, he might. *Breathe.*

"What are your hobbies?"

Grace shrugged. "I've already shared most of them with Brains…I mean you. I'm crafty. I like to read. I like to travel. What about yourself?"

Kyle shook his head but smiled charmingly, taking the sting out of his next words and revealing a cute dimple on his right side. "Not so fast. That's not how this works. I'm not satisfied with your answers. And I need to be before you get to ask me questions. Describe a typical day in your life?"

He settled back in his chair, steepling his fingers and placing them under his chin, listening. Grace giggled nervously. Brains was more unusual than she had ever realized when they had been online pen pals. Most clients didn't want to know about her. They only cared about what she could do for them.

"Okay, let me see. I get up in the morning. I feed Harvey—my bird. Well, you know about Harvey. I don't function well until I have my coffee, so I usually make coffee next. If it's a weekend, I read the paper. Sometimes I make breakfast. I might call my family—you remember my sister lives out of town. If it's nice, I might spend time at the lake, of course."

"And?"

He continued to stare at her, fingers steepled, listening closely. Grace fidgeted in her chair. What more did he want from her? After all, she had shared the pertinent details with Brains. There wasn't much more to tell. But he was her new client. She needed to find a way to humor him.

"And…I might look for beach glass—I must have told you about my collection. I use the glass in my art. Or if it's raining, I might go shopping or catch a movie."

"Alone?"

"Usually." Why was that important? "Sometimes

my next door neighbor, Barbara, comes along." She paused. "Anything else you'd like to know?"

He strode over to the windows, which looked out over a lovely waterfall. "Of course." He responded almost absently, staring at the scene below. "Everything."

"Excuse me?"

He turned suddenly again to face her, walking back to his seat briskly. "Tell me everything. You'll find, Grace, I don't do anything in half measures."

Grace was clearly out of her element. If she had had some warning Brains was also Kyle Willard and soon to be her client, she would have been more prepared. She could have done her homework and researched him. She would have known he was eccentric and been ready for the inquisition. As it was, she felt bowled over by his interest, unsure of what she could possibly say that would pique his curiosity. She didn't think he wanted to date her anymore—not after she had rejected him. There was a reason the papers called him a genius. He obviously liked to know about those he hired to work for them. Grace hoped she passed the test.

Fortunately, Kyle Willard did not rush her, which gave her time to gather her wandering thoughts. Grace wanted the job, and Willard had the money to pay her. Her ten thousand dollar gift from God wouldn't last forever. She'd do her best to satisfy Kyle's curiosity and win the business.

"Well, let's see. I was born in Parma—that's a suburb of Cleveland."

"I'm familiar." He nodded encouragingly.

"Umm…You remember I have a sister, Claire, who

lives in San Francisco—a struggling actress. Our father died young and our mother raised us. I think I told you I have a step-father Glenn."

"Yes, what do you know about his people?"

"Not much honestly. Glenn has a brother in Boston."

"No, your real father."

"Oh, well, I never really knew him. He died when I was two. He was an only child. Adopted."

"Did you father ever exhibit any unusual talents?"

"Well, I hardly know. I mean, I don't really remember him."

"Think about it for a moment."

"Well…my mother did say my father had an uncanny ability to know where she was all the time. She said he was a master at detection, which made him good at his job. He was a police officer."

"Yes, that makes sense. When did you know you were an artist?"

He was back to sitting there with his legs outstretched and his fingers steepled under his chin. His brilliant blue eyes stabbed into her, and she had trouble looking away for long, although she tried. Apparently, the news media were not mistaken about his genius. He had extraordinary listening abilities.

"When I was in fourth or fifth grade. The teacher asked us to draw an advertisement. She showed my entry to the entire class. That's when I first got recognition for my artwork." She paused to collect her thoughts and admitted, "I didn't believe I could do it until much later."

She watched him to gauge his interest. He nodded. "Continue."

"My high school art teacher took an interest in me. She said I had a unique style and submitted a project I created to a local contest. I won."

"Ah." There was a long pause, until she realized he was waiting for her to continue.

"I only won a $50 savings bond. But still it was enough for me to finally get the idea I had a skill I should explore. I decided to major in graphic design in college."

"Where did you go to school?"

"Cleveland State." Her family had not had much money for college. Grace had lived at home and worked in an office supply store to pay for tuition.

"And were you popular in school?"

What did this have to do with her ability to design? "Not really. I was shy. My sister was another story. She was extremely outgoing and popular."

Once again, Grace glanced his way as she explained and found herself pulled in by his stare. "Have you always been jealous of her?"

A sharp pain hit her temples, and she found herself rubbing them while she answered. "Not always. When we were little, we were the best of friends. I love her. But it's hard to be her sister. You'd have to meet her to understand."

"Oh, I do understand. It's hard to be outshone by a younger sibling. But you are close, I see. How would you like to have dinner with me tonight?"

Was this more than business? Had he decided to go down that path again? She was out of her element, not sure how to answer. Before she could respond, he added, "To discuss the project, of course. You said you wanted to know more details."

That she did. She wasn't sure why he couldn't tell her now, but apparently he needed to get to know her before he could trust her with it. She attributed it to the eccentricities of the wealthy. "Okay. Where shall I meet you?"

He smiled. "I'll pick you up at six. Be ready."

He got up and gestured for Grace to proceed in front of him, so she did. It seemed her interview was over. Grace must have fit whatever criteria he was after since he had invited her to dinner.

Surprisingly, Kyle didn't turn her over to Brice's administrative assistant. Instead, he walked with her past the assistant's desk and to the elevator. He pressed the lobby button. He turned to face her and held out his hand. Grace reached out to shake it, and he grasped her fingers tightly. She noted his palms were almost hot to the touch. Her stomach churned and for a moment, Grace seriously thought she was going to lose her breakfast all over his glossy, black shoes.

"Be ready at six o'clock sharp. I'm looking forward to our dinner tonight. You can tell me all your secrets."

Grace was drowning in his eyes. Kyle Willard looked almost fierce, like he was willing her to agree. Grace found herself nodding and saying a bit breathlessly, "Me, too."

Kyle was the type of man it was hard to say no to. Charming and intense, he over-powered her. It was not surprising he was such a success in life. His attention was flattering, but it did not erase the niggling doubt in the pit of her stomach. Men like Willard did not usually give Grace the time of day. They were too driven and successful—more comfortable with a sleek and polished career woman than a struggling artist like herself.

The elevator opened, and Grace stepped inside, while Kyle's gaze continued to drill holes in her back. She turned to face him. He smiled, once again revealing his dimple. "Until tonight."

The elevators doors closed on Grace's reply. She held her hands out in front of her. They were shaking. The stress of the interview had gotten to her.

Chapter Twenty-Three
Portal Be Gone

David was exhausted. He had been pushing himself and his crew to find the hacker, which meant double expeditions over the past three days. Now he was paying the price. He was staying at Geneva's so they could work more rapidly. At the moment, she was bent over him anxiously, trying to deflect the tide of deadheads. The work they were doing was dangerous at all times, but when they were tired, it was more likely he or his men would slip. One mistake could spell death for them all. The stress was wearing on everyone, including Geneva. She had the difficult job of creating a strong enough energy field that would give them safe passage into and out of the mind. David could hear her mumbling obscenities under her breath.

"Damn men and their fucking stubbornness. It serves you right if you end up dead. Are you willing to trade our lives for hers? What's wrong with you?"

David had no energy available to argue, and Geneva took full advantage.

"Don't you know you need eight hours of sleep and three square meals a day? You can't be checking on her David. I know you care about her, but you must conserve your energy or you'll wind up dead."

She paused a moment to take a breath and started in again. "Peter says Grace is no longer in danger. The hacker now knows he can't gain anything from her mind. You need to stay away from her."

That was a struggle. If he couldn't have Grace, he was damned if he would let anyone else have her either. He was pretty sure Geneva would be even more alarmed if she knew the lengths he had gone to already. Good thing he had kept it a secret from her powerful antenna.

David was in no condition now, however, to spy on Grace. He would be lucky if he could check on her forty-eight hours from now. He desperately needed recovery time so they could continue their search for the rogue hacker. They were on the right track—David knew it. Yesterday, they found traces of the hacker's energy in the mind of the president of the Patchwork Company, a multi-million dollar medical equipment distributor. They needed to sift through the Patchwork's customers to find their man. David only hoped his mind defenses continued to hold, because if they failed, it wouldn't matter if they found a whole host of hackers. There would be nothing he could damn well do about it. And he feared no one, not even Grace, would be safe.

*****

The subject of David's thoughts was still reeling from her morning and the odd interview that had taken place. Grace had arrived back at her condo confused and shaken. She was seriously considering canceling her dinner meeting that evening. She grabbed her cell phone several times to make the call and set it down again. Her bills were covered, so she was no longer desperate for work. But in the art world, reputation was everything. And the fact Grace would back out after already agreeing to the job would eliminate the chance of future work from Gallant. It was in her best interests to satisfy their number one client. It was every artist's dream—a client that kept them so busy they didn't have to pound the pavement looking for work. She should be happy Kyle Willard had taken such an interest.

Still, something about the way he'd looked at her, as if he wanted to eat her for dinner, made her nervous. Once again, she pondered the oddness of their meeting. What an unusual coincidence her online friend turned out be Kyle Willard of all people. He had said he wanted to know everything about her. *Why?* Did he normally interview everyone that worked for him personally and take them out to dinner and grill them? It didn't seem likely.

Grace changed her clothes, contemplating Willard's interest. What should she wear? Something conservative and subtle. She did not want to attract any more attention than she already had. Maybe he'd find her boring and leave her alone to work on the design after tonight. It was a reflection of her anxiety that she wished this scenario would come true.

Grace made herself lunch and settled at her laptop to check email and research her famous client. No sooner did she type Kyle Willard in the search engine and press enter, she was staring at dozens of pictures of him and a wide array of websites from Wikipedia to biography.

"Kyle Willard is an American business magnate, engineer, philanthropist, investor, and inventor." Grace read aloud and then scrolled to his early life. *Willard was born in Detroit, Michigan in 1975 to an unwed, unemployed, and disabled mother, Anna Smalley. Throughout his childhood, he and his mother lived in a variety of group homes, until Anna died in a car accident, leaving young Willard an orphan at the age of eight.*

Wow. She'd had no idea he had such a tragic history. She continued reading.

It was this experience, he later said, and reruns of the Six Million Dollar Man and the Bionic Woman, that first got him interested in bionics. He was adopted by the Willard family, who also had three biological children. He excelled in school, scoring close to a perfect 1600 on his SAT and earning a full scholarship to MIT. As a student there he was credited with creating the world's first bionic skin. He holds a patent for this invention.

After graduating, he started Technoderm with a $50,000 loan from his adoptive parents. The firm manufactures and sells the skin for cancer patients and burn victims. The skin is known for its real look and feel to the patients who receive it, as well as smart features, which allow it to adjust its look and feel to the texture and edge of the real skin it is connected to. The artificial skin will never develop cancer or be subject to sunburn, and it will age along with a patient's biological skin.

Grace had read about this skin before. It saved the lives and brought relief to millions of burn victims every year. She arrived at the end of the page. *Willard was cofounder of the Bionic Body magazine. He has been featured numerous times on the cover of Time, Discover, and Popular Science and holds more than fifteen patents.*

The last line on the page caught her attention: *Willard lives in New York City with his long-time girlfriend Kaitlyn Girard.* Interesting he had tried to date Grace with a girlfriend. *Trouble in paradise, maybe.* She supposed it didn't matter with his credentials. Plenty of women would want to date a billionaire who was responsible for such an amazing, life-saving invention. She did a quick search for more dirt on the girl but with little success. Whoever she was, she apparently didn't enjoy the limelight because Grace could not find a single photograph.

"Pretty girl, pretty girl, pretty girl." Harvey screeched from his cage, reminding Grace it was getting late. Kyle Willard had said he would pick her up at 6:00 p.m., and she could not imagine him being late or her keeping him waiting around while she made last minute preparations. She'd get dressed now so she would have plenty of time to calm her nerves before Willard arrived on the scene.

Three hours later, her doorbell rang and she hurried to answer it. She should have known he would send a driver. Grace stared at the man at her doorstep dressed in a suit and tie.

"Are you Grace Woznisky?"

She nodded and said smartly, "Last time I checked."

The chauffeur, Charles, she discovered, smiled and gestured for her to proceed him. "Your ride's out front, ma'am."

Grace had never ridden in a limo and couldn't resist poking into all the compartments and crevices. Charles made friendly conversation with her all the while. "Do you work directly for Mr. Willard?"

"Yes, ma'am. Been driving for him for near ten years now."

"Wow, that's a long time. Do you enjoy the job?"

"Sure do. It's a great job. Course this is only one of my jobs. I also assist with the odd errand here and there."

"And how do you like working for Mr. Willard?"

"I do enjoy it. Especially when I get to drive nice ladies like you around."

"Oh, does that happen often?"

"Yes, ma'am. Mr. Willard is popular with the ladies."

"He's my employer, too." Grace did not want to be compartmentalized as one of 'Willard's ladies' in the chauffeur's mind.

"Oh, yeah? What has Mr. Willard hired you to do for him?"

"I'm an artist. He's asked for my help with a pet project."

Charles nodded but did not say anything, prompting Grace to ask, "Aren't you going to ask me what kind of project?"

"Oh, no, ma'am. That's not my business. I'm only a driver."

"Well, as far as I know, it's no secret. He's opening a museum and wants me to design the artwork for it. That's all he's told me. Do you admire Mr. Willard?"

"Well, I can't rightly say. Me and Mr. Willard aren't exactly bosom buddies. He's just my employer. But I do admire his success. He has come far mighty fast. He's a wealthy man."

"Have you met his girlfriend?"

"Huh? Oh, Kaitlyn. She's not his girlfriend, although the press continues to call her that. Goes to show, you can't believe everything you read in the paper." He chuckled heartily and the sound made her want to laugh along with him. "Kaitlyn's his sister."

"Oh. I did read that Mr. Willard was adopted into a family with three children. Kaitlyn must be one of them."

"Oh, no. I don't believe that's so ma'am. Kaitlyn is Mr. Willard's biological sister."

"But Wikipedia didn't mention anything about a biological sister."

"Yeah, well, again, you can't believe everything you read online."

"Apparently not." She wanted to ask him more about Kaitlyn, but they had arrived at the Ritz, where Mr. Willard was staying while in town. Charles parked the car and got out to open her door. "Will you be the one taking me home?"

"Oh, no, ma'am. Mr. Willard has told me I won't be needed. I suppose he'll be taking you home himself. It's nice meeting you, ma'am." He tipped his hat.

"Thank you Charles." She turned and walked inside, stopping at the front desk to ask for Mr. Willard and was immediately directed to the 21st floor—he had rented the penthouse suite.

Two hours later, Grace realized she was trapped in a hotel room with a mad man. Or at least a seriously disturbed one. It didn't matter he was a billionaire…with an invention…that saved millions of lives every year. Grace wanted out. The trouble was, she couldn't seem to leave. Her mind had a will of its own and right now, that mind had decided she was staying, even though her body had been getting creepy signals for the last hour.

Their evening together had started out innocuously

enough. They spent the first part having dinner and talking about his pet project. He lured her in slowly, plying her with wine and high-priced appetizers. At one point he showed her a horrible burn on his chest and back that had started him on the journey to create bionic skin years before.

Half way through the meal, his sister arrived, and they were introduced. She seemed nice enough, if a bit reserved. She didn't talk much but hung around quietly in the background. That's when things started getting funky. It was like her brain had a mind of its own, revealing personal information she would not normally choose to reveal. Grace found herself conflicted. One part of her mind was encouraging her to let down her guard and get up close and personal with her host. The other part was screaming at her to run and run fast. Unfortunately, that part continually lost. The longer she stayed, the longer she wanted to stay forever. She wanted Kyle Willard. *I mean who wouldn't? He's rich, good-looking, intelligent. What would it be like to sleep with this man?* Bile rose, sharp and burning, her mind rebelling. Grace did not sleep around. What was wrong with her? *I'm not attracted to Kyle Willard...am I? He's too intense and...and scary.* She willed herself to leave, but her legs wouldn't carry her to the door. It was as if she was trapped inside the scary nightmares she had been having—one that went on and on so she could not wake.

"Grace, you aren't listening. You are a naughty one, aren't you? I need you to pay attention. Look at me Grace. Look into my eyes."

Unwillingly, Grace found herself looking. His angel blue eyes seemed to pull her in, like a deep, chlorinated pool.

"That's a good girl. You have something in your mind Grace that does not belong there. Do you feel it?"

Unable to stop herself, she nodded.

"Good. You need to reject it, Grace. Push it from your mind. Only you can do this, Grace. Concentrate and reject it."

She nodded again. But some stubborn part of her she didn't know she possessed was listening, too, and was shouting at her: *Hold on, Grace. Hold on. Do not let go.*

Kyle Willard was growing angrier. She knew he was, even though he did not give the outward appearance of anger. He was trying to control it. He needed Grace to give in. She could put a stop to his anger if she gave in and pushed the ugly thing from her head like he wanted her to.

Grace tried again, but the inner voice was stronger. It continuously urged her not to listen. Back and forth it went, with Kyle commanding her to reject the object in her mind and the other voice rebelling. She was exhausted and finding it hard to pay attention to either side. Suddenly, she couldn't hear anything. There was blessed silence.

When she awoke, it was to the sound of voices raised in anger. Instinctively, she kept her eyes closed and listened.

"Should we push her further? Her mind seems fragile. I'm afraid she'll crack."

"Oh, her mind's strong enough. I tested it myself, remember. She nearly ejected me the first time I entered," the madman bellowed.

"Yes, but you've never pushed her this hard."

"It puzzles me why she is hanging on to it. She doesn't remember him."

"Shhh. Kyle she's conscious."

Grace heard footsteps, and the madman was there, leaning over her. "There's no use pretending to be asleep. We know you're awake. Open your eyes, Grace."

She didn't want to. But like before, she couldn't seem to say no. Her eyes opened to see his grinning face and crystal blue eyes staring into hers. And the nightmare began all over again. This time, she was sure he would win. At one point, it nearly slipped away from her, exciting his triumph. But it was premature. Grace held on, and eventually the portal settled back into place. She clung to it like a dying person to a life preserver.

How long did they stay like that, eyes locked in a mental tug of war? It seemed like an eternity, but maybe it was only an instant. *What am I holding on to? And why? It would be so easy to let go. Let go, Grace. You don't need it anymore. It is worthless. Give it up and the pain will disappear. You'll be able to sleep. The nightmare will be gone. You can go back to your own home.* The dream was becoming more vivid. She could picture her bedroom, all nice and cozy waiting for her. She was so tired. Her pillow looked full and inviting. *I need to let go and lay my head upon it.* She slipped away, like a boat on the water, drifting aimlessly, subject to any bump or wave that came along.

*****

Kyle nearly shook her in his frustration, although rationally he knew his anger wouldn't solve the problem. Why did this woman, of all people, have to prove so stubbornly frustrating? She should have been an easy target. Instead, Grace Woznisky's talent, which he himself had researched so meticulously before he'd introduced himself online, appeared to lie in her resistance. Kyle could only imagine what a formidable foe she would have made if properly trained as a child. Perhaps one of their future children might inherit the talent. Excitement pooled in his belly.

Kyle gritted his teeth. He couldn't take her with another man's portal lodged in her mind. That must go. But after three precious hours, Grace would not eject it. He could almost admire her if he was not so annoyed. He reached out, snagging the ginger ale Kaitlyn had poured for him. The cold fizz helped to settle his stomach. Kyle could not work on Grace while she was unconscious—at least not without causing irreparable damage. For what he intended, he needed her mind intact.

"If you don't watch, you're going to end up with another ulcer."

As if on cue, his stomach gurgled.

"The girl frustrates me."

"I know but you'll make a mistake, like before." She walked to the windows, her short strides reminding him of their mother.

"We were young. We didn't understand our abilities. Our father only taught us the minimum we needed to learn how to use them."

"You were angry. You pushed her too hard."

"I did not." Kyle spoke more sharply than he intended. This was an old argument between them. He reached his hand into his shirt to finger the burn mark on his chest. He could still picture his mother as she lay there, unmoving, after the car she was driving careened off the road and hit a tree. *I did not want her dead.*

I know. I never blamed you. It was an accident. You only meant to give her a small push. You were frustrated because she was making us move again. But when you get angry, it's too easy to make a mistake.

It had been terrifying for all of them. He received a burn across twenty percent of his body, and Kaitlyn had suffered a severe concussion that had nearly taken her life. Their mother had not survived. That's when the bed-wetting began and the teasing had gotten worse. That's when the hitting started, and he first tasted his own blood.

"I paid for my folly." He thought of the crazy old coot who was his first foster parent kicking him down the stairs in the morning.

He was breathing too rapidly. He wrenched his thoughts back to the present. It was a measure of the intensity of his feelings he could not stay focused on his task. A cool hand touched his arm. *Kaitlyn.* The accident had brought them closer. After a series of rotten foster parents they had been adopted by a wealthy family and given every advantage money could buy. Yet, unlike himself, who had thrived, Kaitlyn had not enjoyed their adoptive family and grew rebellious. At twenty-one, she made a request. She asked him to erase fifteen years of memories.

"You've been a good brother to me, Kyle. When I asked you to free me from family obligations, you did. You helped settled me into my own place. And when I was tired of being alone, you offered me a place to live. I don't forget."

He grasped her hand where it lay on his shoulder.

"You never asked me for much of anything. It was the least I could do."

"We have to stick together. That's why you have to control your anger."

Kaitlyn had come to live with him a year ago. His family, and for the most part, the world, believed her to be his live-in girlfriend, and that was fine by him. It didn't seem to bother Kaitlyn either. And he had plenty of women to choose from. He studied Grace, where she lay passed out on the couch. *Too bad the one in front of me is proving to be resistant. I will break her.*

"You must remain calm."

Kaitlyn was right. He settled in the chair opposite, staring at Grace broodingly, hands steepled under his chin—his favorite thinking pose. He had a decision to make. He could send her back to her condo, none the wiser, or he could keep her here a little while longer.

Which shall it be? He glanced at his cell phone. *9:43 p.m. Jenkins will be checking in soon.* The longer he kept her, the greater the risk. He sighed. Nothing was ever easy. *When she's finally mine, I'll make her pay for her stubbornness.*

*****

Grace drifted in a sea of emptiness; her mind could not make sense of anything. At one point there was a bright light, but it faded quickly, sending her into deeper sleep. She awoke much later in her own bed, the whole evening a vague memory. She recalled the first part of the evening well—the chauffeur, the ride to the hotel, the dinner with some new client. That's when everything grew fuzzy. Hadn't she enjoyed a fine dinner and wine? Maybe she had had one glass too many? She remembered getting back into the car, and a man taking her home. She groaned. What a lousy consultant she was. She could not remember one thing about the assignment she had taken on.

*****

The buzzing of his cell phone awoke David. He checked the time. *6:00 a.m.* Peter was always an early riser.

"After twenty years, you'd think I'd be used to these early morning calls." David grumbled. He'd never been a morning person, and he still wasn't. "Hello."

"Rise and shine." Peter wasted no time in getting to the point. "We've searched the database of likely Patchwork customers. I'll give you three guesses who we found."

"Peter Pan? It's way too early for games. Who?"

"Our Chinese friend Thung Yeh."

David thought hard. "So, what does that tell us?"

"Our hacker came across Thung Yeh through the Patchwork Company. That's how he got wind of DuMar's breakthrough."

"Do we have any leads on who the hacker might be?"

"Unfortunately, he's covered his tracks well. No one at the company seems to have a clue. There are hundreds of possible customers. It's going to take us some time to hack into their minds and find him.

"That's what I figured. Call me at a decent hour when you have something more. I need my beauty sleep."

He heard Peter's laugh as he disconnected. Despite the early hour, David could not get the sleep he so badly needed. By his estimate, he had slept a good twelve hours. He knew he needed more, but he must have passed the safe mark or Peter would never have called him.

David's thoughts immediately turned to Grace, and he couldn't resist entering the portal briefly to reassure himself she was okay. Grace was sleeping soundly…no nightmares. *Good.* Everything appeared normal. But David couldn't shake the sensation he was missing a vital piece of information. He hesitated. He should leave. He couldn't afford the drain on his energy supply. Still, it would only take a moment. Decision made, he focused on her thoughts and was immediately drawn into the waves.

Grace was walking through her old house in Parma. Everything was dark—her mother and sister were laughing in the basement. She started toward the voices, but suddenly turned toward the front door and appeared surprised to find it unlocked. He watched as she opened it and slipped out. What did she see? He peered over her shoulder and saw an empty landscape with brilliant, white snow that stretched endlessly into the distance. He nearly alerted her to his presence, barely managing to keep his shock contained. Quickly, he pulled himself back through the portal.

As soon as he could open his eyes, he called for Geneva. She materialized immediately, grasping his hands, her eyes silently willing him to speak. "It's Grace. A good portion of her mind has been wiped by our hacker."

Chapter Twenty-Four
Making Schemes

They were sitting in the home office. Peter, Roland, Rolf, Kevin, Geneva and about every other member of his extended family.

"Tell me again." Peter was asking. "How do you know it's our man?"

"I recognize the landscape. It was the same way in Thung Yeh's mind. Nearly every trace of memory we were after was wiped clean."

"Are you certain?"

David nodded. "Without a doubt."

"He has her."

David found himself shaking his head. "Not yet. He hasn't dislodged the portal I created. It's still there. She's not yet under his control." He struggled for his iron calm, but it was difficult. He wanted so badly to find the bastard and blast him.

"Son, I don't want to tell you what to do." His father laid a calm hand on his shoulder. "I know you care for Grace. But your strong emotions where she's concerned could spell disaster. Your mother and I think you should let Brian handle this one."

"No, it must be me, Dad. She trusts me. Even though her memories of me are gone, some part of her trusts me enough to hang on to the portal. I won't let her down."

His father gave his mother a worried look. The two were clearly exchanging thoughts as they often did. He deliberately gave them their privacy.

"He's right." Peter acknowledged. "As much as Brian would be sure to keep his head, it's unusual the girl has managed to hang on to the portal David created. That leads me to believe on some level, she's tied to David and would respond better to him."

"And I don't relish the thought of being zapped by a techno psychopath." Brian offered, jokingly. "One thing I don't understand, though, is what the nut-job hoped to achieve by wiping an innocent girl's mind?"

"There is something he didn't want us to find." David told him. "Something that would have led us back to him. He is using Grace to get to me. He doesn't care about her. But he knows that I do."

"So what do we do now?" Brian asked.

Peter and David exchanged glances. "No." David shook his head. "It's too dangerous for Grace. The bastard will finish her off."

"It's our only choice. Like it or not, the only way to our hacker is through Grace." Peter's tone became thoughtful. "It may be that's what our friend was after all along. He knows you have strong feelings for Grace. He must realize the likelihood of your slipping up when her safety is involved. With Grace under his control, he will have the upper hand."

"So what do we do?" David reached deep for control to stifle the panic racing through his system.

"We need to set a trap. We have to think like he does. The hacker expects you to rush to Grace's defense. He deliberately wiped her memories so you would be sure to see and react. He wants your emotions to run wild so he can find a way into your mind. Once he does, you'll be under his control. If he keeps you alive, he will have a powerful minion who can do his dirty work."

"If it's all about control," Peter spoke slowly, "let's give him that. Let's make him think he has you when he's under. When he least expects it, in the real world, we spring our trap."

"What will I need to do?"

"As hard as it will be, you cannot rush to Grace's defense. You'll need to sit back and wait for the hacker to show his hand. He will be back, make no mistake. And when he returns, you'll need to make him believe he's won. That won't be easy. To convince him, you'll need to give him some bit of your mind, while hanging onto the controls. Meanwhile, we'll trail Grace. He cannot be doing this at a distance. We'll watch and grab our man."

"Should we bring Grace in on our plan?" Sophia asked.

David shook his head. "That won't help. She doesn't carry memories of me any longer. She won't have a clue what we're talking about and won't believe us once she does. Plus, she's not one of us. She won't be able to keep her emotions under control. Our hacker will know we've been in touch and will use that to his advantage. I'm afraid that wouldn't end well for Grace."

Geneva nodded. "So that's our plan? It doesn't seem right." She glanced at David. "Letting you face him alone and at such a price. Are you sure this will work?"

"Nothing is certain," Peter replied. "Brian will be

nearby, in case. The rest of our crew," he nodded at Rolf, Roland, and Kevin, "will confront the spider in his web."

"We'll also be on watch," Carl Jenkins said, squeezing David's shoulder.

David glanced at his mother. She was nodding at him, but he knew her well enough to know underneath her calm façade she was anxious. Still she smiled and gave him a hug. "We haven't forgotten what to do even though it's been a while."

Peter nodded. "To achieve success, we'll need everyone to be on full alert and ready to take action. Once our hacker thinks he has David and the girl, anything can happen, so let's think like Boy Scouts and be prepared."

Chapter Twenty-Five
Tailed

Something was wrong. Grace's brain was not functioning like it normally did. She couldn't seem to connect her thoughts properly. Why couldn't she remember her important client? She couldn't even remember what he looked like. About the only thing she could recall was the feeling he was disappointed in her. Grace had left something undone but what it was, she didn't know.

Still in her pajamas, she opened the door to get the paper and shuffled back into the kitchen. It was Tuesday. Thank God she could remember that much. The date on the newspaper jumped out at her. *September 5.* Claire's wedding was weeks away. How had that snuck up on her? Grace had her plane ticket and her dress. She felt a twinge of disappointment. *No date.* For some reason, it seemed important she bring a date, but why that would be, Grace couldn't fathom. The last time her sister had almost tied the knot, Grace had still been married. Maybe that was why having a date seemed so important. *Or maybe I want a date to avoid the best man.* She shuddered when she imagined facing James again—she and her tits.

What should she do today? The sky had looked overcast the brief moment she had been outside. Maybe a good day for shopping? Now that she had money in the bank, it was time to spend a little. She wanted to give Claire something special for her wedding day. True, she had gone in with her mom to purchase their dishes, but that wasn't a fun or special gift from a sister. So she had written a poem and had it framed. She would collect it and look for a couple of cute outfits to wear in California.

An hour and a half later she was out the door and in her car, credit cards in hand. She spent a busy afternoon at the mall going from store to store searching for the perfect outfit. She finally found what she was looking for at Macy's and was heading back to her car, when she got a creepy feeling, like someone was following her. She glanced around quickly, but no one was looking her way. She shrugged and got in her car and drove toward the grocery store. She needed milk and OJ and more birdseed for Harvey. Grace supposed she could get that at the pet store, but it would be more convenient to make the purchases while she was getting groceries.

She was pulling into the grocery store when she got the same creepy feeling again. This time she noticed a gray van in her rear view mirror. She did not recognize it or the driver. She pulled into a spot and parked. The gray van did, too. Grace waited for the driver to get out but no one emerged. *Strange.* She shivered involuntarily. *My imagination.* She got out and quickly made her way into the store.

When she came back out again, the van was no longer there. She breathed a sigh of relief. She hadn't realized how anxious that had made her. She seriously needed a vacation. While putting her groceries in the trunk, Grace heard a ping. She checked her phone.

Claire was texting. Grace noticed Claire had also left a voicemail. She must not have heard the ringer when she was in the grocery store. Something was wrong. She put the key in the ignition and returned the call.

"Grace! It's about time you call me back. Where have you been? Never mind…I…I…something is the matter with me."

Claire didn't take the time to say hello. Grace recognized the note of panic in her voice. "What's the matter?"

"I don't know. I'm…having trouble remembering things. I mean I couldn't remember how Tom and I met. And Tom thinks it's the wedding jitters…but, well, it's not like me to forget important details like that. And today at work I couldn't remember the name of the new designer purses we got in to tell a customer. I mean, I knew the name last night, when I put them on the shelf, but today, I couldn't think of it. It was horrible."

Claire was on the verge of hysteria. Could she and her sister be suffering from the same malady?

"I mean, I've always had a great memory, you know? Tom always tells me I'm blessed with both brains and beauty because of how quick I remember my lines. What's the matter with me?" She was softly crying.

"I wonder…Claire does it feel like your mind is fuzzy? Like the thought is clear, but you can't bring it in?"

"Yeeess." Claire sobbed. "How do you knowww?"

"Because whatever you have, I have it too."

"Really? You mean, you can't remember stuff either? Like what?"

"Like the client I had dinner with last night."

"Wow. That's not like you."

"Tell me about it. I must also be suffering from paranoia, too, because I'm at the grocery store, and I could swear someone followed me here."

"What do you mean? Someone in the store? Maybe you swiped the last jar of pickles."

"Not on foot, in a van."

"Why would someone be following you in a van? That's scary. You should call the police."

"Am I being paranoid—like maybe it's a part of my overall brain malfunction, or I inherited the famous Woznisky schizophrenia from Mom?"

"Well, my brain isn't working either, but if I thought someone was following me, I'd go to the police. Aren't they around the corner from where you live? That was one of the reasons you bought your condo, wasn't it? Grace…are you still there?"

Grace had nearly dropped the phone. She had pulled out while they were talking and was heading slowly home when she noticed the gray van again in her rearview mirror. "Yeah, I'm here. Listen, they're back…I…I'm going to take your advice. I'll drive to the police station and make a report. I'll call you when I'm done."

"There really is someone following you in a van?"

"Yeah." She said it a bit breathlessly, nerves thrumming.

"Oh, God. Be careful. Go straight to the station and don't leave until they get to the bottom of it. Don't go home. Maybe you ought to go and stay with Mom and Glenn?"

Grace shuddered. She loved her mother, but the

thought of staying for any length of time with her was enough to cause a panic attack. “I’ll be fine. I’ll go to the station. I’ll call you later.”

“Okay…don’t forget. Write it down in case your brain gives out. I’m doing the same.”

“Good idea.” Grace laughed. “I’m sure it’s my imagination. But I’m nervous enough, I’m going to check it out.”

Ten minutes later Grace pulled into the station. She got out and looked around, making sure to lock the doors. The gray van had veered off shortly before the turn and was nowhere in sight. She took a couple of deep breaths, squared her shoulders, and hurriedly walked into the building to make her report. The lady at the front desk was on the phone and kept her waiting a while until she finished the call. Eventually, she ended the call and looked at Grace. “What can I do for you?”

“Um…I…someone, a stranger, was tailing me in their gray van. I noticed them following me several times throughout the day. I didn’t want to take any chances so I drove here.”

“Did you get a license plate number?”

“Um…no. I’m sorry.”

“Well, I can take your statement, but there’s not much we can do without a license plate number.”

Her voice was monotone, but intuitively Grace knew if she could read her mind, she would hear the officer call her a dumb shit. Why didn’t she get a license plate number? “Can someone at least follow me home? I live a few streets over.”

“Let me see if there’s a patrol car nearby.” She grunted, disappeared for a moment, and when she came back, gave Grace a short nod. “Officer Mack is on his way over and has agreed to escort you. In the meantime, let's get your statement."

Grace gave the woman her name, address and phone number and a description of the van and any other details she could remember. When she had finished, she sat in the waiting area until Officer Mack arrived and followed her back to her condo. The gray van was noticeably absent all the way home.

The long day of shopping followed by the panic attack had been exhausting. Grace was snoring as soon as her head hit the pillow. Moments later, Grace wished fervently she could come awake. But it was too late. The nightmare had returned.

Chapter Twenty-Six
Nightmare

Grace was sinking in a pit of mud. Once again, she was on the beach, but this time she was drowning with no one to save her. The stranger was standing over her, a small smile on his face, his body blotting out the sun. He did not offer to rescue her. Instead, the force of his gaze seemed to send her deeper into the earth. "I have your sister, my dear."

The endearment lent a deadly aspect to his words and yet, they were strangely familiar. Had he said them to her before? She struggled to remember. "She is not nearly as strong as you." He sounded puzzled and a bit disappointed. He shook his head sadly. "Too easy by far. She gave me everything I desire. I'm afraid there will be no wedding for Claire. So sad."

Grace looked at him blankly. What had the bastard done to her sister? Grace wanted to scream for help, but every breath caused her to sink deeper into slime.

"It doesn't have to be that way, you know. I could see your sister walks down the aisle. It all depends on you, my girl. Your sister's happiness in exchange for a small portion of your mind. You won't even miss it."

She stared at him in silent horror. In moments, the earth would cover her mouth and nose and it would be all over. She fought to keep calm but was losing the battle. If she had to go out, she would give him what he wanted in hopes he would leave her sister alone. She loved her sister and wanted to see her happy. She let out a small shriek when two hands grabbed her from behind and hauled her out of the muck.

"Stay calm and let me do the talking." Her savior mumbled, stepping in front of her to face her tormentor. "Let the girl go." He called across the chasm.

"No need to shout," the deadly voice said. "I can hear you clearly."

"It's me you want, not her. Let her go, and you can have me."

"Really? You would give in that easily? She means that much to you?" Grace's tormentor was clearly enjoying himself. "You've got it all wrong, you know. It's not you I want. Grace is mine. I discovered her long before you, which gives me prior claim."

Once again, something about the way the madman spoke sounded familiar to Grace. He must have been familiar to her helper, too, because he stared at the lunatic for a moment as if putting the pieces of an intricate puzzle together.

"You were after Grace all along. Why? She's innocent. What can she possibly offer you? Unless…"

"You don't even understand her true value, do you?" He let out a sinister laugh, pacing on the other side of the pit. "I've had the chance to poke around in her mind a bit. She's strong like your Meg. I'm not letting her go. Which means you must."

His arm flew out from his side, stretching like a giant rope across the gap in the earth and pulling her to him. Her rescuer did not attempt to stop him, and for the first time she got a good look at him. He was tall and broad shouldered but—she drew in a sharp breath—he appeared to be injured. He was holding his left side and she could see a crimson stain.

"Before I intervened, you planned to bury her alive. That didn't appear like you wanted to keep her," he called from his side of the pit.

Her tormentor laughed. "Yes, I suppose it did look that way, but as you know, looks can be deceiving. I was merely ensuring her cooperation and waiting until you arrived."

He laughed again and the sound grated on Grace's nerves. He squeezed her shoulder, as if he would force her to cooperate. "She's an obstinate one. That is not something I can tolerate in my women."

He tightened his grip on her shoulders. To prevent her from running away? Her body was paralyzed. She couldn't make her legs move even if she wanted to.

"I see you ran into one of my traps." He motioned to her rescuer's side. "I can make this quick or painful. Which would you prefer?"

His hands became long whips as he flung them across the muddy pit and into her rescuer's side. He cried out in agony, and the sound made Grace flinch. She could not bear to watch and found herself turning her head into her tormentor's shoulder.

"You see your girlfriend already finds comfort in my arms."

He chuckled and the sound was like dreadful acid washing over her skin. She pulled her head away abruptly, but that did not stop the madman.

"She obviously doesn't share your strong feelings, does she? It will be tragic for her to witness your death. In fact, I'm not sure her mind can handle it. She might never recover. It will be interesting to learn."

"So shield her from it."

"No. My partner must be strong." He bit the words out, and this time his whip-like hands lashed out in succession, throwing her wounded rescuer to the ground.

Wake up, Grace! Wake up!

But her mind refused to obey her, and she remained trapped in the deadly nightmare, forced to bear witness to an innocent man's death.

Chapter Twenty-Seven
Happy Thoughts

"We've got the target."

"Where?" Brian asked quickly, leaning over Peter's shoulder to look at a large electronic map with a blinking red dot. The crew had established a makeshift headquarters near Grace's condo, where they could keep an eye on her coming and going. Peter hung up with Roland who had followed a mental trail, leading straight from the Patchwork Company to Gallant Enterprises and from there to Grace Woznisky.

"The bastard's at the Crown Prince Royal. I knew he had to be holed up somewhere nearby. That was the only explanation of how he gets to her so quickly whenever she is unconscious without a portal in place. We haven't discovered his identity, but we know where he's hiding."

Peter was tapping the pencil he was holding on the table in his excitement. Brian didn't waste any time pointing it out. He and Sophia were needed. Geneva was keeping them apprised of David's situation, and it wasn't good. They needed to get in now, or it wouldn't matter to David or Grace, let alone the men on the rogue hacker's tail. The madman would use the information and power in David's mind to trap them all. Brian held his feeling of impending doom firmly in place—this was no time for panic. He needed to leave it to Peter to coordinate activity in the physical world. His job was to provide a distraction. Brian followed the portal Sophia created for him straight into Grace's mind.

Brian spent a few precious seconds acclimating himself to the scene. David spotted his presence immediately, but the enemy was too busy exacting his vengeance to notice the ripple on the surface of Grace's mind. His arms were whips and he was using them to take chunks from David's arms and legs. Of course, Brian knew those chunks were merely symbols for the damage the enemy was inflicting on David's defense. Grace stood nearby watching in horror, her arms at her side frozen. Clearly, the madman had her well in hand, also. *Time to even the score.*

Brian gathered energy together and threw the proverbial wrench into the mix. The analogy made him smile, but it was only a momentary pleasure. He knew the instant the enemy identified his presence and turned his attention on him. The guy was insanely strong.

A metal barrier formed in front of him. Brian struggled, pushing with his mind to knock it down, but it continued to take shape, chunk by hardened chunk materializing out of thin air. He narrowed his energy as he had been taught, focusing on one spot in the hard steel, but as soon as he created a hole, it filled in again. In that moment, Brian realized he had only bought David a few precious moments. And if Peter and the crew didn't succeed in finding and destroying the rogue hacker, they would be trapped here forever. Their physical bodies would waste away until there was nothing left, and they would be absorbed into Grace's mind or the enemy's once she was fully under his spell.

Brian was helpless. Terrified, he forced the emotion back lest the enemy gain even more of an advantage, and he concentrated on keeping the small chunk open.

*****

Grace watched in horror as the iron wall surrounded the newcomer, trapping him inside. Their tormentor was clearly enjoying himself. Grace was linked to his emotions. Would this nightmare never end? She would not escape, and neither would the innocent men trying to help her, unless she could wake.

Grace pinched herself in the dream, but it did no good. Her anger burned at the injustice, the rage enhancing the enemy's power. The madman's glee overwhelmed her. Instinctively, Grace forced her mind to happy, peaceful thought—imagining the sand on the beach and the sun on her back. Seeing Claire on her wedding day would be amazing. Claire would be a beautiful bride, and Grace would enjoy being a bridesmaid. Her tormentor paused. *It's working.* Grace kept at it. Her mother. She poured on her love and the warm affection as easily as water from the tea kettle. Of course, she worried about Grace and Claire. But Grace knew her mother cared deeply. She wanted her girls to find happiness. *The beach!* There was nothing like the Lake Erie shoreline in summer. Her beach glass collection glittered in an array of colors on her shelf at home… The colors made a dazzling display.

Grace's heart rate slowed to a steady, even cadence. She opened her eyes to see the hole widen around the man who had come to rescue her. He climbed out, facing the madman. On the other side of the great chasm, Grace saw her first rescuer stumble to his feet. He was bleeding profusely but still alive. While she watched, another man stepped behind him, his hand on the first man's shoulder. She glanced once at the madman. He appeared angry at the turn of events. He immediately went after the newcomer, slinging his long arms across the chasm.

Grace closed her eyes and kept at it. *Happy thoughts, Grace. Happy thoughts.* She reminded herself desperately, forcing the image of the badly wounded man out of her mind and the long arms snaking toward him. *Happy thoughts.*

*****

David's tremendous control was slipping. Next to him, his father faltered and fell. David dared not spend any time trying to save him. What little power he had available he was using to shield Grace from the maniac who was slowly tearing holes in his defenses.

It had been three years since he had last encountered the hacker, but still David had not been prepared for the destructive power of the enemy. It was immense, fueled by a maniacal desire to take him over and have Grace as his own. Brian was doing his best at distraction, but it was Grace, herself, who proved a surprising foe. Her mind was resisting the attack. With her help, they had managed to delay the inevitable. The intensity of their attacker's thrusts had diminished. But it was only a matter of time. He could only hope the others had tracked the hacker to his lair.

Chapter Twenty-Eight
Foiled

Kevin, Rolf and Roland raced toward the Crown Prince Royal, but it was nearing 5:00 p.m. on a Tuesday, and the rush-hour traffic was causing a bottleneck on I-90. Rolf kept his thoughts carefully under control, suspecting that at any time he could be sucked into the battle taking place in Grace Woznisky's mind. Would they be strong enough, together, to hold the enemy at bay? He could only hope they would hang on long enough for him and the others to get to the body.

The unknown factor in all of this was Grace herself. Would her mind be tough enough to maintain the battle going on inside it? She surprised them all when Geneva and Sophia reported the change in her energy waves—from jagged and rough to smooth and contained. Their smoothness made them harder for the enemy to use to fuel his tremendous power. She was fighting like a trained mind hacker. Rolf pondered how she knew to do it. He himself had spent many years working on the precision needed to exercise that control.

They continued to crawl through the snarled traffic, until eventually the Crown Prince loomed ahead. Rolf, who had been driving, left the other men at the door while he arranged for valet parking. By the time he joined Roland and Kevin, they had cleared the lobby and were at the front desk. Since they had no idea what name their target went by, they would have to find him by other means. They flashed their badges at the desk clerk.

"FBI. We have reason to believe you have a deadly criminal hiding out in your hotel. We have a warrant for their arrest, but we'll need to search the premises."

The woman behind the counter held her hand out for Rolf's badge. She studied it critically, eyeing them suspiciously. Rolf tapped his hands impatiently on the counter and gave her a mental shove. They had minutes to find their target.

She handed him back his badge. "We have three hundred and eighty-four rooms. Which would you like to see?"

"How many suites do you have and who's staying in your most expensive?"

The desk clerk tapped on keys. "There are twenty suites, all available on the top six floors. The premiere suite is the Jacobs Suite. Let's see. That is showing a Mr. and Mrs. Bill Ford. Would you like to see that one?"

"Yes, hurry." Rolf bit out. "I'll need a key. Kevin, get the names and keys for the other suites and if you don't hear from us, come and find us."

"Roland, come with me." He barked out as the desk clerk handed him a plastic card.

"That's room 2514." She called after them as they took off running toward a bank of elevators.

As luck would have it, the doors opened immediately when they pressed the up button, and they stepped in quickly, punching in floor twenty-five. Rolf hoped to hell they had pegged the bastard for the right suite. Otherwise, they were all doomed.

Within minutes, they arrived at their destination and took off at a run to room 2514. They passed the key over the lock and entered the suite. They went from room to room quickly, but it was soon apparent whoever had been there had left in a hurry. The coffee cup on the table was still three-quarters full. A half-eaten bagel lay beside it. The bed was made, but there was an indentation where a body had lain. Rolf laid his hand upon the surface. It was still warm. His cell phone buzzed. He answered.

"They have resurfaced. Do you have him?"

"Dammit, no."

Chapter Twenty-Nine
Hospital Stay

Grace came to consciousness suddenly, opening her eyes to see her familiar bedroom. She didn't know what she expected to see, but it was not the ordinary items in front of her: Her yellow comforter, the overstuffed chair with yesterday's clothing draped across it, sunlight streaming through the window. Grace took deep breaths to calm her racing heart, but that didn't seem to help. She was weak and frightened, casting glances every few seconds to each corner of the room, fearing a shadow of the man in her dream would emerge from the walls and reclaim her for the nightmare. Grace clasped her pillow and let out an involuntary sob. She maintained a fragile hold on reality, but was close to the breaking point.

There was a knock on her door. "Grace, it's the police, and we have an ambulance. We know you've been through a trauma. Open up. We're here to help."

Grace forced herself to raise her head, but nearly passed out in the process. The urgent pounding continued. "Grace, open the door. We're here to help."

"I'm coming." Her voice was no more than a whisper.

"Grace, stay back. We're coming in to get you."

There was a splintering sound and then the door flew open and police officers and ambulance crew streamed around her. “Let’s get her to the hospital.”

She was lifted onto a stretcher. Someone took her pulse and threw out the number fifty-five which made them spring into action. Her arm stung and a shot of something cold entered her veins. *I’m dying.* Grace felt and heard nothing for a long time.

When she next awoke, it was evening and her mother was in the room. “Oh, thank God. They said you would wake, but I didn’t know when. How do you feel? Are you hungry?”

Grace took stock of her surroundings. “Where am I? What happened?”

“Oh, dear Lord, you don’t know. You are in the hospital, Gracie. Fairview Hospital. They said you experienced a head trauma of some sort. There are policemen who want to question you but not until you’re feeling better. Do you remember anything? Why would someone attack you? It doesn’t make sense.”

Her mother was beside herself.

Grace remembered the terrifying man in her dreams with the abnormally long arms. How was she ever going to explain what sent her over the edge was a figment of her imagination? They were going to need to lock her away. She should be locked away. She was hallucinating. Grace was amazed she still had the mental capacity to realize she was crazy. Tears seeped from her eyes. Grace did her best to convey the urgency of the situation to her mother.

“I’m not…right. I’m seeing things that aren’t real. I need help.” She tried to avoid the word crazy.

Her mother stared at her worriedly but did her best to be reassuring. “It’s going to be okay Grace. Let me get the nurses. They’ll know what to do. You’re gonna be fine."

She went hurriedly into the hall and came back with two nurses. They immediately checked her vitals.

"Everything's looking good," the taller of the two said. She pointed to their names on a whiteboard in front of her bed. "I'm Anna and this is Diane." She gestured to the shorter nurse across from her. "We have the night shift and will take care of you this evening. You've suffered a shock. You'll need to take it easy until your mind has a chance to adjust to the trauma. In the meantime, let's get you comfortable. I've ordered a light meal. Would you like something to drink? We have water, juice, soda…"

Grace nodded. Her throat scratched like sandpaper. "Water's fine."

"Coming right up." She smiled, nodding at Diane who left the room, presumably to get it. When she returned, though, she also brought with her a policeman and another man dressed in plain clothes.

"The police would like to talk to you about what you experienced. Do you feel up to it? There is some urgency."

Grace nodded slowly. Her mother remained by her side, eyeing the police suspiciously.

"Mrs. Ellis, we know you're concerned for your daughter, but we'd like to speak to her alone if you don't mind. We suspect there might be foul play involved and other lives are at stake. It's important we capture the crucial details without jeopardizing anyone else's privacy. We'll only be a moment, and we'll send someone to get you."

Her mother appeared about to argue, but Grace gestured for her to go, relieved she would not have to reveal the details of her mental breakdown to her mother and anxious to share it with professionals who could help. "I'll be okay, Mom." Her voice came out as a whisper.

Her mother hesitated, looking at Grace worriedly, and finally after much encouragement on the part of the officer, and after warning them she would be back in a few minutes, let herself be led from the room by the nurses. Grace turned her attention to the police officers. The younger man spoke first.

"I'm Sergeant Lavillo and this is Chief Brooks." He motioned toward the plain clothes gentleman. "Mr. Brooks works for a special unit of the FBI."

Grace found herself carefully studying them. Why would they be interested in her mental breakdown*? What have I done?* A sudden memory of the unexpected ten thousand dollars in her bank account rose in her mind. Oh, God, she knew it was too good to be true. She'd got caught in a fraud ring. Perhaps, it was a case of mistaken identity. Her confusion and fear must have shown on her face, because the Chief made an effort to calm her.

"Please, call me Peter. Grace, you are an innocent victim. I would like to fill you in on the details of our case. It will explain why you are in the hospital. May I?" He gestured to a nearby chair.

Grace nodded, and he took the chair across from her. For the first time, a glimmer of hope dawned. Could there be a rational explanation for her recent symptoms?

"Officer Lavillo, would you please excuse us?" Peter nodded at the younger man, who immediately left the room.

Grace was alone with the Chief, who seemed at a loss for words. She guessed he was not used to revealing the details of his cases to anyone, let alone a hospital patient. He cleared his throat.

"Your state of mind is extremely fragile right now. I don't want to do anything that will create undue stress for you. But it's important I fill you in on the pertinent details."

He waited until she acknowledged she heard him and nodded her permission to continue. "Your condition makes it difficult for me to tell you everything right away. But we're anxious for you to recover fully. The lives of other good people depend on it." He paused as if searching for the right words, and continued. "You see, your brain has been robbed of critical information, making it difficult for you to cope with any situation, let alone one as complicated as this. Do you understand?"

"What do you mean…robbed? How could someone rob my brain? That doesn't make sense."

"That's the tricky part. I'll do my best to explain." He paused momentarily again to gather his thoughts, rubbing the back of his neck slowly. For a man well into his sixties, he still had a full head of hair, although mostly gray. Married with children or perhaps grandchildren. She found it hard to focus on what he was now saying.

"We have a special unit within the FBI that has experienced some success in the area of mind control. We call it the CMU or Cognitive Mind Unit. This unit has been in existence since the early 1950's. That is when our government discovered a rare genetic mutation, allowing certain families that possessed it, to communicate with one another without words. They could share thoughts and ideas, passed back and forth among them. You can imagine how that might prove useful to our government. It could provide a distinct advantage in a great number of military endeavors."

Grace stared at him blankly. "Did you say, mind control?"

The Chief nodded and continued, as if he hadn't said anything out of the ordinary. "After extensive testing, it was discovered the mutation only transferred to the males in these families. Although both the males and females inherited the same traits, in the males, the mutation was dominant, where in the females it was recessive. I know this is a bit scientific, and I don't want to bore you with an unnecessarily long explanation. Suffice it to say in our studies we learned that although the males inherited the ability to control thoughts, they could not do it well without the females present. The females act as a sort of conduit to the mind, if you would, for their male counterparts.

"Since these discoveries, the government has actively followed these families and encouraged them to use their skills for the greater good. As you can imagine, we have also had to track them in the event any family members turn to a life of crime."

"Are you saying someone—a male family member who has turned to a life of crime—has been in my mind? Why would they do that?"

"Yes, it's what I'm saying. This would not be the first time a civilian has gotten caught in the crossfire." He paused and hesitated, as if he feared his next words would cause her to suffer a relapse. "Does the name David Jenkins hold any special meaning for you?"

Grace stared at him blankly, searching her mind for where she might have heard the name before and finding nothing, shook her head.

"I didn't think so." He continued, still watching her carefully. "You and David started dating several weeks ago. I believe you have feelings for one another. David is a member of one of those special families I mentioned. He's been a member of the CMU since the age of twenty. He's now forty. In our world, he's something of a prodigy. His unique abilities have made him an incredibly valuable member of our unit. But they've also made him a target for an unknown enemy. This enemy wants him eliminated. They want this so badly they have investigated all of David's relationships to determine where he's most vulnerable. They discovered where you are concerned, he's highly vulnerable. So they plundered your mind to get to David."

"This is crazy. This David you say I'm involved with. I have no recollection of him at all. How is that possible?"

"Believe me when I tell you it's not only possible, it has happened. Myself and several others are witnesses. A rogue mind hacker has been in your mind and has tried to kill you. If not for David, he would have succeeded. David saved your life. You have survived only slightly worse off than before. But David has not been so lucky. Even as we speak, he is fighting for his life. We believe you can save him. Will you help us?"

"Even if all this is true, what could I possibly do to help? Last time I checked, I couldn't read minds…could I?" Grace trailed off hesitantly.

The Chief shook his head, giving her a smile. "No, Grace, you can't read minds. Although we are looking into your genealogy. Your mind has proved incredibly resistant to the hacker. This is unusual."

"What are you saying?"

"Grace, what do you know about your father's family?"

"Not much. My father was adopted. He died when I was two. I don't even remember him other than pictures."

"It's possible your father was a hacker. If he was adopted, he may not even have realized. I suspect that your talent was inherited from your father."

"Talent for what? This is crazy. You mean as an artist?"

"It's likely your art talent is closely linked to your psychic talent. Grace, you have the ability to manipulate energy. Because the talent was never developed, you most likely suppressed it, but it would come out in creative pursuits, such as art. I suspect that's why you were drawn to beach glass. Glass and stones store energy. It would be natural for you to want to release the energy, which is what you instinctively do with your designs."

"This is nuts. I don't believe it."

"That's okay. You don't have to. We are doing genealogical research on your father's family and hope to have proof soon enough. But in the meantime, I need you to understand your situation. You can read David's mind if he allows it. That's because he placed a portal in your mind when you and he were getting to know one another. A portal is a sort of instantaneous gateway linking one mind with another. It allows thoughts to travel back and forth freely, without energy escaping. It can only be established between people when there is a high level of trust. Your trust in David allowed him to place the portal in your mind. The rogue hacker sought to remove the portal, but you would not allow him access. Your talent protected you." The last was said with a bit of awe, like she had done something amazing.

"I don't remember anyone sharing my thoughts. I don't remember any talk of portals. Why don't I remember any of this?"

"Because the hacker erased your memories. Haven't you noticed you have large gaps in your recent memories?"

Grace nodded. She had noticed she couldn't seem to remember anything.

"Last night, you had a dream didn't you? And the dream appeared to be real?"

She stared at him wide-eyed.

"The dream involved a man trying to kill you and others coming to your rescue, correct?"

She nodded slowly.

"The dream was real. The battle that took place was real. The men in your dream—all real."

The cruel man's hands had stretched across the great gulf like giant rubber bands. "I saw a crazy man stretch his arms an impossible distance across a great chasm. You mean to tell me that was real?"

"Not in the way you are imagining and certainly not in real life. In the mind, you are limited only by your imagination. Energy travels quickly and across great distances. Your brain needs to make sense of what is happening, so it uses images you will understand so you can follow the energy exchange."

Her heart rate accelerated. Somewhere nearby a machine went off, beeping steadily. "So when the men in my dream were injured, they were injured in real life?"

"That's right." The Chief nodded.

The nurse, Anna, reentered the room and checked her vitals. "Sorry, sir, but your time with the patient is at an end. She needs her rest."

"I need a few more minutes. I'll be quick."

"All right." The nurse Anna agreed, but not before giving him a look. "I have to check on another patient. I'll be back in a couple of minutes."

When she had left the room, the Chief leaned over Grace's bed urgently. "David needs you. He has slipped into a coma, while his brain attempts to repair itself. We are assisting him with drugs known to help the healing process. However, the portal he created in your mind will provide him with a lifeline. We also believe he will fight harder to recover if you are nearby. We would like to have you transferred to our private hospital, where we can easily monitor the two of you and prevent the hacker you dreamt of yesterday from reentering either of your minds to finish you off. Will you do it?"

His voice took on a fierce tone, and Grace realized this request was personal. The Chief must have a strong attachment to David, beyond business.

The man in her dream had taken the thrashing on her behalf. The evil man in her dreams…he could return at any time. The choice did not sound hard. Grace would take being monitored around the clock, thank you.

"Okay, I'll do it."

Grace was surprised at how fast the Chief was able

to set things in motion once she had agreed to his plan. She didn't know what her mother had been told, but whatever it was must have been plausible because she was all for the move as well. She held Grace's hand tightly as they traveled by ambulance to the new facility, which, as it turned out, was on the opposite side of town.

The hospital was small and private, reserved mostly, she was told, for military patients. Within two hours, she was settled in her new room. Before Grace could sleep, though, she was asked to visit David Jenkins. He conveniently was given the room next to hers. They wheeled her by his bedside, prompting Grace to take his hand and have a conversation. She did as they asked. Grace wasn't sure what to talk about, so she explained who she was and how she wanted him to get well. David lay silent in his bed. The only indication he was living was the slight up and down movement of his chest as his lungs continued to draw breath.

Chapter Thirty
Mind Talk

David gasped at the harsh pain and pressure in his head. Someone was holding his hand.

"I think he's waking." A woman's voice called, excitedly. The sound seemed to come from a long way off. "What should I do?"

"Talk to him." A familiar voice responded. "Be encouraging."

"David, it's Grace…Woznisky. Do you remember me?"

David strained to focus on what the woman was saying, but the pain was so sharp, he immediately closed his eyes, slipping blissfully into unconsciousness.

*****

"I'm sorry," Grace said, turning to the Chief. "I tried."

"You did well." He reassured her. "We need to give it time. He'll come to when his mind has recovered enough. Plus, the drugs are keeping him under. We'll wean him and see what happens. Let's get you back to bed. We'll try again tomorrow."

So went the pattern for the next few days. Grace would spend a few minutes with David Jenkins every day, trying to get him to wake and talk to her. Sometimes he stirred, opened his eyes or gripped her hands. Mostly, he was silent. When David did finally speak, even though Grace was not with him, it came as a bit of a shock.

It was only 9:00 p.m. but she lay awake in her bed, afraid to fall asleep lest she get caught in the nightmare and be unable to escape. The Chief had explained the evil mind reader, as Grace privately called him, needed time to recover, too. Plus, he needed to be physically close by to enter her dreams and wreak havoc as he had been doing. Still, she had trouble believing she was safe. Grace vividly recalled the way the madman had looked at her and the punishing way he went after the men who tried to help her. Something told her he wouldn't leave her alone.

He'll be back.

She shivered, a warm rush of tears flooding her eyes. Grace was trying to be brave and strong, displaying a courageous front, but inside, she was frightened. Her mother had come to visit her every day but that was no comfort, since Grace couldn't tell her the truth. Her mother believed Grace had been physically attacked, and they had moved her to this hospital to keep her safe from her attacker, since he was still at large. Lying alone like this late at night, it was difficult to hang onto the illusion he could not find her here. She longed to feel safe. She lay in bed, crying softly, when she heard a male voice.

Don't cry. Please.

The voice was so clear. Was someone in her room? When Grace opened her eyes, she was alone. "Is someone there?" How silly to be talking to the empty room. *Maybe this is the relapse they are all worried about setting off in me.*

I'm deeply sorry for the pain you're enduring. It's my fault.

"Where are you?" Grace asked, looking carefully around the room.

In my bed.

"So how can I hear you so clearly…?"

She gasped as the knowledge hit her. *It's him. David Jenkins. That means it's true. Everything they told me.* Until now, Grace hadn't believed the fantastic tale. Her heart beat hard in her chest. "This is David? You're able to read minds? That's how you're talking to me?"

Yes. But only yours right now. I am not...strong.

"Are you awake in your room?" If anyone would walk in and see her talking aloud with no one in the room, they'd believe Grace had finally snapped.

I can't wake up right now. My body is paralyzed. But I don't need my body to visit this way.

"This is so weird. Is it true, what they told me? You and I…we're…?" She couldn't bring herself to say the word, lovers. But she had forgotten he was in her mind and knew what she was thinking, so she didn't have to. Part of Grace felt violated, and the other part was glad she didn't need to voice her thoughts aloud.

We are. Satisfaction thrummed in the two words. *When I can get out of this bed, I will show you.*

Although she knew he could not possibly see her, her face grew hot. "Yes, well, about that." It was amazing how fast she had adjusted to his mind-reading banter.

Hush, don't worry. Now he was reading her emotions. *Tomorrow or the day after, you will understand more than you do right now. Now I need you to fall asleep so I can get my rest. You are safe. Peter will not let anyone harm you. Although you're a lot stronger than you give yourself credit for."*

"Do you think you'll be able to open your eyes and speak to me tomorrow?"

I'm gaining strength every day. Peter has been cutting back on the drugs they are giving me. That is part of the normal process.

"Peter? Oh, the Chief."

Go to sleep, my love. Come find me in the morning.

And like that, he was gone, and she was once again alone in her mind.

The next morning Grace would almost have believed she had dreamt the whole thing until a nurse told her the friend in the next room was awake and asking to see her. She hurriedly got out of bed, dressed herself, and went to visit. David was sitting and eating breakfast. It was hard to believe this was the same man who had lain in his bed barely breathing a few days earlier.

"Good morning, sunshine. Pull up a chair. Have you eaten? I ordered something for you." He pointed to the tray on the table near his bed. "I hope that's okay?"

She nodded.

"Have a seat." He gestured to the chair near his bed. She pulled it out and sat.

"Does the Chief…Peter know you are awake?"

"He does. He's already been in to see me." He studied her intently, reaching out to smooth a stray curl away from her eyes. "How are you feeling this morning?"

"Better." She was shy, remembering how he had talked to her in her mind last night. Was he reading her mind right now?

“Good.” He grinned. “You’ve nothing to be anxious about.”

“Not easy knowing you can hear my every thought.”

He held his palm out, asking her without words to place her hand in his. She hesitated momentarily and followed suit. It would help him heal if she played along. Gently, he rubbed his thumb back and forth across her palm.

“Relax, Grace. I don’t know every thought. It’s not possible for me to stay in your mind all the time.”

“Really?”

“Really.” He smiled. “And especially after I’ve awakened from a coma. It’s hard for me to focus on anything. Besides, you can share my thoughts, too.”

“Peter mentioned that. Have we done that? Shared thoughts?”

“We have.” He smiled.

“You mean, I read your mind in the past? How is that even possible?”

“It is, and I’ll show you. But not today. I know I look a lot better than I did yesterday, but I’m still not well.” He tapped his forehead with a grin. “The brain takes time to heal.”

A noise at the door alerted them to another’s presence. “Sorry to interrupt, but you have visitors.” The Chief stood there, a large presence in the doorway. “Your family’s here. I couldn’t keep them away, although for your sake I tried. Once they heard you were awake, they insisted on seeing you. Geneva’s here as well.”

Get ready. David’s warning was so clear, but it was

only in her mind as the Chief did not seem to hear. Although she was getting used to his voice making comments or sounding out warnings, it was still unsettling.

Within seconds, it seemed like a large crowd gathered around his bed. David, who still held firmly to her hand, squeezed it gently. The small pressure was reassuring, which is what she knew he intended.

"Grace, let me introduce you to my family. These are my parents. Mom, Dad, meet Grace."

Mr. and Mrs. Jenkins were younger than she expected and greeted her warmly. "Grace, we're so sorry for everything you have been through. You're a brave young lady." His mother leaned over to give her a quick hug. "How are you feeling?"

"Okay."

"Do you remember my daughter, Sophia?" She motioned to a pretty, dark-haired lady next to her.

"No, I don't believe we've met. Nice to meet you."

Sophia and her mother exchanged a look, before Sophia offered a tentative smile. "My husband, Brian, would have liked to have been here, but he's with our kids today, so I could visit with David."

Grace nodded her understanding. "How many children do you have?"

"Two." Sophia smiled. "A son, Alex, and daughter, Georgie."

"How are the rug-rats?" David asked with some affection.

Sophia turned her attention to her brother. "They're worried about you, as we all are. They wanted to come along. It's good to see you sitting and talking, rather than comatose. Welcome to the land of the living. You gave us all a scare. Geneva, especially."

She gestured to a young girl with long, blond hair. Geneva proceeded to sit on the side of the bed, smoothing a hand intimately across David's forehead. David still held fast to Grace's hand all the while, but he did not seem to mind the younger girl's attention.

Jealousy rose, sharp and swift, catching Grace off guard. She pressed her nails into her palms. Geneva was rubbing David's head far too intimately. Grace didn't know why it should bother her. It wasn't like she had any strong feelings for David. Did she?

"Is Geneva part of the family?" Grace asked Sophia in a low voice.

"Not by blood." Sophia replied, studying Grace carefully. "She's a close family friend." If she and David were an item, why had David made no effort to put Geneva in her place?

She's my trainer. David spoke in her mind, and she could feel his concern before she saw it on his face. *Peter did explain about that, right?*

She looked at him, and he gave her a quick smile to let her know only she could hear. She admitted getting information like this was useful, but it was also a bit creepy to know he could come and go in her thoughts whenever he pleased and know her feelings before she had even thought them through. Was it possible to block him out? Grace would have to ask Peter.

You can make it harder for me, but it's not possible to block all your thoughts from me with a portal in place. We call it a mind-meld. That's why they are generally only in use between lovers. He said the last carefully, but David could not disguise the sense of satisfaction from Grace.

There was that word again. *Lovers.* They had been lovers. Looking at him now, Grace could almost believe it. His recent illness could not disguise the handsome lines of his face.

He smiled slowly at her. Clearly, he liked the way her thoughts were headed and could not resist teasing her. *We were and if I have my way, we will be again.*

She blushed and wondered suddenly if the others were reading her mind. She remembered Peter telling her the talent for mind-reading ran in families. As Geneva finished whatever she had been about, she gave Grace a tight smile and stepped back. She turned to the Chief and murmured something Grace was too far away to hear. Whatever it was, the Chief seemed intensely interested, pulling her aside for a quiet conversation.

Geneva is giving him an update on my condition. As my trainer, she's the best one to evaluate my mind's ability to heal itself.

Several of David's cousins stepped forward, and David made sure to introduce each of them to her. The dark-haired man, who looked a lot like David, only shorter, was Roland. The blond, blue-eyed giant was Kevin. Percy was tall and wore glasses. And Rolf was drop-dead gorgeous with brown hair and deep, blue eyes that seemed to look right through her. They were all constrained in their response to Grace, although Rolf politely asked how she was feeling.

David held her hand the entire visit. When she would have tried to move away, he wouldn't let her. Rather than make a scene, she stayed where she was. Eventually, the Chief called a halt to the visit, telling them all David needed his rest. But when Grace tried to leave the room, David wouldn't let her.

"Stay a while."

She looked to the Chief, and he nodded his approval. Now that David was feeling better, she didn't want to be responsible for a backward slip. Grace did as he asked.

They talked about current events, read a few articles in a magazine together and tried to play cards, until Grace quit out of frustration, sure David was using his mind powers to reveal her hand. She supposed she couldn't blame him. If she could read minds, she wouldn't hesitate to use it to cheat at cards.

He insisted he wasn't cheating, but winked and proceeded to call out every card in her hand.

"I'm so going to smother you with this pillow."

He laughed, a happy sound. David was on the mend.

At some point, they ordered and ate lunch. Grace saw David was growing weary and insisted he get some rest. It was a measure of his tiredness that he finally agreed to let her leave. David Jenkins, she was learning, was a bit possessive of her.

Grace's feelings were mixed. On the one hand, David made her feel important—like her opinions and attention mattered. Grace didn't suppose anyone had ever felt that way about her. Her ex hadn't. On the other, David seemed to know her thoughts and feelings before she did. And he took it upon himself to interpret and tell her what to do, which was annoying. She knew it was all a strange fantasy anyway. Grace couldn't stay with David forever. Once they caught the scary man, she would go home where she belonged.

Grace returned to her room in time to greet her mother. "Where've you been?" Her mother questioned, where she stood in the doorway.

"I was visiting the room next door."

"The man in the coma? Has he come to finally?"

"Yes, this morning. They say he will make a full recovery."

"Is he as handsome awake as he is asleep?

"You saw him?"

"Yes, the first night when you came here. The detective mentioned that man fought off your intruder and saved your life. I'm grateful to him. But what was he doing at your place to begin with?"

Her mother was studying her carefully, a slight gleam in her eye. Grace went on full mom alert. "Um, well, yeah that. He's a friend of mine. He had stopped by to say hello."

"That's not what the detective told me."

"What did he say?"

"Well, he said you two had recently met and had been dating. Is that true?

"Yes, well, I mean no. I mean you can hardly call a few nights out dating."

"So is this the online guy your sister says you've been talking to?"

"No, Mom. He's not."

"Well, he obviously cares about you to have risked his life."

Grace opened her mouth to reply but her mother was on a roll.

"I think you should give him a chance, Gracie. He's cute. I know Greg hurt you, but you need to let that go. Look at your sister. You know how afraid she is to tie the knot, and yet, she's giving it a shot."

"She's not married, yet."

Her mother gave her The Look. The one that said if Grace hadn't nearly lost her life, her mother would be all over her case.

"Speaking of Claire, how is she?"

"Fine. There was something she specifically wanted me to tell you. Let me see. Oh, that's right. She said to tell you she's feeling much better. I didn't even know she was sick. It's terrible how you girls don't tell me how you're doing."

"That's because we don't want you to worry, Mom."

Her mother turned her attention to the plant by her bedside, feeling the dirt and grabbing Grace's water glass and dumping it on the soil. "Yes, well, I did want to chat with you about the wedding. Claire is concerned about you. I am, too. Maybe we should delay the wedding until you're out of the woods? I know you're feeling much better, but that—man who attacked you—is still out there and could come back. The detective tells me they are keeping you here for your own safety. I'm not so sure you should be flying to California right now. Especially by yourself."

"Mom, Claire needs to walk down the aisle. I don't want her using me as an excuse. I'm coming to the wedding. I have my plane ticket, and I'm going to use it. Besides, I won't be by myself. You and Glenn will be with me. What could possibly happen?"

"Maybe we should have someone else along…for protection."

Grace should have seen this coming. Her mother was always paying matchmaker. This whole worry about her safety was more worry about Grace not having a date for the wedding. "I'm going to talk to the detective and see what he suggests. We also need to see about your release. You can't stay here forever. Maybe the detective has a few leads on the criminal who attacked you. I'm going to call him after we have supper."

They had dinner in the hospital cafeteria, and true to her word, her mother called Peter. They talked for a few minutes with Grace listening closely to what she could hear of the conversation. From the sounds of it, her mother was winning the battle to have her released to go to the wedding and to have special protection along for the trip.

"Are you sure? Yes, yes. I'm sure Grace would appreciate that, and it would make all of us feel safer. Any leads? Hmm. Uh-huh. I can't thank you enough for all you are doing for us. You and your officers are doing a fabulous job. We're all so lucky to have you on the case. All right. Thank you. Goodbye."

"That Chief Brooks is such a good detective. He told me he wouldn't want you to miss the wedding either. And he plans to have one of his best officers accompany us. Isn't that wonderful?"

"Did he say it was safe for me to travel?"

"He said you would be safer with his officer along." Her mother was a master at evasion when she wanted to be. "He hasn't caught the criminal yet, but he's confident they will. He thinks you can be released in a few more days as long as that's what you want."

Was that what she wanted? Grace wasn't sure. She felt responsible for David's recovery and was loath to leave him while he was still vulnerable. But maybe in a few days, he would be back to normal. Would he still be interested in her?

Her mother was looking at her strangely. “Grace, you do want to go home, don’t you? I would think you would be more excited.”

“Yes, of course.”

Chapter Thirty-One
Happy Place

David came to consciousness suddenly. He knew he needed to sleep as much as possible so his mind could fully recover from the attack, but it was hard to relax with the hacker on the loose. As he recovered, he found himself growing restless. Somewhere out there, an enemy still lurked who wanted Grace. He remained a target, as the enemy sought to eliminate the portal in her mind.

He grabbed a drink from the glass of water by his bedside. The drugs they had given him had kept the hacker from entering his mind and destroying his sanity. But now that they had stopped the drug infusion, their adversary would be back to test his defenses. Geneva had done what she could to repair the damage. His defenses had been weakened but not destroyed. Geneva said his mind was strong enough to withstand the onslaught when it occurred. David hoped she was right. He had never felt so beaten in all his years of service.

The attack on him had been swift and intense, and he had almost cracked under the pressure of the energy stream. The only thing that had saved them was Grace's own unwillingness to yield the portal, and his desire to protect her at all costs, which had resulted in his hanging on despite the thrashing he had endured.

Thankfully, his father and Brian had been spared the intensity of the attack. Neither one would have recovered from the force of the madman's lethal energy waves.

He reached for the portal and entered effortlessly. They couldn't keep Grace here forever, but he needed her near for his own peace of mind. It would only be a matter of time before their friend would strike again.

Grace's wavelengths were slow and steady. David resisted the temptation to linger. He must conserve his strength for the inevitable battle ahead. This time there would be no unknowns. And that would be the key to his success.

He considered the extended energy waves the hacker liked to use. Energy waves like that were hard to manufacture and harder still to control. They had a tendency to develop erratic tails. As long as the hacker had a firm control, they could inflict serious damage. But if the hacker lost control, the waves would become too jagged and could be deflected backward by another strong hacker. Although untested, he was fairly certain he was strong enough to mirror the extended waves.

Control was the rogue hacker's weakness. He struggled to maintain control when he was excited or provoked. Before the hacker had made a sudden exit from Grace's mind, David had seen the hacker lose control of his energy waves. David would use that knowledge to his advantage when next they met. He only hoped he was strong enough to resist the power of the attack.

David pulled himself back through the portal. It was time to bring Grace in on their plan. He and Peter had discussed it in the early morning hours yesterday.

Although he knew Grace was attracted to him, she had no memories or emotions from their previous time together. She was merely repaying a debt and acting the Good Samaritan. Grace would leave when Peter declared her safe. But she wouldn't be traveling to Claire's wedding alone. He would be with her as promised. The hacker would expect her to be at the wedding. Both he and Peter agreed that would be where their adversary would strike next. Grace was vulnerable where her sister was concerned. What better way for the enemy to ensure her cooperation?

Of course, the hacker was unpredictable. He could go after Grace's mother as well. For this reason, the CMU hackers were guarding both the mother and the sister. If the rogue hacker were to appear on the landscape, he would not go unnoticed. To date, though, the hacker had not put in an appearance, or at least he had avoided depositing any energy in his wake.

David rose slowly, cautiously pulling the covers back and swinging his feet over the side of the bed. He stayed that way for a moment, testing his steadiness. When he was confident he was not going to pass out or grow nauseous, he stood. His rubbery legs held. Satisfied, he moved slowly toward the door, out into the hallway, and to Grace's room. No one was in sight. David opened the door and went inside.

The early morning sun cast enough light to see her lying amongst a tangle of covers, like a small child. Her short-cropped blond hair lay matted against her pale face. David reached out a hand, gently rubbing a finger across her cheek. "Grace, wake up." He watched as she came slowly awake, squinting and broadcasting alarm.

"David? Shouldn't you be in bed? What are you

doing here?"

David couldn't stop the smile on his lips. "I came to see you."

"What do you want?" Grace struggled to sit up, as if sensing he had something important to tell her.

"We need to talk."

"It's a little early, don't you think?" She glanced at the alarm clock. "It's 6:00 a.m."

He smiled. "Time to get up. This is important."

"Ok." She grumbled, propping her head with her pillows. "But I haven't had my morning coffee."

"You can get it later. I'll treat you to a hospital breakfast."

"Now that's an incentive. So why the early morning wakeup call?"

David sat on the end of the bed, taking a brief moment, when he realized his presence unnerved Grace, to adjust his energy waves to calm her. "Peter tells me you're ready to be released. I know you plan to travel to San Francisco for Claire's wedding."

"Yes, that's right."

He took her hand, slowly traced the lines of her palm, then chose his next words carefully. "Grace, I know this wedding is important to you, but it's not safe. Our adversary knows about your sister. He will be expecting you to attend the wedding."

Grace shivered, but David wasn't sure if it was from the way he was touching her or the thought of having to deal with the madman again. Maybe a little of both. She knew what he was telling her was logical. She should go into hiding until they caught the crazy son of bitch. But Grace refused to be the reason her sister called off her wedding. Claire would never get hitched if Grace wasn't there to encourage her. David heard: *There's no way in hell they will keep me away.*

"I'm going with you." He said it calmly, as if they were talking about the weather.

"Oh, there's no need for that." Grace sat up taller. "You need to stay here and get well."

"Relax, Grace. I know the idea of us having a relationship is foreign to you. But believe me when I tell you we did have a relationship."

"Yes, but I don't…I can't…"

"No buts or can'ts." David spoke sharply and then took a deep breath. When he spoke again, his tone was calm and reasonable. "Because you can't remember it, doesn't mean it didn't happen—that I don't have feelings for you."

Grace's thoughts were conflicted. David heard: *He did almost die to save me. But he's still a stranger despite what he keeps insisting. But death? Do you want it to happen to him for real this time? To you?*

"David, I know you say we've been lovers. You must understand, I don't remember any of that. You're a…a…virtual stranger to me. I do appreciate your saving my life. That's why I'm here trying to help you. But we aren't going to be able to pick up where we left off. I can't…"

"There's that word again," he grumbled. "No can'ts. I told you I wouldn't pressure you and I meant it. But you cannot expect me to sit idly by while a madman is on the loose."

David's tremendous control slipped. Being near Grace, especially after the recent battle they had endured together, was hard on his nerves. He would not let her shut him out, though. Besides, the fact that she had clung to the portal through it all was a strong statement in his favor. David was in her mind so he knew she was intrigued with him and attracted. Grace couldn't hide her strong emotions. Not from him.

"That's exactly what I expect you to do, David. You need to get well. You won't be able to do that if you're worried about defending me." Grace crossed her arms. "Plus, if that crazy hacker finds me again, you can't do what you did last time. He won't wait to reason with you—he'll kill you."

"Maybe, but I don't think so. He'll keep me alive so he can control me. Listen, Grace. I have a plan. The hacker, whoever he is, has trouble controlling his emotions. Control is essential for a mind hacker. Without it, he cannot manage the energy fields. Believe me, I have seen hackers who can't control their energy die horrible deaths, all because they let their emotions get the better of them when they were under. If we can get our friend to lose control of his feelings, I believe I can wrest control from him."

"If you can do it, why can't another hacker? Why not let Peter choose who should go with me? You're better off staying here and recuperating fully. I don't want your death on my hands when you're so vulnerable."

David smiled inwardly. Grace would never be able to disguise her true thoughts. Not from him. Her worry and fear echoed across his mind, tugging at his heart. Grace needed him.

"Like it or not, Grace, I'm all you have. No one else is strong enough to fight this madman. His energy is so powerful, he would incinerate them. They would never make it back alive. Besides, the hacker is after me. He must defeat me to get to you. After he destroyed my fill-in, he would still come after me, most likely reenergized and even stronger than before. We can't let that happen."

"But you've been so ill."

"I'm not ill but injured and healing fast. Besides, I won't be alone."

She looked at him puzzled. He held her hand tighter and smiled into her eyes. "You will be there, too."

As romantic statements went, it wasn't his best. But it signaled to Grace that they were a team—that he was treating her as an equal partner. That he needed her.

Grace stared at him for a second as if trying to make sense of his words. David knew the moment she gave in fully, her pent up energy releasing all at once.

"Okay. I can see arguing with you isn't going to get you to change your mind. You can come to my sister's wedding. But remember, you're not my date. This is purely business."

David nodded, careful to keep the triumph from showing on his face.

"All right. What do you need from me?"

"We'll need to work on your defense. The hacker will attack where you are most vulnerable—your mother, your sister, a close friend—anyone who means something to you. He's been in your mind, so he'll know. Whatever is important to you, he'll know. It'll be difficult, but you'll need to ignore whatever he threatens and maintain calm. If you can do this, you'll defuse the power he possesses. It will take more energy for him to command your mind. It will help me wrest control."

"How do I do this?"

"You had the right idea before. We'll create a 'happy place' for you. Somewhere you feel calm and that brings you joy. When he attacks, and mark my words, he'll attack again, you will immediately retreat to this place."

"A happy place it is. When can we get started?"

"No time like the present."

Chapter Thirty-Two
On the Move

They ate breakfast in her room and began her training.

"Concentrate on the feeling you have when you are on the beach," David said. "Are you warm, is there a cool breeze, are there seagulls? What are you wearing? What does the sand feel like on your feet? What does the lake water smell like?"

"Quiet. I've discovered a cool piece of beach glass." Grace was lying on the bed, a pillow propped behind her head, eyes closed.

"What does it look like?"

"It's pink, almost translucent like a jelly fish. The edges are smooth and it's big enough to fit in the palm of my hand."

The glass morphed into a red heart-shaped piece of glass. "Hey, how'd you do that?"

David laughed. "A little hacker humor. And while I'm at it…"

Her outfit went from a bright blue one piece, which made her look tanned, to a white bikini that accentuated her bust and behind. A pair of Armani sunglasses magically appeared on her head.

"No fair. This is my daydream. Stay out." Grace re-imagined the blue-bathing suit.

They played tug of war for a while, tussling for

control of the scene, and laughing. After all the stress they had been under, Grace enjoyed the return to semi-normalcy. During that moment, she realized two things: She liked David, and she could not deny the attraction between them. Grace supposed it was possible that they had been lovers, although, she still found it surprising.

David leaned across the bed suddenly and kissed her full on the lips. Too late, Grace had forgotten he could read her mind. The impact of his mouth on hers stunned her senses momentarily. It was as if an electrical charge went straight from his mouth to her heart. She could swear she missed a beat. It wasn't every day a good-looking man, who happened to be a mind reader, kissed her. He was a good kisser. The intensity of the kiss changed, growing more thorough and intimate. She reminded herself to guard her thoughts more closely. It wouldn't do to give him any ideas. He was taking full advantage.

David drew back and looked Grace straight in the eyes. "I told you, it's not possible to guard your thoughts from me with the portal in place. You would need to reject the portal and so far, you've been pretty stubborn about hanging on to it."

Grace responded a bit breathlessly. "How do I go about rejecting it?"

David stared at her for a moment, watching her lips as if he were going to kiss her again. Did she want him to kiss her? Would he get the wrong idea?

Instead of renewing the kiss, David drew away. "It's not difficult. You have to want it gone. Your mind will release it, but you must will it to."

Grace took a deep breath, using the distance between them to gather her thoughts. "But I can't even tell this portal thing exists. How can I possibly tell my mind to release it?"

"Believe me, if you wanted it gone, it would be gone. Instead, you have defended it like a prized possession."

Grace's frustration mounted. David held all the cards. It wasn't fair. Not only did he still have his own memories, but he had access to all the memories in Grace's mind as well. David knew everything, while she remained in the dark.

"Well, I guess I'll need to take your word for it, because I still don't know how I can possibly get rid of something I can't feel or touch."

David studied her a moment, his green eyes glowing with something Grace couldn't identify. She waited patiently for him to respond, but they were interrupted by the buzz of his cell phone. He checked the identity and answered, eyeing her all the while. Grace knew instantly she was the subject of their conversation.

"Yes. Okay. Right. I'm listening." Long pause. "Not good. Yes, I know. When? Today? Are you certain? Okay…no, I'm up for it. Yes, I did, and everything was as normal. She's sitting across from me. Yes, I understand. Yeah, I'll handle it."

David pocketed his cell phone in his hospital gown, his eyes never leaving hers. Something about his stance made her heart beat hard.

"We are being released this afternoon."

"We? I mean, I was expecting to be released. I didn't have a chance to tell you my mother talked to Peter yesterday. But you—are you sure you're well enough? I mean…"

"Yes, we." David grabbed her hand suddenly, pulling her to him. "Our friend is on the move. He's not going to leave you alone. He'll strike soon. You don't think I'll leave you to face him all alone, do you?"

"No, but…what do you mean on the move? How do you know?"

"Because they've found evidence of his energy in a suspected target's mind."

"Who?"

He shook his head quickly, almost impatiently. "Not another hacker."

"Who…?" Something about the way he said the word target, so carefully as if he were afraid to reveal anything by its use, triggered some sixth sense within her. The madman had gone after someone close to her. *Claire.*

He shook his head. "Not Claire. Your mother."

Grace sucked in a sudden breath. *Oh, my God.* Panic welled inside her sharp and deep, like a giant bubble floating to the surface of her mind. Her mother would never survive the psychopath. She's too high-strung and anxious. *He'll kill her.*

David sat suddenly, pulling her with him. "Relax, Grace." He stroked her back. "Put your head between your legs."

Grace complied and immediately her head stopped swimming.

"Try to slow your breathing. Take deep breaths. Your mom is fine. We'd anticipated the possibility. We were able to stop him from entering."

"How?" Grace's voice sounded garbled coming from between her legs.

"We set a trap that was triggered when he made the

attempt."

"A trap—in her mind?"

David nodded.

"So he didn't get in? She's okay?" Grace lifted her head to look at David. She wanted to make sure he wasn't hiding anything.

"Yes, she's fine. But it won't stop him from trying again. He wants to get someone close to you in his power, so he has leverage. Your mother's an easy target, since she's local. Although he can still attack from a distance, it's much harder for him to generate the energy he needs, and he can't stay under as long. If he's on the move, we must be, too. This hospital is out of the way, but if he has the resources we think, it's likely he's tracked us. Peter suspects he's nearby, waiting to strike at the first opportunity. We need to leave. Now. Go pack your things. And call your mother and let her know your attacker is at large and the police are coming to get her. Tell her they will put her and Glenn in a safe house for a few days, and you'll call her once you're settled." He turned to go.

"But wait—where am I going?"

"With me. You're not leaving my sight." David cocked one eyebrow at her, as if daring her to argue. When she didn't immediately, he turned and left the room. "Get packed." He called back over his shoulder.

Grace sat for a moment after he left, still stunned by the knowledge the hacker had tried to attack her mother. Her anxious mother would be overwhelmed by the experience. The nasty man would prey on her worst fears, telling her that her girls were in trouble.

The room spun, causing Grace to close her eyes for a moment. She had forgotten her secondary concern:

How would David be able to save Grace when he had barely saved himself the last time? One more battle would surely do him in, wouldn't it? The look in the madman's eyes. How did he take her over, paralyzing her ability to move? Her only defense had been to keep calm and resist his advances. It was clear she would need to draw on that inner strength again to find her happy zone. Grace prayed by the time the real attack came, she had a happy zone to draw on.

Her phone beeped, distracting her with an incoming text. *Claire.* Grace glanced at it apprehensively, fearing that Claire would use her so-called accident to call off her wedding. She hated that all of her troubles could be the cause of another failed wedding for Claire.

11:15 a.m. How are you feeling? Up for a phone call?

She thumbed. *Yes, feeling great. Going to be released today.* Immediately her phone buzzed and Grace answered.

"Hi, Claire. How's everything?"

"I'm fine. It's you I'm worried about. Any leads on the man who attacked you?"

"Not yet, but I know they're working on it. I'm not the only one he's gone after."

"Oh, yeah. I heard about the cute guy next door that saved your life. Mom was a bit hysterical when I talked to her. Called him a hero or something. What's he like?"

"Yes, well, she's not far off. He felt like a hero to me. He's nice but…I mean…I hardly know him…well…"

"What's the matter?"

"Oh, nothing's wrong. It's…I've decided to bring

him to your wedding." This last was said on a rush, as if she were afraid Claire would argue.

"You mean your knight in shining armor? Oh…my…gosh. I'm so excited. Mom said you were dating him and he's cute."

"We're not dating. And I'm not bringing him to your wedding as my date. It's more of a bodyguard thing."

"Sure, sure. You're bringing a bodyguard that is recovering from a serious accident to my wedding—and he's not your date. Really, Grace, it's okay if you want to call him your boyfriend. I don't mind. So are you still flying in on Friday as planned? I can't tell you how excited Tom is to finally meet you and Mom."

"We're excited to meet him, too. Everything's set. Mom and Glenn are meeting me at the airport. We're flying United and our plane is due into San Francisco at 4:10 p.m. I didn't have a chance to find out from David where he plans to stay, but he's a little paranoid about leaving me alone right now. Are you able to put him up?"

"Of course, and I think it's a good idea anyway. After all, he did save your life. It's the least we can do."

Grace would never admit it out loud, but with a lunatic at large, she did feel a bit safer with David around. Even though the man could read minds. "Does he like cats?" Claire continued. "He's not allergic is he? Daisy has the roam of the place, you know. Wait until you see her. She's gotten so big."

Daisy was Claire's baby. She had gotten her as a stray kitten after her last breakup. "I don't know. I'll have to ask him. As far as I know, he's fine with cats. But honestly, I don't know that much about him."

Except the fact he could read minds. Grace crossed her fingers. No way would she be telling Claire that. It would be a real test of Claire's charm if she could flirt with a mind reader, and he found her irresistible.

"So are you going back to your condo or will you stay with Mom?"

"Neither. I'm going to be staying in a safe house for a while. Mom, too."

"Really? Who's taking care of Harvey? Barbara?"

"Yes. Mom called her when I first got to the hospital, and Barbara has him at her place."

"I can understand why they might want you to go somewhere safe, but for heaven's sake, why would they want Mom to go to one? Unless—do they think the creep will go after her, too?"

"Yes, they do. In fact, they think he's already made an attempt, although she doesn't know that so don't say anything."

"Oh, my God. Of course not. But this is terrible. I'm so glad they're making her go with you. But that will only be for a few days, and you'll be visiting. I can't imagine he would try and track you to California. Do you think?"

"No, I don't think so." Grace lied.

"Can you believe in a little more than a week I'll be a married lady? I cannot believe it."

Grace couldn't keep pace with the steady stream of thoughts, so she stopped trying. She was grateful that Claire was still on track to say "I do." She had gotten within a week of the big day and was still in the running. More and more Grace was convinced Tom must be the right groom for her sister. Now, if they could only make it down the aisle.

Chapter Thirty-Three
Energy Shard

It didn't take Grace long to pack her bags. By 4:00 p.m., she and David had completed their paperwork and were released into Peter's care, who informed them her mother and Glenn had already been safely ensconced in a safe house.

"What's their address?"

"We won't give it out." Peter spoke with quiet authority. "We don't want our rogue hacker to track them."

"What if something happens and I need to get in touch with them?"

"Roland knows their location. You may call your mother once you arrive at your destination."

Grace didn't recognize the man and woman that came to escort her and David to the safe house. She was told it was critical the hacker would not recognize or follow them, so they sent what looked to be a middle aged couple. The woman had a neck brace. It wasn't until hours later, when they were finally in a remote location, Grace discovered they were young and distant cousins of David. She and David had also been given elaborate disguises. Grace laughed when she saw the gray hairpiece he would wear, making him look like an elderly gentleman.

"You look like my Grandpa Woznisky. All you

need is a cane."

"Like this?" He pulled a black cane from under the pile of garments, and she giggled. He held a pair of ripped jeans and a tattoo kit. "It will be interesting to see what you look like in these."

She eyed the wigged ponytail. "It looks like I'm meant to be your granddaughter."

"C'mon, we'd better get these on and get a move-on. Let me know if you need any help." He winked, causing her to blush, and took off to his bedroom to change.

An hour later, they left with at least a dozen others. Grace was instructed to spend time in her happy place so the enemy, if he were watching, would have a harder time sensing her energy. It must have worked because they made it to the safe house without incident. The cousins didn't stay long afterward. David told her they were an accountant and teacher in real life and needed to get back to their day jobs.

The house was less of a house and more of an apartment complex set next to rows and rows of what appeared to be other similar apartment complexes. "The walls of this building are insulated with a compound that absorbs energy," David said. "It will help to prevent a hacker from infiltrating."

Grace followed him inside, where she discovered plenty of private bedrooms and bathrooms, a big central kitchen and lounge area and even an exercise room. The building itself looked like it had been built in the 1950s, but it was well maintained.

"Make yourself at home. We'll be here until Friday."

"What time will we meet my mom and Glenn at

the airport?"

"Oh, about that. There's been a slight change of plans. Peter has arranged for a private flight to San Francisco. A commercial flight is too risky, since it would be easy for our hacker to monitor all the commercial flights out of Cleveland into San Francisco. We cannot chance it."

"Wait a minute. That ticket was expensive. When was he going to tell me?"

"Don't worry Grace. You'll get a full refund. The CMU is generous that way."

"How about Mom and Glenn? Will they join us on the flight?

"That's the current plan. Also, and don't be upset by this, but we can't have you staying with Claire. That would be too dangerous."

"Can I at least call her and tell her where we are staying? Come to think of it, I don't even know."

"And that's a good thing. The less you know, the safer you'll remain."

David had become quieter and more guarded since they had donned their disguises. Grace found herself missing the earlier David who had teased her and laughed out loud. She didn't recognize the tightly wound and dangerous man next to her. Watching him, she could understand why he had gained a reputation as a powerful mind reader. No hint of emotion crossed his dark features as he sat across from her, practicing some sort of mental exercise he told her was necessary. Geneva arrived shortly afterward, giving Grace a quick nod and leaving with David, presumably back to his room. Grace pretended to read a magazine until they were on their way. If David was her lover, the girl would be the first to go. Something about her calm exterior and the way she constantly had her hands on David set off alarm bells. And who the hell was Meg? Grace hadn't forgotten how the evil hacker had referred to Meg as belonging to David.

Grace didn't know whether she resented David's high-handedness at rearranging the details of their trip or if she were grateful. On the one hand, he had not consulted her on any of the particulars nor bothered to tell her of the arrangements he had made with Peter until they were already on their way. He preferred to keep her in the dark. On the other hand, it was nice to know David was concerned for her safety and was taking steps to protect her. Grace had gotten better at guarding her feelings from him, but her thoughts were a bit harder to control. The "portal," as he called it, seemed to allow David to know what Grace was thinking whenever he wanted. And he wanted a lot. When she asked for her privacy, David refused, telling her it was his "job" to alert the rest of his crew if their enemy found a way to infiltrate her mind. Although they did not expect the hacker would make an attempt before the ceremony, they needed to be prepared in case he decided to mount a surprise attack. And so Grace had to deal with David as a shadow in the back of her mind. It was downright annoying and a whole lot embarrassing. There were certain thoughts a girl preferred to keep private. As far as Grace was concerned, Friday couldn't arrive fast enough.

*****

David knew the exact moment Grace shut him out. Geneva was making some adjustments, and he had let his mind wander to the portal. Grace's energy waves were soft and even. It required more of an effort for him to pull them in. He didn't protest or give any indication he knew what she was doing. But he had to admit, he had grown used to understanding her emotions, along with her thoughts, and he hated the distance between them. At the same time, he recognized she was gaining mental ground. If she could cloud his view with a portal in place, then it was likely she could reduce the enemy's power over her and limit the amount of destruction he could carry out.

Since David had been in the hospital, his team had been working to track the hacker. They had thoroughly investigated the hotel staff where they knew for certain the hacker had been hiding out, but the effort did not generate any new leads. The problem seemed to be the enemy was skilled at erasing thoughts without leaving evidence of his presence behind. It was only when implanting thoughts, which was a far more risky procedure, he could not always contain his energy, particularly when he was excited.

The weekend wedding. David could not stop thinking about it. Once again, he was forced to use Grace as bait to draw the enemy out. He hated that. But Peter had convinced him it was the only way. Logically, he knew they couldn't stay in hiding forever. It was always better to have the enemy attack where and when they were expecting him, rather than wait to be ambushed. The trouble was David could not shake the feeling he was missing something. It had all been too easy—their escape from the hospital and arrival at the safe house. Roland reported Grace's mother had arrived at her location without any difficulty either.

Unknown to Grace, tonight the team would be

going on one more scouting mission before David, her mother, stepdad, Peter, and Geneva flew in to San Francisco Friday afternoon. He mulled over the details even as he readied his mind for the trip. Rolf had been tailing Claire. She had kept him busy for much of the day, visiting a hair salon, a tanning bed, and a major shopping outlet. On the surface, everything appeared normal. But David had paid Claire a nocturnal visit yesterday and caught errant energy waves in her mind, indicating the hacker had been there before him and more than once, too. David wondered when and which of her many thoughts the enemy had implanted. There was only one way to find out for sure. He would pay Claire another visit.

Geneva stepped back from where he lay on the couch with a nod. Since the attack, they had been taking extra precautions to make “the trip in” less taxing for him. One way was to make sure their target was fully asleep before their arrival, which had been verified by Rolf about fifteen minutes earlier. It was important David conserve what power he could in the event of an unexpected confrontation with the enemy.

“Ready?”

David gave Geneva a mental thumbs up. The portal yawned in front of him, and he made the familiar descent. Within seconds, David was through, nodding to Roland and Brian who joined him. Together, they made short work of a limited number of soldiers, allowing him to narrow the landscape, and navigate the energy fields with little effort.

David did not immediately notice anything alarming. Claire’s thought patterns were even, her mind waves indicative of a normal dream state. He searched carefully for any clue that would indicate their enemy had been there earlier. It wasn't long before he spotted a familiar jagged tail. David examined it carefully. The hacker who had created it had been extremely excited at the time. The energy at the tip was raw and unrefined. David filed it carefully with past samples. There was nothing in it he could use except the knowledge the rogue hacker had trouble controlling his power.

David continued the search. *Nothing. Time to quit.*

As he was about to exit, David noticed the wave ahead contained a slight warp, indicating a foreign energy deposit. He pulled it in, carefully containing his excitement so he did not contaminate the shard. He could not be sure until he examined it more closely. But he was fairly certain he had it…a clear deposit. One he could trap, analyze and perhaps, tap into without the enemy's knowledge. The hacker had been careless. That mistake might prove his undoing. *Time to leave.* David signaled to the others, exiting in a smooth pattern and with little expenditure of energy.

"A shard?" Geneva asked excitedly the minute he opened his eyes.

David nodded.

"Usable?"

"I'm fairly certain but will need to take a closer look."

He began his review shortly after, carefully deconstructing the energy pattern and reformulating it, until he was confident it could be duplicated. He struggled to contain his excitement. The time had come to go on the offensive.

Chapter Thirty-Four
Messages

"I don't understand," Grace asked him for the third time. "Why can't I contact Claire? You promised I would be able to once we got here. I'm sure she's worried sick."

Grace had eaten breakfast alone, thinking she would let David sleep, until she had grown bored and restless and went to search him out in his bedroom. She found an empty room, his bed still neatly made. Her mood darkened.

Grace eventually found him, squirreled away in a room they were using as an office, Geneva and Peter by his side.

"I've told you. It's no longer safe. We can't risk it. We'll have Rolf call your sister in the morning."

"But why's it no longer safe? If I understood what was happening, maybe—"

"The less you know the better. You have to trust me."

Grace groaned. She was sick and tired of being treated like a child. She was safe in their hideaway. What had changed since last night? What wasn't he telling her? Grace stared at David angrily across the room, not caring if Geneva and Peter were silent witnesses.

"But if I knew what was happening, I could help

you. Listen, if this battle is going to take place in my mind, I'd like to at least be privy as to what to expect."

David was dressed in a pair of faded blue jeans and a forest green shirt. Despite frustration, some part of Grace registered and resented how it brought out the green in his eyes. She didn't want to find him attractive. He smirked, and Grace gritted her teeth, the fragile edges of her temper fraying. She snarled. "Get out of my head."

David chuckled and strolled across the room until he was staring at her, his expression calm and emotionless. "Make me."

Grace gasped at his audacity. Behind him, she heard Geneva snicker. She stamped her foot in frustration. A major temper tantrum was about to erupt, and it wouldn't be pretty. They were laughing at her. Grace didn't recognize this man, who claimed to be her lover. It couldn't be true. She would never fall in love with someone so controlling and insensitive, would she? The fact that David, along with his so-called trainer, made fun of her was like a match to a fuse. Grace couldn't dampen the flames unleashing inside of her.

"Oh, I would if I could, believe me." She spat the words in his face, uncaring that he towered over her. "Go ahead, have it your way. Don't tell me what's going on. Keep your little secrets. I'll be in my room. That is, if I'm allowed to go to my room?"

She drew out the question, letting it hang between them. Her body shook with the force of her rage. To her horror, in the silence that followed, she let out a garbled sob.

David drew in breath, but Grace didn't wait for

him to speak. Instead, she slammed the door with such force, it bounced open again, and dashed to her room, where she cried her frustrations into her pillow. Grace was pretty sure she hated David right now—all of them. She was like a recalcitrant child who had confronted a stubborn parent. David had another thing coming if he imagined she was ever going to resume their so-called relationship. Grace didn't care how many minds he hacked, he wasn't going to convince her otherwise.

*****

"C'mon big boy, don't let it get to you. She'll come around again, once the game is done."

Despite Geneva's reassurances, David wasn't convinced. There was only one thing that might restore her faith in him, and he could not risk giving it to her yet. Rationally, David was certain Grace didn't hate him. Far from it. If she hated him, she would relinquish the portal they had established between them. Even so, it was a struggle not to run after Grace and provide comfort. It would go better for her if she believed she hated him. If David won, he could explain it all later, when she was in his arms again. And if he lost—David forced himself to consider the distinct possibility. If he lost, she'd be lucky to stay alive, let alone have any feelings to spare for him. The enemy would seize control. David shoved the thought aside. He wouldn't lose. They were all depending on him.

*****

Alone in her bedroom, Grace's angry tears subsided, as she became aware of a steady beep. Her cell phone! She still had it. Grace hadn't charged it in a while, so the battery was low. What would the harm be in texting Claire she was okay? A single text would not give anything away, would it? It's not like the mad hacker could infiltrate her cell phone and take her over.

Grace shivered, scrambling for the phone in her purse, anxious to try it now the idea had surfaced. She used a new tactic that seemed to keep David out of her head. Grace recited nonsense words repeatedly, all the while searching her purse frantically for the phone. Once she found it, she composed a hurried text.

11:16 a.m. I'm safe. Will arrive in San Francisco Friday afternoon. Everything is great. I will see you at the rehearsal dinner. Mom, too. Don't worry about us. We'll be there.

Grace reread it and hit send before she could change her mind or David got wind of her plan. Her phone returned an immediate error message: Unable to Send. *What the hell?* She copied the message and tried again. Same thing. *Damn him.* He must have done something to her phone, for God's sake. Did he think of everything? Didn't he ever make a mistake? As rhetorical questions went, they were good ones, but they weren't going to help her get word to Claire. She needed another idea.

Grace paced the floor, all the while continuing the mental gibberish in her head. If the idiot wanted to keep her in the dark, there was nothing she could do about it. But she didn't have to sit idly by and watch her sister call off her wedding because she was worried about Grace and their mother, especially if Grace could prevent it with a simple text or telephone call.

C'mon Grace, think of something. For once in her life, the positive self-talk worked, because the most brilliant idea came to her. Grace couldn't prevent her grin of satisfaction. She would show mister mind control he wasn't the boss of her. So her phone was dead. There was wireless Internet in the joint. David had given her the lengthy password when they first arrived, telling her she could surf the Internet and check email messages but she couldn't send them. But that didn't mean Grace couldn't access some application that allowed a chat feature. And she knew the very one.

Grace found her charger, plugged it in and looked for the open wireless signal. *Success.* She opened her favorite game. The familiar blue logo popped up, along with the chat feature. She and Greg used to challenge one another in this game all the time, and Grace knew she could easily send him a message. He and Claire had recently been in touch, too, so it wouldn't be hard or alarming for him to send Claire a message. Decision made, she typed.

8:31 p.m. Hi, I'm having cell phone/texting issues and having trouble getting in touch with Claire. Could you please call her and let her know I'm all right but won't see her until the rehearsal dinner on Friday? Thanks so much. I'll owe you one.

Grace studied the message a moment with a frown, and went back and crossed out the "I'll owe you one." *I owe him nothing, even if he's doing me a huge favor.* She hit send at the same moment Grace realized she was no longer alone.

A cold fear raced through her system. She glanced over to see David, propped against the door frame, studying her. Grace didn't need to read his mind to know he was angry. She waited in silence for him to lash out. Predictably, he was quiet.

Several uncomfortable seconds ticked by. Grace grew self-conscious. If only he would yell at her and get it over with, like a normal man. Instead, she had to endure his quiet condemnation and probes into her head. Finally, when Grace was about to scream and storm out of her own room, David held out his hand. Grace was surprised he would want to hold her hand, until she realized her embarrassing mistake. He was after her phone. She didn't dare protest but quickly handed it over. David pocketed it and came inside the room to once again tower over her.

"So who did you send a message to?"

"You didn't get that?" Grace joked, trying to diffuse his anger. Silence. She swallowed nervously. "My ex-husband." Her voice came out with a squeak.

"Of course. Because the hacker doesn't know you used to be married and so will stay out of his head, right? No, don't answer that." He interrupted, not allowing her to speak. "You do realize what this means, don't you?"

"What?"

"You mean you haven't figured it out yet? My-my. Now who's a little slow?"

Tiny pinpricks of moisture formed, as Grace fought back tears. She wasn't used to sarcasm from David, and his bitterness took her aback. It hurt. Maybe Grace liked David more than she realized.

David sighed and sat next to Grace on her bed. He reached out and took her hand. "I'm sorry, that was small of me. I am…worried. Your text means our enemy will now know for certain you will show for the rehearsal dinner."

"Are you saying we can't go to my own sister's rehearsal dinner?"

"I wish." He sighed, running a hand through his

dark hair. “Listen, Grace, I know you’re angry with me, thinking I’m keeping you out of the action. What I’m trying to do is keep you safe. Listen, if you don’t know anything, he can’t steal anything from you. You of all people know what that’s like. Do you really want to go through it all again?”

David didn’t wait for her response but kept talking, almost to himself. “No, perhaps it’s better this way. Our friend will use this to his advantage. He now knows you’re flying in tomorrow, and it won’t be hard for him to get the details of the rehearsal dinner. I suspect he had this information anyway. We’ll have to expect the attack to happen on Friday. Less time to prepare, but we’ll manage.”

As it dawned on Grace what David wasn’t saying, remorse filled her. He still needed time to heal. He had needed the extra day.

“David, I’m so sorry. I was worried about Claire. I should have realized you were still recovering.”

David smiled, joking. “So you do care.”

Grace found herself smiling back. “Of course, I care. I don’t like being treated like a child. You should’ve told me you were worried about your ability to fight. I would have understood that.”

“I’m not worried about myself.”

“What…?”

“I have an idea but it hasn’t been…tested. We were working on that when you saw us earlier.”

It was evident David was not used to revealing his plans to anyone. The fact he did spoke volumes. Grace was touched. He pulled the hand he was holding to his lips and kissed it tenderly. Grace shivered. He looked at her, and she saw the play of emotions run across his face. *I worry for you.* He whispered the words, but his lips weren't moving. It was a caress in her mind.

David bent to kiss her but stopped right before their lips touched and breathed her in, his hands tenderly cupping either side of her face. This time he whispered the words out loud before his lips dropped to hers. "I worry for you."

The words, followed by the familiar, day-old stubble on David's face and the scent of his aftershave had Grace trembling. The tip of his tongue outlined hers before plunging inside to devour the inside of her mouth. All the while, he whispered endearments in her head. The effect was mind-blowing. The pun was not lost on Grace. If this was how he kissed, what would it be like to make love to this man? The thought seemed to unleash something powerful in David, as he devoured her lips. His hands smoothed down her backside, bringing Grace tightly to him.

"I hate to break up the party, but might I remind you we have work to do?" Peter stood in the doorway, his words like a bucket of cold ice water dumped on their heads.

David pulled away from Grace slowly, and she shivered at the loss of heat. He continued to stare at her hungrily, though, his breathing heavy. Finally, he spoke, all the while looking at her and not at Peter. "I'll be right with you. Grace and I have reached a new understanding."

"I gathered that." Peter spoke dryly. Grace cheeks burned. "You've got five minutes. Come find us." He turned abruptly and walked away.

"Don't mind Peter." He told her, reading her thoughts once again. "He likes you. We have a lot riding on this."

He tossed a hand through his perfect hair and stood up, pulling her with him. "I do have to get back. He wasn't lying when he said he would return in five minutes. He has his stop-watch going as we speak. Grace, I'm not going to be able to stay away from you when this is all over. So don't make the mistake of thinking we'll go back to being strangers."

"David, I…who is Meg?" If they were going to have a relationship, then she needed to understand the competition.

"No one you need to worry about."

"But David, I…"

He put a finger to her lips to stop her from speaking. "Shhh. Trust me, please. There is no competition. You forget…I'm in your mind. Despite your recent efforts to block me out, I can still hear your thoughts."

Grace was effectively silenced. *Damn him and his mind-reading abilities.* It wasn't fair.

"You look so cute when you're frustrated." He tweaked her nose, giving Grace a brief kiss before heading out the door. "Try not to get into any more trouble, would you? We'll depart at 10:00 a.m. tomorrow for San Francisco. Practice going to your happy place. If Peter's right, you'll be paying it a visit tomorrow evening."

David disappeared, leaving Grace more confused than ever. Not for the first time, Grace wished she had her memories of their previous time together. Maybe they had been a legitimate item after all.

Chapter Thirty-Five
Diversion

Kyle Willard leaned back in his soft leather chair, steepling his fingers, as was his custom, and contemplated the scenery outside his penthouse suite. There were no skyscrapers in San Francisco, due to earthquakes, but he had a lovely view of the city. Somewhere out there, right now, Grace existed, deeply engrossed in her lover-boy. In a few hours, he would see her again. Had she thought of him since their last encounter? His memories of her were still vivid. Grace had fought him hard, but he would still conquer her in the end. What would Grace be like when she was under his control? Would she be like all the others, no match for his superior strength? Or would she continue to resist, while he stripped her clean of all barriers? He couldn't wait to find out. The sooner, the better.

Kyle had been making preparations for this moment ever since he was forced to exit prematurely during their last go around. He had had difficulty controlling his anger. A few minutes more, and he would have conquered. To be so close to victory and to see it shattered. Well, no matter. He shook off his disappointment. Kyle could not afford the distraction if he were to succeed this time. He looked at his watch. In two hours and twenty-two minutes Grace would be his, and he'd finally rid the world of David Jenkins. There would be no stopping him.

A soft knock sounded. The door behind him opened and closed. He saw his sister's reflection in the window and quickly sent a mental message. *Any snags?*

No. They all understand their orders.

Good. Let's get started.

He took off his jacket and shoes and loosened his tie. It wouldn't do to be uncomfortable. He lay on the bed and closed his eyes. A familiar scene rose in front of him. He twisted the energy waves going in so he immediately seized control of his target's mind. *Such a weak creature I am forced to use for this job.* It was difficult to ignore the feeling of distaste and condemnation that built inside of him, threatening to spill over into the target's mind. That would never do. He forced it back inside and bent to his task. He needed the target alive for a little while longer, until he was, like all the others, expendable.

Kyle studied the scene through the weakling's eyes. He was pleased to see his earlier instructions had been followed to a tee. Long strips of pantyhose had been cut to an exact size. They lay neatly beside him, waiting for his order. He wanted her to be fearful but unharmed—at least for the time being.

"Find her and tie her up."

Immediately, the target grasped the panty hose and moved to do his bidding. Kyle quickly and efficiently over-powered the brief resistance. "Now."

Within minutes, it was all over. The girl was bound and gagged and tied to the bedposts. The target lay on the bed as instructed. Kyle spent a few moments planting the desire to sleep. He exited, coming back to his body swiftly. Kaitlyn worked over him with quick efficiency. She alone knew how distasteful this task was to him. *I am far too powerful to have to spend time in the minds of underlings.*

Kyle had set the plan in motion. Now it was time to watch and wait for the right opportunity. He brushed Kaitlyn away hurriedly and checked his watch. One hour and fifty-seven minutes. He had only been under for twenty-five minutes. He was ahead of schedule. The lack of precision annoyed him.

Not long now. Adrenaline pumped through his system, causing his palms to grow hot. This would not do. *Contain your excitement!* Kyle inhaled, slowing his heartbeat and dimming his energy. He must contain his power until he needed it. *I will have her under my control in no time. And I'll have the hacker.*

Chapter Thirty-Six
Sneak Attack

Grace checked her cell phone anxiously. David had charged it and returned it to her before they left their hotel with strict instructions not to contact anyone. *4:30 p.m.* If the driver did not hurry, they would be embarrassingly late.

David was sitting next to her working his own cell phone with quiet authority. Geneva sat in the back, mostly staring out the window when she wasn't exchanging mental messages with David. Grace knew they were talking because periodically, she would let a real word slip out.

Grace still had a hard time comprehending the exact dynamic of Geneva's relationship with David. She glanced at him for at least the tenth time since the driver, who she did not recognize, had come to take them to the rehearsal. David looked sophisticated in his navy blue suit and pinstripe tie. Not a hint of worry showed on his handsome face. Other than Roland, Grace wasn't sure who he was getting updates from, but his phone seemed to buzz with a new text every few moments. As usual, David appeared calm and in control. Roland, she was told, had escorted her mother to the church. David relayed they had arrived safely and everything seemed normal. Claire and Tom had not yet arrived, but her mother was forty-five minutes early.

This was by design. If the enemy were watching, he would believe her mom had arrived alone and anticipate Grace might miss the big event.

That was another plan that had been scratched without her knowledge, Grace thought. She had expected to meet with her mother at the Cleveland airport. Instead they had flown to San Francisco on separate flights and with different arrival times. David explained they didn't want to be expected. The key was to keep the enemy guessing for as long as possible. Since they knew the hacker had to be located nearby to mount an attack, their plan was to scout him out quickly before any damage could be done. Once they tracked his physical body, they could prevent the attack and take him into custody.

Grace looked out the window at the snarl of traffic leading into the city. David had reassured her they would arrive at the rehearsal practice in plenty of time. She hoped he was right. It was frustrating how he had taken charge of her life in such a short space of time. Grace hated that she had let him. But like it or not, she needed David. When this was all over, Grace was going to have to show David he couldn't boss her around. She shivered. If they survived. It was hard not to remember the hacker who stalked them, and the pain he was capable of inflicting.

David's phone buzzed again but this was a call, which was unusual, so she listened closely to the conversation. "Hi…yes. Damn…not good. Okay. Right. I'll wait to hear." He glanced at Grace watching him.

"What?" She asked anxiously, but his response was directed to the driver.

"Derek, take us back the way we came." Derek

nodded, immediately making a right-hand turn at the corner.

"What happened? Why are we turning around?" Why did he always keep her in the dark?

He placed his hand on her arm and immediately Grace heard David's voice in her mind. *Stay calm. Claire and Tom did not leave their apartment, and they should have by now. Roland is investigating. It may be nothing.*

Before Grace could protest, he added. *"I don't like the way this feels. Something's wrong. We can't risk it."*

It dawned on her, David wasn't voicing his thoughts out loud because he did not want Derek to overhear. Derek must not be a hacker. *Oh, my God. Do you think he has her?* It was difficult not to vocalize her concern, but Grace managed to keep it to a thought. Immediately, he responded.

We don't think so. Roland has been watching their apartment carefully, and no one has entered the premises.

His cell phone buzzed again, interrupting their conversation. Grace listened intently. Geneva was also focused on the conversation taking place. "Roland? Uh-huh…uh-huh… Not alone…you'll need backup. Okay…okay…yes that's what I'm thinking. Ten minutes."

What now?

We go back to our hotel and wait.

His worry battered at her mind. *Is Claire okay?* Grace thought anxiously.

We don't know, yet. The door was locked, but your sister's car is still in the driveway.

Oh, dear God, when will this nightmare end?

Steady, Grace, breathe. You must control your feelings.

She tried to do as David asked, imagining the beach and sand and the warmth of the sun, and it did seem to help a little.

Within minutes, they pulled into their hotel, parked and went inside. Grace, David and Geneva were in the elevator, heading to Grace's room when her cell buzzed indicating an incoming message. Out of habit, she opened her email and stared in surprise at the sender's address, *brainsmp@gmail.com*, and the subject line, *Hello*.

What could he possibly want? It had been many weeks since they last exchanged texts.

What is it? David questioned in her head. Since they had left the hotel the first time, he had placed himself in her mind and would not leave.

"Welcome to San Francisco." She read the cryptic message aloud, showing him the email.

"It's the hacker! Catch her, David!"

Geneva motioned frantically to David, who said something in response, but Grace could no longer hear. A buzzing sounded, growing in intensity until her head would split in two. Dimly she heard Geneva issuing orders, while Grace slipped, falling into a black abyss with no end in her sight.

Grace came to consciousness suddenly, for a brief moment aware she was in her room, curled in a ball on her bed, David beside her. The buzzing receded, and the room spun away, leaving her to face the madman across a pool of water. Grace looked, but the water was dark, and she could not see the bottom. Something moved in its depths. *A crocodile? A shark?* Neither one brought comfort. Grace let out a startled gasp, as someone squeezed her palm. *David.* She was not alone. She clung to his hand, willing herself to remain calm.

Happy thoughts. I'll handle the rest.

Grace closed her eyes, imagining herself on the beach.

*****

While Grace was busy in her happy place, David quickly took stock of the enemy's energy waves. Already the jagged edges were forming. He was growing excited. *It will not be long.* Geneva, he was sure, was giving the others an update. David must put his carefully laid plan into action.

The first strike was harder and faster than David remembered from the last time—or perhaps his defenses were weaker. The water below him swirled and coiled, like a serpent. The wind lashed them from all sides, and he was aware of giant trees surrounding them, bending and swaying in as if they might break.

"You cannot win, you know." The hacker shouted over the wind. Lightning struck a nearby branch and sent it tumbling into him. David backed away in time, pulling Grace with him. "I'm faster and stronger."

The madman thrust his hands out like a conductor and hurled rocks, mud, and other debris at them. One of the stones struck David in the shoulder and another on his ankle. The shock of the blows in quick succession stunned his senses momentarily.

He needed to put a stop to this and quickly or it would not end well for him or Grace. David focused his energy into the jagged pattern of the enemy and threw a spike into the mix. The effect was like a boomerang, wreaking havoc within the force field and bouncing back to him. He pulled the energy wave in and prepared himself to fire again.

The wind, which had been blowing fiercely, settled, and the enemy took a step back on his side of the pool. “You think to challenge me.” He snarled the words. “It’s not possible. You will lose.” Once again, he drew his hands together and punched a long arm across the cesspool, but instead of targeting David, the enemy’s fist was headed straight toward Grace.

Grace, look out!

David yelled in her mind. She responded immediately, opening her eyes and backing quickly to miss the fist in front of her. That response elicited another crow of delight from the hacker, who immediately came at her again, fist raised to strike. Grace gasped and covered her head but the blow never connected. David had forced a jagged energy pattern again and threw it in front of the long arm, stopping it in mid-air. The effort it took felt like a punch to his gut.

Back to your happy place. David shouted at Grace with a mental push for good measure.

Thankfully, Grace didn’t panic but calmly closed her eyes and obeyed. Unfortunately, the enemy wasted no time in using the distraction to his advantage. His hands had become two long whips, flashing in the wind and taking a gash out of David’s previously injured side. He gasped at the pain but concentrated on constructing another jagged wave. If he could mirror the enemy’s waves exactly and his aim was good, he could not only put a stop to the power coursing through the air, but he could draw on that energy source himself to magnify his own strength. David could take control of the fight.

The wave grew in intensity and power, until the familiar jagged, black edges took shape. He trembled under the weight of the force and hoped he had the strength to manage it. Casting a silent prayer into the universe, David once again hurled the manufactured wave into the mix. This time the spike caught and held in place, interfering with the enemy's energy pattern.

Power coursed through him like a live wire. Although intoxicating, some part of David realized the emotions he was feeling were not his own. He could not get caught in the energy field or he would be sucked inside and the battle would be over. Instead, he must slowly take over the pattern, alternating it bit by bit until he wrested control from the hacker opposite.

David focused carefully, containing his fear and anger and concentrating instead on the calm at his center. Slowly, the waves took on his rhythm. He was winning!

Rage, sharp and deep, echoed across the energy field. David magnified the waves until they were beyond the hacker's control. He had him.

Reaching out a giant arm, David plucked the hacker from the shoreline and hurled him into the shark-infested waters. There was a shout and instantly, the jagged energy waves settled, modifying themselves to David's steady rhythm. A deep joy rushed through him. *I've won!* But the moment of victory was short-lived. Grace lay on the ground motionless. A familiar buzz and ping sounded—the warning sign for a hacker to get out fast. Instinctively, David reacted, ejecting himself through the portal. But it was too late. Something snapped in his mind, causing an agonizing pain. Everything went black.

The first thing he became conscious of was a sound, short and steady. At some point, David realized he was in a hospital and the sound was a monitor, checking his vital signs. *Where's Grace?* He panicked and tried to call out, but no sound would come. He was dragged into a dark abyss.

David stayed there for a long while, floating in and out of shades of darkness. It was the voice he first became aware of—a maddening sound that would not let him rest. It whispered to him incessantly until he wanted to scream. But still it continued. For a long time, David couldn't make out words. It sounded like a roomful of people whispering. He heard his name. *"David."* He listened hard, afraid it was his imagination. *David.* He heard it again. The voice was familiar.

I'm here.

Thank goodness. Focus on me. Keep talking to me.

How is she? How's Grace?

She's fine. Don't worry about Grace right now. Worry about yourself. We nearly lost you.

Joy swamped his senses. Grace would be okay. They had won. He fought hard to concentrate on Geneva's voice.

We're all working to help you. Relax. The energy you generated was more than any of us have ever managed on our own. Sophia is here and your mother, too. You'll be okay. We won't let you go.

David recognized the precarious nature of his position. It was only Geneva's voice keeping his mind intact and tethered to his body. Which explained why she needed help. If Geneva were keeping him here, she would need the others to remove the deadheads. And given the amount of energy generated in Grace's mind, David was surprised her mind had held on as long as it had before rejecting him.

How are you feeling?

Better. He said and realized it was true. Geneva's voice no longer sounded like a whisper but had a steady tone. David's thoughts turned to Grace. How had she survived the massive amount of energy generated in her mind? *Amazing...a miracle.* He needed to know she was okay.

David noticed the light first. Granted, it was still far away from him, but it was there. "I'm surfacing."

David, no. You aren't ready. Grace is fine. She's here with us. Stay under a while longer. It'll be easier for you if you do.

His impatience grew. *I'm coming up. Be ready.*

David needed to see Grace for himself. He had a hard time believing she had survived the energy coursing through her brain. That ping had meant her brain was having trouble. He needed to see, touch and connect with her himself.

David focused on the light, his mind rising to the surface. At one point dizziness struck, and he stilled the forward momentum while he steadied himself. Afterward, David moved at a frustrating crawl, until eventually, he made it to the top and simply climbed out. As soon as he did, he was able to open his eyes.

David looked anxiously from Geneva to Sophia to his mother. They were exchanging worried looks with one another. Of course, they would be worried about him, but he guessed it wasn't their primary concern. He opened his mind to speak but couldn't form the words.

In his panic, he quit and sent an urgent, mental message to his mother. *Where, Mom? Don't lie to me.*

His mother sighed and brushed her hand across his forehead. *She hasn't surfaced yet.*

David turned accusatory eyes to Geneva. *You lied.*

I had to, David. We needed you to come back to us. We were afraid you never would.

Where is she?

David, you need to rest. We aren't done here. You won't be any good to Grace until we are.

I need to see her. Take me to her.

The three women exchanged nervous glances. "You'll have to be able to sit in a wheelchair. Can you manage that?" Sophia asked.

David wasn't at all sure, but he nodded anyway, careful to keep his thoughts concealed. If he didn't see Grace now, while he could, she might slip away. David couldn't let that happen. He finally found his voice. "Where's my cell phone?"

"Right here." Sophia pointed toward the nightstand next to the bed. "I put all your personal items there, where they would be safe." She opened the drawer, pointing to his cell phone and wallet.

David spied a familiar piece of glass. How many times had he fingered that glass? It was a symbol of all he had to lose. They had come so far. He would not let her go.

He held out his hand, and Sophia promptly handed him the contents. Thankfully, his hospital gown had large pockets where he could safely store the items.

His mother propped the pillows behind him, helping him to sit. She was gentle, but with each movement, hard fingers jabbed his brain. The buzzing and vibrations became more pronounced, as they helped him into the wheelchair. When David was finally in the chair, he was sweating and breathing heavily. He leaned his head back and closed his eyes. Geneva and Sophia hovered over him and their combined touch helped to deaden the buzzing. After several moments, David nodded, and they rolled him out the door and into the room next door.

Passing through the doorway, déjà vu struck him. This time, David was the patient that had fared better. He had failed to protect her. David had known this was a possibility when he was plotting their course of action, but in his plans he had had more time to coordinate their defense. The real event had happened so abruptly David had barely registered they were under attack. Roland and Rolf should have been with him when the battle took place, but there had not been time. He stared at Grace as she lay in her bed, her face pale and her breathing shallow. Her mother sat in a chair next to her bed. She looked their way as they entered the room.

How long has Grace been like this? David sent the message to Geneva telepathically so as not to alarm Grace's mother.

It's been three days since the attack.

What are her chances?

They don't believe she'll come out of it. Kyle Willard deliberately targeted her when he realized you had gained control. He wiped most of her mind before you ended it. That's why you were ejected.

Willard the billionaire?

Geneva nodded.

Of course. Willard would have been keenly

interested in robotics. And he had the means to go after those secrets. He also recalled the memory in Li Su Yeh's mind. The gentleman with the blond hair was Willard. *What have you told her mother?*

She believes the two of you were in a car accident.

Take me to her bedside. Push me close enough so I can hold her hand.

They did as he asked. "I'm sorry." David nodded at Grace's mom.

Her makeup was smudged from crying, but she managed to nod at him in recognition. "Glad to see you up." Elaine Ellis attempted a wan smile. "Oh, David. I'm so worried about Grace. She's in a coma. The doctors don't know if she'll come out of it."

"They're doing everything they can to help her." David paused. "I hate to ask this of you, but do you mind if I have a few minutes alone with Grace?"

"I…can't leave her. I'm sorry. I'm so worried."

He grasped her hand, and she looked at him. "You need a break if you're going to be any good for Grace. Stretch your legs or get yourself something to eat or drink. I'll stay here until you get back."

Elaine nodded, her look confused. "Okay. Thank you, David. I won't be more than ten minutes."

"Take all the time you need."

She left, but Geneva, Sophia, and his mother remained. The effort cost him. David's head pounded. Immediately, Geneva laid gentle hands upon him.

"David, are you sure this is wise?" his mother questioned.

"Mom, I have to see for myself how bad it is."

"You know the doctors are well-trained. They've done careful analysis. There's nothing you'll be able to do to help her until you yourself are well. You may make things worse."

An unfamiliar panic ripped through him. He couldn't lose her now! Not after they had won, and he could finally claim her as his own. Fate would not be so cruel, would it?

"David, Mom's right." Sophia used his panic to her advantage. "There's nothing you can do for Grace right now. If you're going to be any help, you need to be well, yourself."

He fingered the glass in the pocket of his hospital gown. Perhaps there was something he could do for her. It was a long shot. David had no idea if it would work. It could backfire, and he would pay the penalty. Plus, he would need a full day's rest at a minimum and Geneva's help. It would be much easier, and David would be more likely to succeed if he were fully recovered, but that could take weeks, and Grace may not have much time. Fifty percent of the time a mind that was fully wiped would stay in a comatose state forever. The other fifty percent of the time they went crazy. So far, it appeared Grace was on the comatose end of the spectrum.

David studied Grace where she lay like a white ghost in her hospital gown against the pale sheets. With deliberate calm, he reached out a hand and grasped hers. Her warmth was reassuring. If Grace still had a pulse, she was alive and her brain was active.

He focused on the portal. It was but a dim light. In his weakened state, David would not be able to use it to enter. He needed a night of deep sleep and Geneva's support if he was going to have a chance in hell of saving Grace. The night of rest he thought he could manage. Geneva was more problematic. David would have to bring her in on his secret, and she was not going to like it.

The strength in his arms was returning. After taking one last look at Grace, David wheeled himself back to his room. He could not even visit her mind tonight as he'd done the previous nights.

Chapter Thirty-Seven
Restoration

David awoke quickly, his mind clear, to find he was not alone. Peter was sprawled in a chair, eyes closed. “You won’t change my mind.” His tone was sharp, prepared for battle.

Peter opened his eyes. He had not been sleeping. “Of course, not.” His voice was gruff. “I wasn’t even going to try. If you can do something for Grace, by all means, do it. But be smart about it. The docs aren’t holding out a lot of hope.”

David hesitated, not sure if he could handle the answer to his next question but needing to know anyway. “What do you believe her chances are for some kind of recovery?”

“Slim to none.” Peter didn’t believe in beating around the bush. “I’m sorry. I’ve seen this before.”

David did not care for the reminder. “What about her sister and fiancé?”

“They’re fine. Of course, they were in complete shock. We were forced to tamper with their memory slightly—you have Rolf to thank—but as far as they know, they were on their way to the rehearsal when they heard about the ‘car accident.’ The wedding, of course, was postponed. The sister is a mess. You would think she was the one that faced the hacker. Be prepared. She has been here visiting every day since and is staying nearby with her mother."

He nodded. "What happened while we were under?"

"He was in the room across the hall. How he knew where we were staying is beyond me. But he had the resources to have eyes watching and to bribe or manipulate the hotel staff. We suspect Willard has been stealing secrets, undetected, for many years, which explains all the technological advances of his companies. Apparently, he was part owner—a quiet partner—of Gallant Enterprises.

He cleared his throat. "From what we've gathered so far, Willard spent millions of dollars on a database he was using to track your kind. He was after a suitable partner to father his children but needed an off-the-grid talent. Willard had been tracking adoption cases, which is how he stumbled on Grace's father. From there, he found Claire, but when she didn't show any signs of psychic talent, he went after Grace. There he struck gold. He'd already had an earlier run-in with you, and now you were in the way.

David nodded, thinking back to Willard's fanatical pursuit of Grace.

Peter continued. "It took us a while to find him and his trainer. She's in our custody—his twin sister by the way. Willard, of course, is in a coma. His recovery is doubtful. We're still completing our investigation, but it appears he had a rough upbringing—several sets of abusive foster parents before he was adopted by a loving family. That may explain his rogue behavior. No one seems to know the father, but it's assumed he and his sister inherited their abilities from the paternal side. The sister has refused to talk by the way. But as you know, we have ways around that little problem. A bigger issue is what to do with her."

David nodded impatiently. He didn't care what happened to the sister right now. He had more urgent matters to think about. "Peter, I need your help." He stared at him, his focus unwavering, until the older man looked away.

"What are you going to do?"

"I need access to Grace's mind, and I'll need Geneva's help for that. I'll also need to be alone with her for an extended period."

"You do realize that would not be wise? Her mind, or what remains, is fragile. All it'll take is one wrong alteration to see it collapse. You would be trapped, most likely, forever. You were lucky to escape this last time unscathed."

"I know. But I need you to let me take that chance. Will you help me?"

Peter sighed, but his answer was fast in coming. "Of course."

David gazed at the older man with affection. "Thank you."

Peter checked his watch. "You can meet with her around one, and I can give you until five. Will that be enough? It will be difficult to keep her family from her after that."

He nodded. Peter rose, stretched his long legs and hesitated. "I've spoken to Alan. Of course, he is suitably grateful for your latest service. You will be compensated accordingly."

David shrugged. He would have no use for any amount of money without Grace by his side. Ever since she had been out cold, and he could not enter her mind, he felt bereft, like a lonely raft at sea. He needed her well again.

Peter was uncharacteristically hesitant, strolling to his bedside and staring at him without saying anything.

"Okay, old man. Out with it. I don't have the strength to surf your mind right now."

Peter cracked a smile, but it was brief. He leaned awkwardly and patted David on his shoulder. He cleared his throat. "I'm not one for a lot of fine words, as you know. But in case this task you have set yourself doesn't turn out the way you'd like, I want you to know you're the best…" His voice broke, and he cleared his throat and tried again. "The best hacker I've ever worked with. I don't have children but if I had had a son…"

He trailed off awkwardly but David grasped his hand with affection. "I won't fail."

Even as he said the words, David knew he would be forging new territory. As far as he knew, no hacker had ever attempted what he was about to do. But no other hacker had as much to lose. David had known this moment might come long ago…had, in fact, planned for it. Failure was not an option he would allow himself to contemplate.

David spied his clothes in a bag on the couch opposite. He would get dressed and leave to clear his head and prepare himself mentally by envisioning every step of the task ahead. He could not afford a single error.

After Peter departed, it took some energy and time to convince Geneva to help him. She had resented Grace from the first moment she understood how David felt about her. Those feelings had softened but were still there.

"I won't do it. Her life is not worth yours."

He stared at her stubbornly, asking her without words to relent.

"Consider, David. Your chance of saving her is maybe…ten percent. Think of all the people who will be devastated when you're gone. Your mom, dad, sister, me."

"I have considered. I need your help. Please."

He would not budge on the course he had set. Grace's life was worth the risk, no matter what Geneva believed. David would accept the consequences. If Geneva wouldn't help, he would find someone else who would.

She stared at him a silent minute more. David could feel the long tentacles of her energy waves reaching out to brush his mind. He allowed her entrance so she could understand the depths he would travel to rescue his Grace. Geneva frowned and shrugged.

"All right. It's clear I can't sway you from this mad course you've set."

"Thank you, Geneva. I'm grateful."

David glanced at his cell phone. He had lost forty-five minutes of precious time. They would have to move quickly. He figured they needed a good two hours with Grace and some. But if they didn't get a move on soon, even David would not be able to help her.

They took a taxi back to the hotel, where they booked a room and spent the next hour deep in meditation, which improved his energy level and focus. By noon they were on their way back to the hospital. Although it was only ten minutes away, he wanted to start at one on the dot.

David had forgotten Peter's warning about Claire until he nearly ran into her in the corridor outside Grace's room, causing her to drop a magazine she had been carrying. He recognized her immediately.

"Sorry," she said, giving him a wide-eyed look and studying him with interest. "Are you here to see my sister? Are you a friend?"

"I am."

"You wouldn't be the great David Jenkins now, would you?" she asked with a wink and a small smile.

David inspected her. Her face contained the same shape as Grace's but there the resemblance ended. Grace was shorter, curvier and had a unique shade of blonde hair and deep gray eyes. Claire was tall and willowy. Her hair was platinum blond and her eyes a bright blue.

"I would be." David gave Claire a slight smile. He discovered it was important to him he make a good impression.

"Wow, you're much handsomer than either Grace or my mother told me. Why would they keep that from me, I wonder?"

When she smiled, he could see a blinding row of perfect white and straight teeth. The effect was not lost on him. Claire was flirting, while her sister lay comatose in the next room. David remembered vividly what Grace had told him that first afternoon. How her sister always went after the same things she did. Was that what this was about? He did not have the luxury of time to figure it out. Besides, he gathered she was on her way downstairs, summoned by the staff to keep her out of Grace's room.

"I'm sure they've had more important things on

their minds. Please excuse me."

He strolled into Grace's room, feeling Claire's eyes on his back. David did not bother to turn around to confirm she was watching.

While he waited for Geneva to return from the ladies room, David took a moment to study the woman he now knew he loved unreservedly. Once again, he had to prevent feelings of anxiety and panic. What he was about to attempt would take a cool head. No hint of emotion could leak from him to her. It would be difficult—almost impossible. If there was one thing his association with Grace had taught him, it was even he had powerful emotions.

Grace looked so still and small where she lay in the hospital bed. David took the familiar heart-shaped glass from his pocket, offering a silent prayer for her full recovery. His heart ached at the silence. So much to share. So many more memories to make together. He must succeed.

Geneva breezed in, closing the door behind her and interrupting his ruminations. "Are you sure you won't change your mind?"

David fingered the glass in his palm, ignoring her. "Let's get started."

Geneva gazed at him, her look one of pity. He thought she would launch another argument, but she did not. Instead, she plopped herself into a chair nearby and gestured to the recliner next to her. "Your throne awaits, your majesty." She smirked.

David sat, reclined the chair and lay back, eyes closed. He positioned himself comfortably. He knew hackers who were forced back into their bodies prematurely because an arm or leg had fallen asleep.

"Here goes nothing." With her usual flair, Geneva opened a large portal in front of him.

He slipped through effortlessly, David surveyed his surroundings. As expected, only the shell of her thoughts remained. The enemy had wiped whatever he could in those few seconds he had directed his tremendous energy Grace's way. He didn't have much time. Her brainwaves were already growing erratic at his forced entry.

David seized control by focusing a narrow energy beam to counter the erratic pattern. At first, there was no change, but gradually the waves calmed and settled. Quickly and evenly, he created tiny pulses of light, forcing them into a steady pattern. This was a crucial step. He held his breath, waiting for the familiar hiss and ping. It did not come. Grace's mind held and responded. Ignoring the overwhelming relief flooding his mind, David forced himself to contain the rise in energy. Once her brainwaves stabilized and held the pattern he had created, David signaled to Geneva and withdrew through the portal. *Part one successful.* He breathed a sigh of relief.

"She's unlikely to make a full recovery David."

He did not respond immediately. He glanced at the alarm clock beside her bed. Nearly three. They did not have much time. Geneva had already begun the process of neutralizing his energy waves. David needed her on his side.

"We aren't done."

"What do you mean? Anything more and neither one of you will survive. Do you have a death wish?"

"I can restore her memories."

"Are you crazy? You can't restore her memories.

They're gone."

"No. They're not."

"What do you mean?" Geneva watched him as he lay there fingering the ruby glass. She gasped as understanding dawned. "Is that glass…charged? You stored them?"

He nodded.

"How…when…?"

"Never mind all that. Trust me. I have them. But I need your help or it'll never work."

"David, this is risky. Even if you are able to restore them, her mind may not take them back."

He waited, willing her cooperation. "I need to try. Will you help me?"

Geneva sighed, biting her lower lip, clearly torn. To his great relief, she eventually decided in his favor. "All right. Never let it be said I kept you from your one true love. What do you need from me?"

"Lots of energy and to hold a steady focus. If all goes well, I'll need about two hours. He glanced again at the clock. "We'd best get started."

"And if it doesn't go well?"

"You may need to pull me out. I doubt I'll be able to do it myself."

"Why haven't you asked the cousins for help?"

He shook his head. "Too risky. It's one thing for me to take this chance. Grace's life is worth my own. But I can't ask it of the rest of my family."

Geneva nodded. "Okay, then. We'd better get a move on. Ready?"

David clasped the glass in the palm of his hand, closed his eyes and prepared himself to unlock its secrets. "As I'll ever be."

The orange gateway yawned in front of him, a much narrower opening than before. He re-entered cautiously. The foundation he had set had strengthened. *Promising.* David readied himself for the transfer.

Over the next two hours, he painstakingly added to the foundation, bit by bit. The work challenged him mentally and physically, since he had to absorb each wave from the glass, examine it for flaws and carefully match it to the succeeding thought. All the while, David waited to hear signs Grace's mind rejected him. At last, he pulled the final energy wave from the glass and deposited it safely back with its rightful owner. He had succeeded!

Summoning his energy reserves, David managed to pull himself back through the narrow opening with Geneva's assistance. He lay there sweating and feverish for some time, his breathing labored. The massive energy expenditure after his recent ordeal had been costly. Cool hands touched his forehead. Geneva. David pried his eyes open.

"Sleep, David." Geneva soothed. "I'll keep an eye on her. You need to rest."

"Time?" He managed to croak.

"4:59 p.m."

A slow smile spread over his face. Peter would be proud. David grasped Geneva's arm urgently, eyes closed. "Wake me if there's any change in her condition."

He could not wait for a response. His mind and body were shutting down. Saying a final prayer for Grace's recovery, David let himself slip into darkness.

Chapter Thirty-Eight
Awakening

Grace floated in a dark place. For a long while she did not particularly know or care she floated. Time passed slowly. Occasionally, voices spoke, but Grace did not know what they were saying or if the words were meant for her. Gradually, one voice separated itself from all the rest, distinct in its persistence. Grace tried ignoring it, but it would not relent, calling at her through the vast emptiness, forcing her to turn toward the sound. Soon the dark turned into gray, the gray into blue, until she moved toward a distant light. Grace tried desperately to still the forward motion, preferring the safety of the darkness. Too late. The voice would not let her go. It joined her there in the darkness, urging her forward, shouting in her mind so Grace could not rest. As she drew closer to the light, she grew afraid. Grace was aware of two things simultaneously: A man's voice called to her. The man surrounded her in the darkness.

Don't be afraid. He told her, his voice familiar. *I will not let anyone hurt you.*

David?

That's right! She heard the relief in his tone. *You remember me.* David appeared in the darkness.

Where are we?

You're sleeping. But this isn't a dream. You've been in a coma, while your mind heals, but sweetheart, it's time now for you to wake.

How are you speaking to me?

David reached for her hand and held it. A shock ran through her system at his touch. *Think, Grace. Remember who I am.*

Grace thought and scenes flooded her memory banks like sparks lighting the night sky. David meeting her in the coffee shop…on the beach…his cottage…the first time they made love. His telling her about his profession.

You remember.

How could she have forgotten? David could read her mind whenever he chose. He could talk to her in her head. Panic raced, frightening in its intensity.

Grace, he's dead.

What? How?

You don't remember it because he erased many of your memories. But, he's gone. I promise. He can't hurt you or anyone else anymore.

How'd you do it?

Not me, Grace, we. We did it together. I'll explain all, I promise. But it's important you come to consciousness. Your mind will recover faster that way. Can you push toward the light?

Grace faced the light surrounding them.

Don't be frightened. We'll do it together. You won't be alone.

Okay. She summoned her courage to leave the safety of the darkness.

In unison, they pushed toward the surface where the light was strongest. Grace became aware of other voices.

"She moved her hand. She's waking up," Claire

said excitedly.

"Dear God." Her mother cried out. "Oh, holy God."

Grace opened her eyes. Her mother stood over her, tears streaming down her face. "Claire, do you see…do you see! She's awake. Grace is awake. I prayed. Oh, thank the good Lord my prayers were answered. Gracie you sure know how to give us all a scare." She scolded. "Do you know who we are? This is Mom. And this is your sister Claire."

Grace's lips spread apart in a smile. "It would take more than a coma for me to forget you two."

Her family was surrounding her bedside, but the large hands still holding hers belonged to David. He was staring at her intently, love shining from his gray-green eyes.

I don't want to let you go, but the doctors need to examine you.

Grace nodded shyly. Awake, it felt strange to hear David talking in her head.

You'll get used to it. He said it gently, releasing her hand and standing so the doctor could get close to her bedside.

The doctor looked into her eyes with a bright light and had her answer a series of questions. When he was done, he smiled and nodded. "Everything is looking fantastic, Grace. Your recovery is amazing. We do see this sometimes, particularly with those patients who have supportive loved ones. We'll continue to monitor you, but your vitals are wonderful for someone who has endured the head trauma you have."

He turned to the rest of the group. "She'll need to be watched for another forty-eight hours, but it appears the worst is over folks. I expect our patient to make a full recovery. Where's Mom?"

Her mother raised her hand, and the doctor preceded to rattle off instructions. No loud noises or sudden movements. Rest as much as possible. Gradual physical activity. She'll need to learn to do some things again, so be patient with her. Grace grew tired.

"Let's continue the conversation out in the hall," she heard David say. "Grace needs her rest."

I love you, he told her silently, as he ushered her family out the door.

The words spoken in her mind carried with them a rush of warmth and affection. He loved her. He would protect her at all costs…sacrifice his life for hers. He did not want to live without her.

It was her last conscious thought before exhaustion overtook her and Grace slept.

When Grace awoke next, it was early morning and she was not alone. "It's about time you woke again. I've been dying to talk to you."

"Hi." Grace smiled at her sister, reaching out her arms for a hug. "So are you the new Mrs. Walters?"

"Promise me you won't freak out first. I don't want to do anything that will send you back into a coma. Your David has warned us to go easy."

"Oh, yeah?"

"Yeah, and he's pretty intense. I don't dare disobey." She laughed. "Seriously, though, he's not like Greg at all, and that's a good thing."

"You mean you flirted with him, and he didn't take the bait." Grace said wryly.

"He only has eyes for you, and I mean only. He practically glared at me when I suggested he join Mom and me for dinner yesterday. It was almost like he knew I was testing him, and he didn't like it."

Grace had reached for the water glass beside her bed but nearly choked on the contents. "Yeah, about that, I wouldn't test him. He's pretty intuitive about stuff like…that." She trailed off lamely.

No way could she tell Claire David could read minds. As soon as Claire knew, so would their mother and the rest of the world. Grace hadn't forgotten Sophia's warning about what the government would do to those who didn't keep their mind hacker unit a secret.

"So I take it you didn't walk down the aisle?"

Claire laughed. "No, we didn't, but we will," she added quickly, seeing Grace's frown. "We delayed it until you could be part of it. I couldn't get married without my maid of honor present, now, could I?"

"Really, it's delayed? Where's Tom?"

"He had to go back to work. He only had so much vacation time, and he couldn't afford to burn it all if we were going to need it later when you were well enough to attend the wedding."

Grace nodded her understanding.

"So, is David the one?" Her sister asked hesitantly.

"Yes, he is."

"He's handsome, I'll give you that, but he seems a bit…controlling. I mean, he wouldn't let anyone come near you the other day, not even Mom, for about half the day. The doctors said they thought it would help if someone who knew you intimately could spend some time with you. I guess that made sense, but it was hard to take he was the one who could help you and not us. I mean, we've known you forever. You've only known him for a few months." Claire was trying, but she couldn't keep the hurt from her voice.

"Claire, I know it seems weird. And it's true I've only known David a short time. But…I love him. He's a bit overbearing and direct at times, but that's one of the things I love about him. David cares about me. Truly cares. He's shown me over and over again he's willing to do anything to protect me. I think…I think I struck gold, Claire."

"Wow. Really? Wow. You never talked that way about Greg. So, he's the one, huh? Does this mean you guys will get married?"

"Well, I don't know. David hasn't asked me." Grace frowned. "I mean there hasn't been time. And I'm not looking to rush into anything. But if he does ask me, I might say yes. We'll see."

"Wow."

"Is that all you can say?"

Claire laughed. "Sorry, it's such a surprise. But I'm glad for you. I am. Hey, maybe we can have a double wedding?"

Chapter Thirty-Nine
Ghost

The pace of Grace's recovery surprised even the doctors. They marveled at how swiftly she regained full body movement. Within days, Grace was walking around, and two weeks later, she was released for good.

Grace, David, her Mom and Glenn flew first class back to Cleveland. David sat next to her on the airplane. He tried to disguise it, because he knew how much Grace hated when he was in her head, but David watched her carefully for signs of trouble. Grace had gotten good at thinking certain thoughts to get a rise out of him. Sometimes, she imagined famous people naked—that always seemed to do the trick. Grace grinned when David flinched next to her. Apparently, her current image of Barack Obama in his birthday suit was not a pleasant sight.

"Keep it clean, darling."

Grace found herself smirking. Paybacks were wonderful.

It was noon when they landed at the airport. Her mother and Glenn collected their suitcases and departed, but not before Grace was warned repeatedly to rest and not do anything strenuous.

"I don't want you to suffer a relapse," her mother cautioned. "Let David take care of you. He seems to do it well." She gave David a hug. "Call me from time to time. You know how I worry."

"I will," Grace promised. "Are you sure you don't want to join us at Sophia's?"

"No, no, you kids go ahead. I need to unpack and relax. Plus, Claire's going to call me later this afternoon so we can finalize her new wedding date."

"Okay, Mom. Thanks for everything." She fought back a sudden rush of tears. Why she was crying wasn't clear. Lately, it seemed like tears were always a bit close to the surface. David wrapped an arm around her, pulling her close.

Together, they waved her Mom and Glenn safely into a taxi and met Sophia and Brian, who had insisted on driving them to their home. Grace and David had agreed to stay with them over the next six weeks, while Grace completed her convalescence. This was a compromise to David's original plan, which was to have Grace all to himself at the cottage. His sister's home was much closer to the clinic, where Grace was expected to travel for regular physical therapy, and was large enough to accommodate a small army. She and David would have plenty of privacy.

On her first day there, David's extended family joined them for a reunion of sorts. It was a crisp, fall Saturday, and the leaves were in full color. Sophia made chili and hotdogs, and they sat on her back patio around a chiminea that held a small fire, eating. Eventually, the male cousins played a game of tag football, while the girls chatted about nothing in particular, and the kids ran wild.

"So, will we hear wedding bells anytime soon?" David's Mom asked, a smile on her face. Clearly, she was anticipating an announcement. Grace blushed.

"I don't know. You'll have to ask David."

Sophia and her mother exchanged glances. "Yeah, about that," Sophia said. "David's not one to reveal his plans. We know he cares deeply for you, of course. But don't count on him to tell us before he tells you."

Grace nodded. She liked that about David. She watched the backyard football game with interest.

"You must wonder about us," Sophia commented, watching Grace as she gazed at the football action. "Like how could they not use their abilities to win the game?"

"Okay, I'll bite. Are they mind controlling one another?"

Sophia laughed. "Yes, they are. Well, most of them," she said, eyeing the field. "Except they're all so powerful, no one is winning. David could even the score pretty quickly if he chose to do it. He doesn't usually exploit his gifts like that, though."

Suddenly, David caught the ball and took off running down the field, dodging Rolf who had closed in for the tackle. "Well surprise, surprise," Geneva commented wryly. "He aims to impress his lady."

A familiar, ever-present blush took root and held. Grace was still getting used to their strange way of slipping in and out of one another's thoughts. David said he could teach Grace how to share her mind…that she possessed undeveloped psychic talent. But until then, she remained on the outside, looking in.

She watched David run the ball in for a touchdown. Would David ask her to marry him? Would she say yes like she had told Claire? If Grace did say yes and they had children, would their children be gifted? Would they be forced to be mind hackers? What if they didn't want that career, would they be able to choose something else for themselves?

The questions were non-stop in her head, and it didn't help that Grace carried memories that were not her own. Who was the angelic woman she kept seeing…this Meg…and why did David miss her so? Grace did not know the rules in the strange new world she had entered. She didn't suppose she ever fully would.

After making a touchdown, David dropped the ball in the end zone and headed her direction. Grace watched the confident way he ambled across the field, his lanky form creating a dark shadow behind him as he walked. Grabbing a bottle of water from the cooler, he plopped himself next to Grace, catching her hand in the process. Reassuring energy waves coursed through her system. David had settled in her mind again. Grace wished she had a clearer idea of when he was making an entrance and exit. It was disconcerting. She had asked him repeatedly to give her warning, but it came naturally to David, and he could never seem to do it.

Look at the kids. Don't they look like normal kids, having fun? Any children we have together will be special, and like any other kids, they'll have a choice to use their gifts for the greater good or not. It'll be our job to teach them right from wrong and how special they are.

The children had raked a large pile of leaves and were taking turns jumping in it. They appeared happy and joyous like kids everywhere in the fall. They did not look like mini mind hackers.

Grace noted David had refrained from offering any reassurance on the marriage front. Instead, he turned to eye Rolf, who was heading their way. The other cousins and Brian trailed in Rolf's wake. Rolf plopped himself next to Geneva with a sigh. Grace noticed Rolf seemed to gravitate to Geneva whenever they were together. Oddly, she refused to pay him any attention. In fact, as Grace watched, Geneva turned her back to Rolf and talked to Kevin.

It's a complicated relationship. Rolf's a little obtuse where Geneva is concerned. Strong trainers like Geneva don't take kindly to being dictated to.

What will Geneva do now that you're officially retired?

She'll keep working. She's been paired with Rolf, but she's not happy about it. Rolf will need to tread carefully. Geneva's family can be a bit over-protective, and he hasn't earned any points with them over the last year.

What did he do?

A temporary lapse in judgment.

You mean, Rolf cheated on Geneva?

Well, you can't call it cheating if you're not dating to begin with. But yes, he had a brief fling with Cynthia Torra.

"Why does that name sound so familiar?" Grace remembered. Cynthia Torra was the blond bombshell on channel five. She did a local segment called '10 at 10'—ten bits of advice for women on a variety of practical topics. Cynthia Torra was some hefty competition. Grace didn't blame Geneva for being upset.

Grace stood. For some reason, she felt close to tears again and needed a time-out. They had put their bags inside earlier, so she knew where to find their room in the massive house. David stood with her.

"What's wrong?"

"I'm a bit tired. I…I need to lie down. You stay here, though. I can find my way." Grace hoped she sounded convincing. She needed time to process what David had told her without his psychic antenna listening in.

David's eyes swept her length, lingering on her face. After a few uncomfortable seconds, he nodded.

Grace fled in a hurry, finding her room and throwing herself on the bed, where she let the tears flow freely. Grace loved David, but she wasn't sure she could marry him. Not that she wanted to be a mind-reader, but she would always be the outsider—even from her own children. And he could cheat on her, and she might never know it! She thought of the pain Greg had inflicted on her. All David had to do is change her thoughts and bingo, Grace would be blind to his indiscretions.

David gave her exactly thirty minutes before quietly knocking on her door and opening it. Grace was a mass of quivering emotions and anxieties. She pretended to sleep. Why she thought that would work with David, Grace didn't know. He lay next to her, taking her into his arms. He seemed to know instinctively holding her had a power all its own.

"Grace, sweetheart, I would cut off an arm before I'd cheat on you. You know this. I've shown you my thoughts. Where is all this insecurity coming from?"

"I don't know." Grace gulped, swiping at tears. "Wh…what's to stop you from messing with my mind? If you do cheat on me, how would I even know it? I'd be trapped."

Grace buried her head in his chest. He smelled of aftershave and something else, something undefinable, a scent uniquely his. David rubbed her head gently, his breath warm on her cheek. "The others wouldn't allow it, you know."

"How could they stop you? Sophia told me you're off the charts."

"Sophia doesn't know everything. My cousins and Geneva all have unique abilities. Together, they could stop me. They would not allow you to be hurt in that way. But I would never hurt you. Why can't you believe me?" He sighed, the small expulsion of air warm on Grace's cheek. "What's bothering you isn't this at all. What you want, I am not sure I can give you."

David knew. So much for keeping secrets. "Who is she, David?"

He shook his head. "Who she is doesn't concern you. That's in the past. You, Grace, are the future."

"Why, David? Why's she so important to you? What happened?"

"You need your sleep," he said, rising from the bed and heading toward the door.

For the first time since Grace had known David, he couldn't get away from her fast enough. After all they had been through together, his rejection hurt. Grace believed David loved her. But he had loved the girl, too. She needed to know how much and why.

An hour later, David found her and apologized. "I love you, Grace. You're the most important person in my life. Try not to worry so much. I'm not going anywhere."

Grace believed him. But still, he didn't reveal the

identity of the girl she kept seeing. She bided her time and waited, and they spent the next few weeks in relative harmony. In the end, however, she made a decision.

She loved David. She truly did. But she would not marry a man who loved a ghost more.

Chapter Forty
Escape

Keeping secrets was not easy when your boyfriend was a mind reader, especially one as powerful as David. Only Grace's long-dormant psychic talent, which she had spent the last several weeks honing, had allowed her to keep this much to herself.

Still, she needed to keep thoughts of her plans to a minimum.

She took a good look around the bedroom, where she had been staying, and wheeled her suitcases into the hall. It was time to get her life back in order. She couldn't stay here forever. The Uber car she had booked from her cell phone was waiting in the drive to take her to her condo and Harvey. She missed the old bird.

This morning, when David had announced lunch plans with Sophia and Brian and the cousins and asked her to go with him, she had declined, pleading a headache. He had given her a concerned look, but Grace had focused her thoughts on the image of nails driving into her skull, and somehow his psychic antennae had not detected the lie. He'd encouraged her to get some rest and left with Sophia and Brian thirty minutes ago. Grace had the place to herself.

Where are you going?

Damn. Apparently she was wrong about that. *I...I*

need to check on Harvey.

I told you I would take you back to your place any time you wanted. I'm coming back to get you. Wait for me.

David, no.

Silence.

David, don't come for me. I need...I need space.

Silence.

I'm leaving now. I will call you. But you need to give me time to think. I appreciate all you've done for me, and I care about you, I do. But, well, it's time for me to go home.

Grace opened the front door and walked briskly toward the waiting car, dragging her suitcases behind her. She was not a prisoner here. She was free to come and go. So why did she feel like a traitor?

The driver popped the trunk.

Don't you dare lift those yourself.

Grace looked around. His voice was louder. He was getting closer. Defiantly, Grace reached for her bags, but the driver was there before her. "No ma'am. Let me get those for you."

Stop it! Quit making people do things for me. And don't follow me, please. I'll call you, I promise. I just need some time alone. To think. Alone. So stay out of my head. Please.

No answer. Grace sighed and fastened her seatbelt. It wouldn't matter if he followed her. She was not going back. Not with the ghost between them. Not for a long while. Maybe not ever.

"Twenty-one Daphne Road in Lakewood, right?"

"Yes…no…please, can you drive to Edgewater Beach, instead?"

The driver, a young boy who told Grace it was his first week on the job, agreed, and they eventually pulled into the parking lot at Edgewater. Grace left her suitcase by a park bench and strolled to the water's edge. Out of force of habit, her eyes narrowed on the golden stretch of beach to look for glass. She would need to get back to earning her living as an artist.

She had only been searching for a few minutes when a dark shadow fell across the sand in front of her. "When were you going to tell me?"

Grace straightened and turned. David stood facing her, his expression impassive. What was he thinking?

"I did tell you. I said I was going home. That I needed time away. I asked you to respect that."

"I meant about the baby."

Grace gritted her teeth to keep from swearing aloud. So much for keeping secrets. This was not how she wanted to tell him. And tell him she would have, but in her own time and way. "I suspected you would figure it out yourself before too long. And see…you did." She turned away and made her way to her perch. "I didn't know myself for sure until a week ago." And what a week it had been, fraught with all sorts of conflicting emotions. The baby, in part, was also her reason for leaving. She would not be tethered to a man simply because she bore his child. She had more respect for herself than that, and she would not use the child to tie David to her under any circumstances, but especially when there was so much unresolved tension between them.

He'd followed her, and was now leaning a broad shoulder against the rock. "It's a boy, Grace."

She stared at David, shocked and more than a little

miffed. Clearly it hadn't occurred to him that she might not want to know the sex of her child. He could have at least asked. But then the wind gusted and one dark lock of hair fell carelessly to the side of his green eyes, and she felt an impossible urge to brush it away. A boy? Really? She was having a boy?

Would he look like David?

"How can you possibly know such a thing?"

"You're thirteen weeks along. The baby has a heartbeat…thoughts."

Grace sagged against the rock. "You…You're reading its mind?"

"Him, Grace. We're having a boy." David reached a long arm out and wrapped it around her, pulling her to his side. "A son."

Grace stiffened and held back. "David…I…I can't do this anymore." Her voice cracked.

He stared at her in disbelief. "You're going to walk away? Just like that? After all we've been through together? No words, no explanation?"

"I haven't…I…I don't know, David."

"We've created a child, Grace. I'm the father. I don't know what kind of man you think I am, but I can't walk away from you…or our child."

David's hurt and anger was like a punch to the gut. The force of his emotions rushed in and grabbed at her heart. What was happening? Why this, and why now?

"We are linked, Grace. When I feel strongly, you do, too. You can't be upset, or worried or frustrated without me knowing. So, why not tell me what's on your mind rather than make me work for it?"

Grace bowed her head and sighed. "Dammit. Why do you do this to me? You won't like it."

She had purposely kept herself from thoughts of the girl because whenever she did David's face tightened and his body stiffened—she glanced at him—like it was doing right now. If he loved her, why was it so hard for him to open up to her? "Who is she, David? The girl? Why won't you tell me about her?"

"It was a long time ago," he said tightly, dodging her yet again. "It wouldn't serve any purpose to bring it up now."

The hell it wouldn't. "I know you don't want to share her with me. She was that dear to you. But that's exactly why I need to know about her. If you love me like you say you do, you'd trust me. How can I be with a man who loves a ghost more than me?"

He took his hands from his pockets and rubbed his forehead. "You're wrong, Grace. I do love you. And I'm not angry with you for wanting to know. It's not that. It's…Meg is…I have trouble reliving it."

He was showing a chink in his armor. She couldn't let the opportunity slip away. "I promise if you tell me, you'll never have to talk about it again. I won't pester you about it. But David, you have to understand. I have these memories that aren't mine, and I need closure. I need to know what happened. Who is she to you? How does she fit into your life, your past? I'd ask Sophia or your Mom, but I need to hear it from you."

Holding her breath, Grace crossed her fingers behind her back. David looked out to the lake, the choppy waves matching his expression. He glanced her way and sighed.

"I don't suppose you'll be happy with anything but the full story?"

She smiled, hoping she looked encouraging. He

inhaled, his nostrils flaring, and looked back toward Lake Erie. "All right. What do you want to know?"

"She's dead, right?"

"Yes."

"And you feel guilty. Why?"

He put a hand across his forehead, shielding his eyes. "Because I killed her."

"How can that be? You loved her. She was dear to you. You grew up together. I see…I see you as children. Was she your childhood sweetheart?"

"Yes, but not in the way you're imagining. We were…a team, Meg and I."

"She was your trainer."

"Yes." He nodded. "But more than that, she was my twin."

"Oh, my God. David, I'm so sorry…"

He waved off her reaction. "You wanted to know. And I'm only going to say this once. Twins are a rarity in my family. When they happen, everyone knows they'll make a strong team. We were groomed from the beginning. And we were incredible together…" His voice cracked, and he paused to collect himself before continuing. "Unstoppable. Meg always knew when I was upset. She knew how to calm me and keep me focused."

Grace's heart broke for him. "She sounds wonderful," Grace whispered.

"She was…she is…very special." He turned and made his way to the nearby rock, leaning against it as if it were propping him up. "The day Meg died…" He shuddered. "It was my fault."

Compassion drove Grace straight toward him. "Impossible," she denied with conviction. "You would never hurt her."

David was silent, his expression inscrutable. Grace allowed him a few moments more to collect himself before asking quietly, "What happened?"

He didn't tell her. He showed her. Grace still had trouble getting used to the way David could share his mind with her. But she had to admit, it made it easier for her to understand. Memories flickered by like a rolling film, and Grace was a horrified, silent spectator as the sister he loved more than life itself put herself in harm's way to rescue David. He'd made it out. The rest of the crew and his twin had not.

Now do you understand? Grace knew he did not vocalize the words because he couldn't.

She was having trouble speaking as well. She had no doubt it was Kyle Willard who had killed David's sister. The same madman who had tried to kidnap her and kill David. She put her hand on David's back, rubbing softly. "Oh, David. You blame yourself for something you had no control over. You didn't kill Meg. You loved her. And she loved you. She would not want you to blame yourself for her death. She would not want you to be in so much pain."

David was silent, his body hunched. Grace moved closer and took his face in her hands, forcing him to look at her.

"David. I saw what you did. You barely got out alive. Would your sister have wanted you to die, too? You know she wouldn't. You did everything you could to save her. The situation was out of your hands."

He didn't speak, didn't react.

She tried again. "Do you remember when you told me I might be falling for you, but I wouldn't acknowledge it?"

Grace took his faint nod for a yes. "I knew I loved you then. But I didn't trust you…didn't believe in my good fortune. Do you remember what you told me?"

David remained silent, but Grace knew he remembered by the flicker of recognition in his remarkable eyes.

"You told me I didn't have to believe you, but you wouldn't let me shut you out. Well, you don't have to believe what I'm telling you, but if you want to be with me, you can't shut me out. You have to learn to trust me as well, David. Or we have nothing."

Strong arms reached out, pulling her close. "You're stubborn, but that's why I love you."

He held her for a long moment, then pulled back to touch her face. "Of course I trust you. I'm just not…used to sharing my feelings with anyone."

"David…"

"Control has been drilled into my head since I was a boy, Grace. It's a very hard habit to break."

She nodded, trying her best to understand.

"But I can see I'm going to need to start sharing if I want you," David added sagely. "And I do want you, Grace Woznisky."

He leaned down and kissed her, his mouth firm on hers. She savored the moment, savored his newfound trust in her, savored the slow heat of desire building between them. But she was not done with this conversation yet.

Pulling her head away, she spoke quietly. "You're not responsible for your sister's death, David Jenkins. Do you hear me? The hacker took that from you. And he tried to kill me, too. You prevented that. I know one does not cancel out the other, but it's past time to let go of the guilt you feel. You did everything you could for Meg. Just like you did for me. To protect me."

After a long, tense moment of consideration, he smiled at her. "Meg would have loved you." He reached for her hand. "C'mon, let's get your stuff and go to the cottage."

"I wish I could have met Meg," Grace said, as they reached the bench holding her suitcases. "But I feel like I have, through you. She's part of who you are, David—your brave and honorable spirit."

David moved to collect her luggage, then paused instead to bend and pick up a small piece of green glass next to her feet. Staring at it in his hand, he said softly, "Meg was with me for every important event in my life, and I feel like she's with me now." He paused, handing Grace the glass. "Now do you believe me when I say you're the only one for me?"

Grace nodded, happily.

"The day Meg died, she wondered if either one of us would ever fall in love and get married. She believed in happily ever after. And you know what? So do I."

Without warning, David slowly dropped on bended knee, pulling a small box from the pocket of his trousers. Grace's stomach took a nosedive and her heartbeat soared, as she realized what was happening. She couldn't help but look around wildly to see if anyone was watching them, to see if there would be any witnesses to what she both hoped and feared was about to happen.

They were alone.

David smiled, as if he knew every careening thought in her head. "Grace Woznisky, I have been carrying this ring around all month, waiting for the right moment to give it to you, and I feel like it's now. Will you do me the honor of becoming my wife?"

He waited patiently, his green eyes watchful, his smile firm and steady. Grace thought she might pass out from the excitement.

"I thought you'd never ask," she finally blurted, pulling him up and into her arms so he could hold her steady.

Laughing, he did just as she wished, surrounding her with his strong, solid arms. As they continued to gaze at each other, smiling and silent, tears misted in her eyes as a deep joy filled her heart. Then, tenderly, David released her to place the sparkling emerald cut diamond ring on her finger.

The orange portal glowed and beckoned between them, and he entered. *I love you, Grace Wosnisky. Will you marry me?*

Yes, my beloved David. Oh, yes.

David smiled again, then bent his head and kissed her there on the beach, until Grace was positive they'd better get inside.

"David," she finally managed breathlessly as he turned his attention toward nuzzling the side of her neck in that sweet, sensitive spot just below her ear. "Do you think we ought to check on Oliver?"

His warm, knowing grin sent waves of love cascading through her. "You read my mind."

A word about the author…

Amanda Uhl has always had a fascination with the mystical. Having drawn her first breath in a century home rumored to be haunted, you might say she was "born" into it. After a brief stint in college as a paid psychic, Amanda graduated with a bachelor of fine arts in theatre and a master's degree in marketing. Over the past twenty years, she has worked as an admissions representative and graphic designer, owned her own freelance writing company, and managed communications for several Fortune 500 companies, most recently specializing in cyber security. Amanda is an avid reader and writes fast-paced, paranormal romantic suspense and humorous contemporary romance from her home in Cleveland, Ohio. When she's not reading or writing, you can find Amanda with her husband and three children, gathering beach glass on the Lake Erie shoreline or biking in Cuyahoga Valley National Park.

For a sneak peek at the second book in her
Mind Hacker Series, Geneva and Rolf's story,
please visit Amanda online at
www.amandauhl.com
www.facebook.com/amandauhlauthor
Twitter at @AuAuthor